The Maggody Militia

Other books by Joan Hess

The Maggody Series

MALICE IN MAGGODY

MISCHIEF IN MAGGODY

MUCH ADO IN MAGGODY

MADNESS IN MAGGODY

MORTAL REMAINS IN MAGGODY

MAGGODY IN MANHATTAN

O LITTLE TOWN OF MAGGODY

MARTIANS IN MAGGODY

MIRACLES IN MAGGODY

The Claire Malloy Series

STRANGLED PROSE

MURDER AT THE MURDER AT THE MIMOSA INN

DEAR MISS DEMEANOR

A REALLY CUTE CORPSE

A DIET TO DIE FOR

ROLL OVER AND PLAY DEAD

DEATH BY THE LIGHT OF THE MOON

POISONED PINS

TICKLED TO DEATH

BUSY BODIES

CLOSELY AKIN TO MURDER

The Maggody Militia

AN ARLY HANKS MYSTERY

Joan Hess

A DUTTON BOOK

DUTTON
Published by the Penguin Group
Penguin Books USA Inc., 375 Hudson Street,
New York, New York 10014, U.S.A.
Penguin Books Ltd, 27 Wrights Lane, London W8 5TZ, England
Penguin Books Australia Ltd, Ringwood, Victoria, Australia
Penguin Books Canada Ltd, 10 Alcorn Avenue,
Toronto, Ontario, Canada M4V 3B2
Penguin Books (N.Z.) Ltd, 182–190 Wairau Road,
Auckland 10, New Zealand

Penguin Books Ltd, Registered Offices:
Harmondsworth, Middlesex, England

First published by Dutton, an imprint of Dutton Signet,
a division of Penguin Books USA Inc.
Distributed in Canada by McClelland & Stewart Inc.

First Printing, April, 1997
10 9 8 7 6 5 4 3 2

 REGISTERED TRADEMARK—MARCA REGISTRADA

LIBRARY OF CONGRESS CATALOGING-IN-PUBLICATION DATA
Hess, Joan.
    The Maggody militia : an Arly Hanks mystery / Joan Hess.
        p.   cm.
    ISBN 0-525-94236-X
    I. Title.
PS3558.E79785M26   1997
813'.54—dc20   96-42518
                                                        CIP

Printed in the United States of America
Set in New Baskerville
Designed by Jesse Cohen

PUBLISHER'S NOTE
This is a work of fiction. Names, characters, places, and incidents either are
the products of the author's imagination or are used fictitiously, and any
resemblance to actual persons, living or dead, events, or locales is entirely
coincidental.

This book is printed on acid-free paper. ∞

This book is dedicated to the memory of Ellen Nehr, who was a treasured friend and confidante. Her perspicacity, wit, and boundless knowledge of the mystery genre will be missed.

A great deal of my information came from *Armed and Dangerous: The Rise of the Survivalist Right* by James Coates (Farrar, Straus and Giroux, 1987; revised edition 1995). Mr. Coates was gracious enough to consent to a telephone interview and answered a lot of really stupid questions. Margaret Maron generously shared her impressive array of research material. Other information was unwittingly provided by pawnshop owners, dealers at my one and only gun show, and such publications as the Paladin Press catalog and books written (I use the term loosely) by devotees to the cause.

From *The Starley City Star Shopper,* November 1:

What's Cooking in Maggody?
by Rubella Belinda Hanks

I'd like to thank the wonderful folks at the *Star Shopper* for asking me to write a weekly column about happenings here in Maggody. It'd be nice if they were paying me more than $15.50, but I reckon it's better than a kick in the backside, as my great-aunt used to say before she had that stroke that froze up her face like a dried apricot.

For starters, the Four-H Club at the high school took second prize at the county fair for their display on kitchen appliance safety. Lottie Estes asked me to remind you all of the bake sale next Saturday in the home ec room right across from the welding shop.

Last Sunday afternoon Eileen Buchanon hosted a baby shower for her daughter-in-law, Dahlia, who's expecting toward the end of the month (although it's hard to tell on account of her being on the large side to begin with). At the shower were myself, Estelle Oppers, Elsie McMay, Millicent McIlhaney, Joyce Lambertino, Mrs. Jim Bob Buchanon, and Edwina Spitz and her sister Teddi Witbreed, who's from Hagerstown, Maryland. Eileen served spicy cider and sponge cake, and a good time was had by all.

A warm Maggody welcome to our newest addition to the community. I suppose someone ought to go out to the edge of town and change the sign to "Population: 756" one of these days, but then when Dahlia and Kevin's baby comes, it'd have to be done all over again. Anyway, for those of you who've been off visiting kin, Kayleen Smeltner will be opening a pawnshop in the old hardware store. She bought the Wockermann property out on

County 102 and is staying at the Flamingo Motel while she's having the house remodeled. Kayleen tells me she's originally from Dallas, Texas, and was living over near Malthus when her husband was killed by burglars that broke into the house. Kayleen's hobbies include needlework, fishing, and gardening. She hasn't decided which church she'll attend. Everybody's invited to drop by and get acquainted. I don't want to name names, but I've been told one local resident has been spotted at the doorstep with flowers and a box of candy.

Edwina Spitz had herself a real nice trip to Branson, where she attended three shows and ate lunch at the Country Catfish Café.

Leslie and Fergie Bidens will attend Fergie's sister's wedding in Kansas City the day after Thanksgiving. Leslie will preside over the guest book at the reception.

Elsie McMay is visiting her niece in Blytheville for ten days. Lottie Estes is dropping by Elsie's house every day after school to feed Stan, Elsie's cat.

Estelle asked me to announce that she'll be running specials all this month, including a ten-percent discount on perms and festive holiday tints. Give her a call at Estelle's Hair Fantasies.

The Voice of the Almighty Lord Assembly Hall will be the site of a Thanksgiving pageant presented by the Sunday school. Brother Verber's not real sure of the time and date yet but is leaning toward the Wednesday prayer service the week before Thanksgiving.

Bismal Buchanon is home from the hospital after having surgery of a personal nature. His wife wants to thank everyone for the cards, casseroles, and prayers. Bismal expects to be back at work by the end of next week, as long as his hemorrhoids don't flare up.

Until next time, God bless.

Eileen's Spicy Cider

1	cup packed dark brown sugar
1	cinnamon stick
1	tablespoon whole cloves
2	cups water
1½	quarts apple cider
⅓	cup lemon juice
4	cups orange juice
1	lemon, sliced
1	orange, sliced

Put your sugar, spices, and water in a saucepan and heat to boiling, stirring until the sugar dissolves. Simmer for about ten minutes, then strain the syrup and throw away the spices. Add cider, lemon juice, and orange juice, and when it's back to simmering, garnish with the fruit slices.

CHAPTER 1

"You didn't say anything about the sale on beauty accessories," Estelle said as she tucked the *Star Shopper* into her purse. "I just got in three dozen bottles of fingernail polish in an exciting variety of colors." She held out her fingers. "This is Pumpkin Patch Pizazz. I think it'll be my best seller."

Ruby Bee finished wiping the bar and dropped the dishrag into the sink, where the water was as dingy as the sky outside. Her face, normally pink and plump as a baby's bottom, was puckered with some unexpressed worry. "I'm not supposed to be giving folks free advertising," she said with a shrug. "I'd end up with a whole column of nothing but used pickup trucks for sale. Raz would expect me to announce his moonshine prices, and Jim Bob'd start telling me about his two-for-one specials on paper towels."

"Well, excuse me, Miss Lois Lane." Estelle finished her sherry and picked up her purse, but put it back down. It didn't seem neighborly to leave Ruby Bee all by herself in the gloomy barroom, especially when anyone with eyeballs in the front of their head could see how blue she was. "Maybe I'll have another piece of apple pie,'' she said, just so Ruby Bee would have something to do.

Ruby Bee gave her a sharp look, but obliged without commenting on certain people's gluttony. After all, Estelle was as skinny as a fence post, although darn few fence posts had bright red hair in a beehive teased a good eight inches high. You didn't see many with violet eyeshadow and cherry-colored lipstick, for that matter. Imagining Estelle out at the edge of a field, holding a strand of barbed wire, brought a flicker of a smile to Ruby Bee's face.

Estelle mentally congratulated herself on the success of her ploy. "So who's this mysterious suitor sniffing around Kayleen?" she asked. "I'd have thought you might have told me right away instead of leaving me to read it in the newspaper. Didn't I tell you when Millicent McIlhaney let it slip that Darla Jean came home drunk and threw up in her pa's boot?"

"I don't want to be accused of spreading gossip. The woman's only been in town for a week, and she might get her feelings hurt if she finds out everybody's talking about her behind her back."

"So who is it?"

Ruby Bee leaned forward like she thought a tabloid reporter was hunkered down in the booth in the corner, taking notes. "I just happened to be setting out the garbage when I saw Brother Verber come sneaking around the corner like a schoolboy with a toad in his pocket. He liked to drop the box of candy when he saw me standing there. He stammered out some foolishness about how he was calling on Kayleen to invite her to go to the Assembly Hall this Sunday. Maybe he thinks I'm as near-sighted as Lottie Estes.''

"Brother Verber?" said Estelle, stunned.

"I was a little surprised," admitted Ruby Bee, "but if you think about it, why shouldn't he come courting? He's a bachelor, after all, and it could get a mite lonely over there in the rectory. Kayleen's been widowed for more than a year now. There's nothing unseemly about her entertaining callers."

"But he's so . . ."

"I'll be the first to say nobody's gonna confuse him with Rudolph Valentino, not with his red nose and squinty eyes and flabby lips. It's not hard to guess who's first in line for dessert at the Wednesday night potlucks, either."

Estelle took a sip of sherry while she considered all this. "I suppose there could be another side to him, although he sure keeps it hidden behind his blustery, self-righteous sermons and unhealthy interest in exposing depravity. What's Mrs. Jim Bob got to say?"

"Nothing as of yet, but you can bet the farm we'll hear something before too long."

"Amen," said Estelle with a snort.

"The woman is nothing but a common tramp," Mrs. Jim Bob (aka Barbara Ann Buchanon Buchanon) told her husband as he came through the back door. "Did you wipe your feet? The last thing I need right now is mud tracked all over the house. Edwina and Millicent are coming over in the morning for coffee, and Perkins's eldest hasn't been here to clean in a week. She says she hurt her back, but it's more likely she's pretending to be poorly so she can collect welfare checks and sit around all day in her bathrobe."

Jim Bob froze in the full wattage of her glare, even though he was carrying two hefty bags of groceries. "Is that why she's a common tramp?"

"I was not referring to Perkins's eldest." Mrs. Jim Bob opened the oven door to check on the pork chops, then slammed it closed and resumed glaring. "It's that woman staying in the motel out behind Ruby Bee's Bar and Grill. A good Christian would never open a pawnshop."

"Why not?" he asked curiously.

"Because it is not the Christian thing to do." She shifted her attention to a saucepan on the stove while she searched her mind for a more insightful explanation. She knew perfectly well that there was something sinful about pawnshops. She finally thought of an old movie she'd watched a few weeks ago when Jim Bob had claimed he was working late at the supermarket. "Pawnshops lure in criminals who want to get rid of stolen property. We've had more than our share of wickedness here in Maggody since Arly Hanks took over as chief of police. I told you when you hired her that it was not a suitable job for a woman, especially one that struts around in pants and has a smart mouth."

Jim Bob set down the bags on the dinette and ran a hand through his stubbly gray hair. As far as Buchanons went, he was on the more perceptive end of the continuum. "Did you and Arly have another run-in today?"

"No, and I don't have any more time to waste trying to help her get back on the right path. I can't count the number of times I've prayed for her, tried to counsel her, and invited her to attend church and join the Missionary Society. Living in New York

City swelled her head and corrupted her soul. If she doesn't mend her ways, she and that Smeltner woman will be on the same express train to eternal damnation.''

"If you say so," he murmured, wondering if there was any way he could slip back out to his truck and sneak a swallow of bourbon from the pint bottle in the glove compartment. Probably not, he concluded. Mrs. Jim Bob's piety had given her a keener sense of smell than a bloodhound's. He didn't have any idea why she was so fired up, but he sure as hell wasn't going to give her another reason to lecture him. Not when he and the other boys on the town council were planning to play poker Saturday night.

"I may have to work late this weekend," he said as he started for the living room. "I was gonna have Kevin do it, but the boy's just too stupid to trust with the receipts. I caught him this morning on the loading dock, staring into space like one of those department store dummies. I had to whack him upside the head with a broomstick to get his attention. You'd think he was pregnant instead of that cow he's married to.''

"I will not have that kind of language in this house, Jim Bob. What would someone walking by think if he heard that coming from the mayor's house? We have an obligation to the community to maintain the highest standards." She came to the doorway, her beady eyes narrowed and her mouth pursed. After a moment, she said, "I assume you'll be working late this weekend in Jim Bob's SuperSaver Buy 4 Less instead of in the backroom of Roy Stiver's antiques store.''

He snatched up the remote control and aimed it

at the TV set. "You get the craziest ideas of any woman I've ever met. What would I be doing at Roy's on a Saturday night?"

Kevin was no longer on the loading dock, but he was far from being bright-eyed and bushy-tailed. He'd been mopping the same square yard of linoleum for the best part of ten minutes while he dreamed about fatherhood. Back when Dahlia had first told him she was in the family way, it had seemed so far-fetched that it hadn't sunk in. Now, with less than a month to go, with the crib in the room next to theirs, with the stacks of nighties and diapers and cotton blankets on the dresser, with the smell of baby powder in the air, he was beginning to realize that he, Kevin Fitzgerald Buchanon, was gonna be a father. He was gonna be presented with a warm little bundle to love and protect.

Without thinking (which he rarely did, being on the opposite end of the aforementioned continuum), Kevin dropped the mop and cradled a four-pack of toilet paper in his arms. Babies were soft and squeezable. They arrived all pink so you'd want to kiss their tiny toes and tickle their little noses.

"Excuse me," said an old lady with a cane, "but could you tell me where you keep the toothpicks? I've been up and down all the aisles."

Kevin replaced the pack and gallantly escorted her to the right spot. Rather than return to the mop, however, he dug a dime out of his pocket and went to use the pay phone in the employees' lounge.

He waited patiently for a dozen rings, imagining his beloved heaving herself off the couch and moving majestically across the room. A stranger peering through the window might not guess she was within weeks of having a baby. What weight she'd gained blended right in with the three hundred odd pounds there'd been of her to begin with, and she'd refused to wear outfits with storks and cute messages about the current location of the baby. Kevin's ma had found one that might have fit, but Dahlia'd turned up her nose and kept on wearing her regular clothes.

"What?" she growled into the receiver.

Kevin realized he might have interrupted her in the middle of one of her soap operas. "Nothing, my sweetums. I just wanted to call and ask how you was doing. Is there anything I can bring home this evening?"

"You know darn well I'm on this awful diet. What are you gonna do if I ask you to bring home two gallons of ice cream and a carton of Twinkies?"

He gulped unhappily. "I was thinking more of crunchy celery and that real tasty low-fat yogurt." His beetlish brow, common in varying degrees to all members of the Buchanon clan, crinkled as he struggled to make amends for setting her off again. "Or a magazine! The new issues just came in this morning. I don't recollect exactly, but I think there's one with ideas to decorate a nursery."

"When am I supposed to sew curtains and paint stencils on the wall?" she said with a drawn-out sigh of pure misery. "I have to poke my poor finger four times a day on account of this diabetes. The sight of my blood bubbling up makes me sick to my stomach, so I have to get a sugar-free soda pop and lie down until I stop feeling queasy. Then I haft to listen to that tape they gave us and make silly noises. When I'm not doing that, your ma's hauling me to the clinic so I can put on a paper dress and wait until that weasel of a doctor finds time to pull on plastic gloves and smear petroleum jelly on—"

"I gotta get back to work," Kevin said as his knees buckled and sweat flooded his armpits. "Why don't you have yourself a nice nap on the sofa? After all, you're sleeping for two."

He made it back to the mop and bucket, but it was a long while before he started sloshing dirty water down the aisle.

"Am I disturbing you?" asked Kayleen Smeltner as she came into the PD and paused, her expression cautious.

I put aside my pocketknife and the block of balsa wood I was trying to coerce into resembling a marshland mallard. I keep it in a bottom desk drawer for those stretches of time when the rigors of upholding the law in Maggody are less than burdensome. Some peculiar things have happened since the day I arrived home to pull myself back together after the divorce, but mostly I run a speed trap out at the edge of town, pull teenagers over for reckless driving, beg the miserly town council for money, and try to stay in my mother's good graces by pretending that my only goal in life is to acquire another husband, a vine-covered cottage, and a lifetime subscription to *TV Guide*.

In her dreams, not mine.

"Have a seat," I said to Kayleen. "The bank robbery's not scheduled until five o'clock, and the extraterrestrial invasion won't start until midnight."

She sat down on the edge of the chair across from my desk and unbuttoned her coat. "Maggody doesn't have a bank."

"I know," I said. "It doesn't have a landing pad, either." I'd met Kayleen at the bar, of course, in that I was in there two or three times a day, sometimes four if I made happy hour. She appeared to be in her early forties, maybe ten or twelve years older than me. Her makeup might have been a tad heavy-handed, but it went well with her long, wavy blond hair and slightly masculine features. She was nearly six feet tall and carried a few extra pounds beneath well-tailored silk and linen dresses. The leers and wolf-whistles that greeted her in the barroom implied the overall effect was that of a 1940s Hollywood sex goddess.

She finally gave up trying to figure out what I'd said and relaxed. "I want to give you a copy of my license to buy and sell firearms, just so you'll know everything's legal. I applied for it a few months after Maurice was killed."

"Maurice?" I echoed.

"Everybody called him Mo, but I always called him Maurice on account of how sexy it sounded, like he was from France instead of Neosho, Missouri." She took a tissue out of her purse and dabbed the corner of her eye. "He left me his gun collection. I had to sell it, and I found out real quick that dealers end up with most of the profit. Pretty soon I had a brisk business going, some mail-order but most of it out of my home. When I got tired of having strangers tromp through my living room, I decided to open a pawnshop. This way I can keep my private life separate from my business one."

I leaned back in the worn cane-bottomed chair and asked the question that had been buzzing around town like a deranged hornet. "Why Maggody? Wouldn't you do better in a larger town? The only walk-in trade you'll get here is from the drunks across the street at the pool hall, and I doubt any of them owns anything of value. Traffic consists of tourists heading north for the country music halls of Branson, or heading south for the self-conscious quaintness of Eureka Springs. The only reason anyone slows down going through here is to throw litter out the car window. If anyone actually stopped, we'd all go outside to stare.''

"I stopped here once upon a time," she said in a dreamy voice. "I was on my honeymoon. Jodie and I were fresh out of high school, driving an old car his grandfather had given us, down to our last few dollars. We didn't care, though. We were heading for Texas when we had a flat tire four or five miles down the road from here. It turned out the spare tire was flat, too, and Jodie was setting off to walk back to Maggody when this man pulled up. He drove Jodie to a gas station to get the tire fixed, then brought him back and insisted we stay for supper. It was the kindest thing anyone's done in my whole life. I guess I've thought about coming back here ever since then.''

"What happened to Jodie?"

This time she put the tissue to serious use. "We scraped together enough money to put a down payment on a little farm west of Texarkana. Less than a year later, Jodie was killed when the truck he was working on slipped off the jack and crushed his chest. I was pregnant at the time, and miscarried the next day. I couldn't stand living in the house filled with his memories, so I sold the property and moved to Dallas. Sometimes I pull out my old high school yearbooks and look at his picture, wondering what my life would have been like if . . .''

I was touched, although not to the point of asking to borrow her soggy tissue. "I still think you may regret opening a business here," I said to change the subject before she whipped out wedding pictures (or an urn filled with ashes). "And you may regret buying the Wockermann property, too. The reason the house is in such disrepair is that it's been empty for a couple of years. The real estate market's not booming in this neck of the woods. It's not even pinging."

"Maurice left me enough to get by on," Kayleen said with a small smile. "I'll have my mail-order business, although I guess I'll have to drive into Farberville to use the post office there. Besides, big cities are frightening these days. You don't know your neighbors. If you need something fixed, you have to let a stranger come inside your house. He could be a rapist, or a psychotic, or even a government agent."

"A government agent?"

"You never can tell. These are dangerous times we live in, Arly. Don't think for a minute that the government doesn't know how much money you make and how you spend it down to the last penny—and I'm not talking just about taxes. They know who you talk to on the telephone and get mail from, and which organizations you belong to."

I raised my eyebrows. "There're more than two hundred and sixty million people in this country. I can't imagine the government keeping tabs on all of them. Mobsters and drug dealers, maybe—but not ordinary citizens. Why would they bother?"

She gave me what I suppose she thought was a meaningful look, although it didn't mean diddlysquat to me. "Keep in mind that the media are regulated by the government, so they can't say things that might expose what's happening in this country. Come by the shop and I'll show you some interesting material about what you can expect sometime down the road."

"Okay," I said uneasily, then took a shot at changing the subject once again. "Maurice was your second husband?"

She promptly teared up again. "He was murdered a little more than a year ago."

"Murdered?" I said, mentally kicking myself for bringing up another painful topic. "What happened?"

"One night we heard glass break downstairs. Maurice took the thirty-eight from the bedside table and went to investigate. Three shots were fired. I called the police, then went to the top of the stairs. I saw men run out the front door, but it was too dark to get a good look. All I could tell the police was that there were three of them, wearing dark coats and ski masks. I've had some training as a practical nurse, but there was nothing I could do to help Maurice. He bled to death before the ambulance arrived."

"Were the men caught?"

Kayleen grimaced and shook her head. "The police interviewed all the local ne'er-do-wells, but nobody was acting guilty or bragging in the bars. I think the men must have been from Springfield or maybe Kansas City. Maurice was a well-known gun collector. He advertised in magazines, and we used to go to shows as far away as Chicago and Houston and Santa Fe. It wouldn't take a college degree to figure out there'd be valuable guns in the house."

I resisted the urge to launch into a lecture that would not amuse card-carrying members of the NRA. Sure, I have a gun (and a box with three bullets), but

I keep it locked away in a filing cabinet in the back room. I'm a cop, after all, and may be called upon one of these days to shoot a rabid skunk or an Elvis impersonator. I can't imagine myself shooting much of anything else, even though Hizzoner the Moron has tried my patience on occasion.

I settled for a vaguely sympathetic smile. "It doesn't sound like you've had much luck with husbands."

"It's a good thing I'm not afraid of living alone," she said as she stood up, buttoned her coat, and pulled on hand-sewn leather gloves. "I need to run out to the house and find out if the electrician ever showed up. I just thought it'd be nice if you and I got better acquainted."

"Drop by any old time," I said, my fingers crossed in my lap. She seemed perfectly nice, if a little bit odd about wily government agents. A little bit odd barely rates a mention in a county with Buchanons as plentiful as cow patties in a pasture.

I watched her drive away in a creamy brown car, genus Mercedes, species unfamiliar. I turned off the coffee pot, collected my radar gun, balsa wood, and pocket knife, and was almost out the door when the telephone rang. Despite my instincts to keep on going, I turned back to answer it.

"Get yourself over here," whispered a voice I recognized as that of the proprietress of Ruby Bee's Bar & Grill.

"I can't," I whispered back. "I have to nab speeders at the edge of town so I can earn my minuscule salary at the end of the month. Maybe later, okay?"

"You got to come right this instant, missy."

I was going to inquire into the nature of the

emergency when I realized I was listening to a dial tone. It could have been an armed robbery, I supposed, but it was more likely to be a mouse in the pantry or a snag in her panty hose. My mother dishes out melodrama as generously as she does peach cobbler.

I left the radar gun on the desk, and ambled down the road, pausing to wave at my landlord, Roy Stiver, who was hauling a spindly lamp into his antiques store. I live in an efficiency apartment upstairs, although I've begun to wonder if I ought to find something less cramped. It had seemed just fine when I first arrived from Manhattan, even though it was quite a step down from a posh condominium with a view of the East River and the Queensboro Bridge. My current residence has a view of the pool hall and a couple of vacant buildings with yellowed newspapers taped across the windows. It also has cigarette burns in the linoleum, mildew on the walls, and a toilet that creaks to itself in the night.

As a temporary refuge, it was adequate. I sure as hell hadn't planned to stay any longer than it took to let my bruised ego recover from the divorce. Now it seemed as though I'd never left town, that the blurred memories of cocktail parties and art galleries were nothing more than scenes from a movie I'd seen somewhere.

Shivering, I went into the barroom to find out what, if anything, had provoked the call. The provocation certainly had not come from the trucker snoring in the corner booth, or from the rednecks in the next booth, who were arguing about breeds of hunting dogs.

This narrowed it down to a lone figure on a stool

by the bar. There were no antennas bobbling above his head, and he was wearing a camouflage jacket instead of a sequined suit from the Graceland souvenir store. Ruby Bee was standing in front of him, listening while she dried a beer mug with a towel. I couldn't quite decipher her expression; she was nodding politely, but there was a certain rigidity to her features that suggested she was keeping her opinions to herself.

Which was unusual, to put it mildly.

When she saw me, she dropped the towel and chirped, "Here's Arly. She took her sweet time getting here, but that doesn't mean she's not interested in meeting you. Did I mention she happens to be the chief of police here in Maggody? The mayor's wife was real annoyed when the town council hired her, but there wasn't a line of candidates begging for the job." She took a much needed breath as I came to a stop at the edge of the dance floor. "I was just telling General Pitts about you, honey. He's in town to visit Kayleen, but she's not out back in her room."

I crossed my arms. "If you'd told me you wanted to file a missing person report, I would have brought the forms with me. Before I round up a posse to search the ridge, however, I might mention that Kayleen left the PD about ten minutes ago on her way to the Wockermann place. Something about an electrician."

"General Pitts, this is Arly. Her real name is Ariel, which I chose on account of it having a nice ring to it. She used to be married, but when she got divorced, she decided to take back her maiden name, which is the same as mine. How long ago was that, Arly?"

The man slid off the stool and spun around in a

neat, controlled movement worthy of a ballroom dancer. He had short gray hair, close-set eyes, and thin, taut lips. A jutting jaw gave him an air of belligerence. That, or listening to Ruby Bee dither about me as if I were the hottest thing since sliced bread.

"I'm Sterling Pitts," he said.

"Okay," I said, figuring he knew pretty much everything about me from kindergarten to court. "Would you like directions to the house Kayleen bought?"

"Eventually, but why don't you allow me to buy you a soda?"

I glanced at Ruby Bee, who was rolling her eyes and wiggling her mouth at me as though a bug was crawling up her back. "A beer sounds good," I said as I brushed past him and sat on a stool.

He frowned at the badge on my shirt. "Are you allowed to drink alcoholic beverages while on duty, Chief Hanks?"

"I'm not on duty," I said as I took off the badge and put it in my pocket. "My shift ended fifteen seconds ago when I decided to have a beer. I can deputize Kevin if the bank robbers show up."

Ruby Bee banged down a mug in front of me. "Mind your mouth, Arly. General Pitts may not think you're as funny as you do."

"That's right," Estelle said as she came out of the ladies room and perched on her customary stool at the end of the bar, where she could eavesdrop without spilling her sherry. "What's more, you ought to take some interest in your appearance when you're on duty. I just got in a shipment of lipstick that might give you some color. Why don't you come by and let me give you a complimentary makeover?"

I ignored her. "You're a general?"

"It's really more of an honorary title," he said, flushing. "It was bestowed on me by the members of a group that I organized several years ago. We adopted military ranking in order to provide internal structure."

Ruby Bee gave him a disappointed look. "Oh, I thought you were a real general, like Eisenhower and Patton. Go ahead and tell Arly what you're aiming to do next week."

Pitts clearly was not pleased to have his rank dismissed so nonchalantly, but after a brief moment of pouting, he turned to me and said, "Please rest assured that our activities will take place outside your jurisdiction, Chief Hanks. Furthermore, we are law-abiding citizens with no desire to disrupt the community or cause alarm. We simply ask to be allowed to exercise our constitutional rights without undue interference."

It didn't sound as if he was planning to stage a beauty pageant to select Miss Stump County—or anything remotely that innocuous. Then again, he'd hardly tell me if he were plotting to overthrow the town council and put in a dictatorship (as if we'd notice).

"Just what do you have in mind?" I asked, setting down my beer in case I needed to put myself back on duty.

"I am the leader of a small group concerned about protecting the American way of life. We are preparing ourselves to fight back in the face of an invasion of foreign troops or even an attempt by the federal government to declare martial law and deprive us of our rights. Should push come to shove, we will not be led to the slaughterhouse like bleating sheep. We will resist."

"How are you preparing yourselves?"

Pitts gave me a smile that oozed superciliousness. "Through rigorous physical training, as well as education and networking with others who share our beliefs. We will establish an encampment at the far edge of Kayleen's property in order to perform military maneuvers in the more rugged terrain on the ridge. We will perfect survival techniques in anticipation of the day when resources are controlled by the enemy. We will eat off the land."

Ruby Bee winced. "You're gonna eat roots and berries when you could have a nice blue-plate special right here? Wouldn't you prefer chicken-fried steak with cream gravy and your choice of three vegetables?"

"We are not ignorant savages," he said. "We will simply make do with game or fish, if necessary supplementing it with provisions brought with us. One of the women handles those duties while we focus on important matters."

"You can't make decent biscuits over a campfire," stated Ruby Bee, who clearly fancied herself to be an authority of the same stature as Julia Child.

He gazed coldly at her. "Sacrifices must be made in order to defend the Constitution of the United States of America."

When he didn't burst into the national anthem, I said, "I'm not sure it's wise to play G.I. Joe in the woods next week. Deer hunting season starts this Saturday. A lot of guys stick a bottle of bourbon in their pockets and go stumbling around, shooting at anything that twitches a whisker. There are one or two

fatal accidents every year. I wouldn't set foot out
there, even if Raz Buchanon offered to carry me
piggyback to his still."

Pitts climbed off the stool and took a step back,
his shoulders squared and that same damn smile on
his face. "There are worse dangers than drunken
hunters. Now, if you'll tell me how to find Kayleen's
house, I will be on my way. I'm sure you have more
important things to do than sit here and make idle
conversation."

"You'd think so, wouldn't you?" I said without
enthusiasm. After Ruby Bee had given him directions,
no more complicated than left out of the parking lot,
right on County 102, he marched out the door. I finished my beer and stood up. "Did Pitts say where he
lives when he's not stalking squirrels and godless
communists?"

Estelle snorted. "Farberville. He owns an insurance agency."

"Then I hope he has a hefty life insurance policy," I said as I headed for the door.

"Do you think there's anything to what he said?"
asked Ruby Bee. "Could the government up and take
over the country?"

"About the time Marjorie sprouts wings," Estelle
said with another snort.

I kept on walking.

CHAPTER 2

Brother Verber was slumped on the couch in the silver trailer that served as the rectory for the Voice of the Almighty Lord Assembly Hall. It was so small that it was a miracle he didn't run into himself in the hallway that led to the bathroom and bedroom. What's more, it lacked the cozy touches only a woman could provide, like doilies on the armrests and china knick-knacks on the table. The counter of the kitchen alcove was cluttered not with the makings for buttermilk biscuits, but with dirty dishes, crusted pots, and empty sacramental wine bottles.

It hadn't seemed so awful a week ago, when he was resigned to being a bachelor for the rest of his life. He had his pulpit and his congregation, his subscriptions to magazines that kept him informed of any new trends in sexual deviancy, and occasional trips to Little Rock to do personal research into such matters. Still, there'd been times when he wondered if he was missing something.

He put down the plastic tumbler to clasp his hands together and find out what, if anything, the Lord would think about all this. " 'Two are better than one because they have a good reward for their labor. For if they fall, the one will lift up his fellow, but woe to him that is alone when he falleth, for he hath not another to help him up.' " He paused, then added, "That'd be from Ecclesiastes, in case You couldn't quite put Your finger on it."

The Lord didn't seem to have a response, so Brother Verber went to the refrigerator and refilled his glass with the last of the wine. Rather than resuming his prayerful posture on the couch, he looked out the window at the Assembly Hall, a metal structure that bore a vague resemblance to the rectory. Kayleen had agreed to come to the Sunday morning service, but she hadn't promised to join his little flock on a permanent basis. He imagined her in the first pew, her face rosy with religious fervor and her skirt hitched up just far enough to permit a glimpse of her muscular thighs.

He took a handkerchief out of his bathrobe pocket and blotted his forehead. This wasn't anything to do with lust, he told himself. It had to do with warm, loving companionship as they traveled down the road to the Pearly Gates. There was nothing wrong with that, surely. They were both too old to go forth and multiply, but that didn't mean they couldn't partake in a few worldly pleasures of the flesh.

Sweat was dribbling into his ears and his eyes were glazed with the particulars of his fantasy when he heard a knock at the door. He shoved as many wine bottles as he could into the garbage bag under the sink, took a last swipe at his forehead, and opened the door.

"Why, Sister Barbara," he began in what he hoped was a voice of surprise and delight, "I wasn't expecting to see you this afternoon. Why don't you—"

"You're not dressed," Mrs. Jim Bob said as she swept past him. "Shouldn't you be out visiting the sick or over in the Assembly Hall working on your sermon? The devil finds work for idle hands, as you well know."

While she took off her coat, he snatched the tumbler off the kitchen table and stuck it in the nearest cabinet. "I was headed for the county nursing home this morning," he improvised, "but then I started feeling like I had a touch of the stomach flu. Not wanting to inflict my germs on those feeble old things, I came right home where I could pray for them without endangering their health."

"You do look kind of damp," she said as she sat down on the couch. "If you're still feeling sickly tomorrow, I'll make a pot of chicken soup and bring it over here."

"You are so selfless," he said, sitting down next to her so he could pat her knee. "That's why you're such an inspiration to the congregation."

"I understand you've been doing some recruiting."

"It's my duty to bring sinners off the street and into the bosom of the Lord, Sister Barbara. I know for a fact that the angels burst into song whenever a lost soul finds salvation through prayer and Bible studies."

"I assume you remember how Jesus ran the moneylenders out of the temple, saying it had become a den of thieves. You wouldn't want that to happen at the Voice of the Almighty Lord Assembly Hall, would you?"

Brother Verber was more than a little mystified by her remark. "I should say not," he said, trying to sound emphatic. "In this sea of wickedness that surrounds us, the Assembly Hall is our lifeboat, and you, Sister Barbara, are right there at the helm beside me."

"I'm glad to hear we have an understanding." She removed his hand from her knee and picked up her purse. "I'll be by tomorrow with the soup."

"God bless you," he called as she went out the door, then retrieved his wine and watched her drive away in the pink Cadillac Jim Bob had bought for her after she found out about his relationship with a divorcée living at the Pot O' Gold trailer park.

Thinking about that reminded him of Kayleen, with her shapely figure and loving nature. He wouldn't rush her, of course, but instead give her time to learn to appreciate his finer qualities, like his compassion for the little heathen children in Africa, his spirituality, his sacrifices to battle Satan's soldiers.

Imbued with optimism as well as wine, he sat down on the couch and considered when it would be fitting for him to drop by the Flamingo Motel again. He'd give it a day or two, he decided as he took a swallow of wine and let it dribble down his throat like diluted honey.

The sun was shining the next morning, but the wind was frigid. I kept my hands in my coat pockets as I hurried across the road to the PD, accompanied only by skittering leaves and litter. As soon as I'd made coffee and was settled at my desk, I called the sheriff's department in Farberville and asked to speak to Harve Dorfer.

"Is there something goin' on out there?" asked
LaBelle, the dispatcher. "More Martians?"

"No," I said, struggling to keep the irritation out
of my voice. LaBelle covertly runs the department,
deciding whose calls to put through and whose to
leave indefinitely on hold. She was enough of a pain
in the rear that I almost would have preferred voice
mail: "If you're in the act of committing a felony,
press one."

LaBelle sniffed. "Sheriff Dorfer's been real busy
these last few days, what with the upcoming election
and all. He's speaking at the Rotary meeting at noon
about all the drug busts he's made in the last year,
then he's supposed to—"

"Just put him on, okay?"

"Yes, ma'am," she retorted, no doubt already
plotting her revenge.

When Harve finally came on the line, he sounded
as if he were rehearsing his speech. "Good to hear
from you, Arly. It's important that law enforcement
agents work together to keep crime out of Stump
County so our children won't be sold drugs on the
playgrounds and our senior citizens can sleep at
night, knowing their houses won't be vandalized."

"Save it for the Rotarians," I said. "I need someone at your end to run a check on a guy named
Sterling Pitts. I'd estimate his age at fifty-five to sixty,
gray hair, a propensity for khaki. Purportedly, he has
an insurance office over there."

Harve chuckled. "Sounds like a dangerous char-
acter. Did you nab him for running the stoplight?"

"He hasn't done anything—yet." I told him
about the conversation in the bar the previous day,
then added, "The last thing we need is a bunch of

weekend warriors crawling around in the woods during deer season. You're not going to win any votes if
half of them are carried out in body bags.''

I heard the scritch of a match as he lit one of his
infamously vile cigars. "You have a point," he said
slowly, "but do we have a leg to stand on here? If they
have the property owner's permission—and you're
saying they do—I don't see what we can do about it.
It may be stupid, but it's not against the law.''

"Just check out this guy. Maybe we'll get lucky
and find an outstanding warrant to dangle over his
head. I don't care if they want to sleep in caves and
eat bark for breakfast; I just don't want them doing it
during deer season. We have to protect our reputation.''

"Your reputation?'' He guffawed as if I'd related
a tasteless joke involving politicians and barnyard animals. "Are we talking about the same place that had
Bigfoot sightings last spring?''

I waited until he quieted down. "Gawd, I'd forgotten about Diesel. The last I heard, he's still up on
Cotter's Ridge, biting heads off rabbits and squirrels.
He won't take kindly to being surprised by some
wacko in an army helmet. And what about Raz? He
keeps a shotgun in his truck in case he finds someone getting too close to his moonshine operation.
How many stainless steel tables do they have at the
morgue?''

"I reckon you've got yourself a problem," Harve
admitted as he wheezily exhaled. "I'll check out this
fellow when I get time, and I'll also have a word with
the county prosecutor. It won't make a skeeter's ass
of difference, but at least we'll have tried.''

He promised to call me later, then barked at

LaBelle to fetch him a fresh cup of coffee and hung up. I leaned back, propped my feet on the corner of the desk, and tried to remember if anybody else besides Diesel and Raz frequented the ridge. The high school kids preferred the gravel bars along Boone Creek for their beer binges; there were enough aluminum cans scattered in the weeds to support a recycling plant. When the more mature philanderers desired privacy, they gravitated toward the trailers at the Pot O' Gold or the seedy motels at the edge of Farberville.

Cotter's Ridge was almost inaccessible by car; the steep, overgrown logging trails were rutted and often blocked by fallen trees. Robin Buchanon's shack remained standing (or leaning), and the odiferous outhouse behind it, but no one had lived there since she'd been murdered and her children dispersed by social workers. As far as I knew, Raz and Diesel had the ridge to themselves.

Until next week, anyway.

I shuffled through the mail, made a second pot of coffee, and examined the stain on the ceiling until my neck began to ache. I knew Harve wasn't going to call back anytime soon, but I wasn't in the mood to run a speed trap out past Purtle's Esso or lurk around the corner from our one and only stoplight. I wasn't in the mood to deal with Ruby Bee, either; she'd be in a dither because I hadn't shown up for breakfast. The last thing I needed was a lecture about common courtesy and the value of good nutrition (as if biscuits and sausage gravy were applauded by the surgeon general).

I finally decided to accept Kayleen's invitation to

drop by the pawnshop and look at whatever material she claimed would lead to my enlightenment. The building that had once housed a New Age hardware store and then a short-lived "souvenir shoppe" was only a block away, but I took my car in case I spotted a getaway car idling in front of the charred remains of the branch bank. The radio rarely did more than snap, crackle, and pop, and the siren sounded like a dying donkey, but the heater was working for some mysterious reason.

I parked beside the Mercedes. There had been no grand opening as yet, but lights were on inside and presumably Kayleen was busily arranging her lethal display. In reality, the main room was barren and cluttered with the debris left by the previous occupant. I continued into the office, where I found Kayleen talking on the telephone.

"Hold on," she said into the receiver, then looked up at me. "Can I do something for you, Arly?"

"I'm hoping you'll answer some questions," I said.

"Sure." She told whomever she'd been talking to that she'd call later, then hung up and moved some files off a second chair. "I heard you met Sterling Pitts yesterday. Could that be why you have questions today?"

"You obviously have some sort of involvement with this paramilitary group Pitts mentioned. I'd like to know more about it."

"Sterling has an unfortunate tendency to get carried away when talking about what amounts to a small social club made up of people who enjoy camping. They don't exactly share the left-wing philosophy of the Sierra Club, but they're harmless. Otherwise, I wouldn't have agreed to allow them to use my property.''

''Pitts was talking about military maneuvers,'' I said, unconvinced. ''That tends to imply weapons.''

''They use paint pellets instead of bullets. I've known Sterling for a good ten years, and I can promise you he and the others are no more sinister than your basic outdoors enthusiasts.''

''Are you aware deer season starts Saturday?'' I persisted. ''Why is Pitts determined to do this at a time when the ridge is crawling with overgrown boys who can't see straight?''

''It's when most of them can get a few days off work. I'm not happy about it, either, but Sterling's the one who has to accept the responsibility if someone gets hurt. I'm just letting them use the back pasture.''

''Then why let them use it?''

''Sterling can be as stubborn as a mule, and he kept badgering me until I agreed. In the past, they had a place over near Yellville, but the guy who owned the property got sent to jail for tax evasion and his wife refuses to let them come back. I don't think you should worry about this, Arly. They've been going out during deer season for the last five years, and nobody's ever had more than a bellyache from eating the wrong kind of berries.''

''I wish you'd change your mind,'' I said. ''They're risking not only the very real possibility of being mistaken for a buck, but also hypothermia, snakebite, and encounters with our local moonshiner and an unbalanced hermit—all so they can be prepared to defend themselves from a mythical foreign army.''

"Sorry, but they're old enough to know their own minds, and they won't be breaking any laws. Sterling's always careful about that. Just ignore them. Nobody else in town will even know they're here, and at the end of the four days, they'll go back home to their microwave meals and warm beds."

I could tell I was wasting my breath, so I stood up. "You mentioned something yesterday about some material you wanted me to read."

She herded me toward the front door. "I do, but I forgot it's in a cardboard box in a storage cubicle over in Malthus. When I get everything hauled over here and sorted, I'll drop some tracts off at the police department." She accompanied me onto the porch and glanced at the silver trailer across the road. "He's an odd bird, isn't he?"

"Brother Verber? You could say that without any fear of being contradicted by anyone with a lick of sense, which includes everybody but the most witless of the Buchanons."

"He's kind of sweet, though," she continued thoughtfully. "Even though I was brought up Baptist, I said I'd come to the Sunday morning service. It's good to start putting down roots, meet my new neighbors, learn the local traditions. I'm glad I decided to move here. I think it's gonna work out real well."

It was not a sentiment often heard inside the city limits. I left her standing on the porch and drove out County 102 to make sure nobody had run off the low-water bridge or stolen the sign that continued to claim the population to be in the mid seven hundreds. It hadn't been changed since my high school days.

Not much else had, either.

Sterling Pitts was back in his office after lunch with his fellow Rotarians. Most of the time it didn't seem worth the trouble, but today he'd had a chance to get Lou Gerkin aside to discuss a group health proposal. Lou'd promised to think it over, which was all you could expect with a speaker droning on about drugs in the schools. As if drugs were the pivotal threat to society, Sterling thought with a sigh. One of these days the pudgy sheriff would be asking himself why he was living under martial law and taking orders from a member of an inferior race.

Missy came to the doorway. "Your wife called while you were out, Mr. Pitts. She said to tell you she's playing bridge tonight and won't be home till real late."

"Anybody else?" he asked, wondering what it'd take to convince the girl to write down messages on paper and leave them on his desk. She seemed to prefer to brief him as if she was a platoon leader.

"A man named Reed, but he wouldn't tell me his last name or what he wants. Is he a client?"

"No, Missy, he's a mechanic at the garage where I take my car. He's got an estimate for some repairs. Now go call the home office and find out what claims adjuster we're supposed to use while Durmont's laid up. And shut the door, please."

He waited until a button lit up on the telephone, then utilized a second line to dial a number that was answered not at a garage, but at a squalid apartment.

"I told you not to call my office," he began grimly. "Security is essential to our success. Your line could be tapped at this very moment."

"Yeah, but I got to talk to you, Pitts."

"I'll be home alone tonight. Park down the block and come in through the back door. I'm beginning to suspect my house is being kept under surveillance; an unfamiliar car has been parked across the street periodically for the last week."

"Then why don't we meet someplace else? My place, or at a bar or something? It's not going to help our cause if the feds link the two of us."

"Come to the house at 2200 hours." Sterling banged down the receiver, frustrated by the necessity of dealing with those of so little discipline. How many times had he stressed the need to follow the procedures laid out in the manual? Calls were to be made only from telephones known to be safe. Names were never used in communications, only designated code words, but Red Rooster had said Pitts's name in the course of the brief conversation. Of course the feds could figure it out without too much trouble, since Reed had dialed the number of Pitts's Tri-County Patriots' Insurance Services.

Instead of plunging back into group health policies or paperwork from the state commission, Pitts opened his drawer and took out a slim book. *The Ruger 1022 Exotic Weapons Systems* was as soothing as a glass of warm milk. Smiling, he flipped to the chapter on how to transform a Ruger 1022 into a selective-fire, close-combat gun—*all without modifying the receiver or trigger housing in any way!*

Reed "Red Rooster" Rondly was staring at the blank television screen when Barry "Apocalypse" Kirklin came into the apartment and dropped a six-pack of beer on the scarred coffee table.

"Thought you was supposed to work late today,"

Reed said as he leaned forward to wrench a beer out of the plastic holder.

"What the hell difference does it make to you? Oh, I get it—Martha Stewart's coming over to give you some decorating tips for Thanksgiving."

"Who?"

Barry opened a beer, then went into the kitchen to look for something to eat that wasn't covered in fuzzy blue mold. "God, you're a pig," he said as he came back to the living room with a bag of chips. "I don't know how Bobbi Jo put up with you as long as she did. You heard from her since she got to her parents' house?"

"I don't want to talk about her—okay? She's gonna be real sorry she went off like that, taking the car and the VCR. She probably would have taken the refrigerator if she could have figured out how to jam it in the backseat."

Barry flinched as his friend crumpled the beer can and threw it at the television set. Reed was a couple of inches shorter than he, but considerably more muscular and prone to getting into brawls with frat boys slumming at places like the Dew Drop Inn and the Exotica Club. They'd both gone into the army straight from high school; four years later Barry'd come out with a healthy regard for self-preservation. Reed had come out with a dishonorable discharge and the disposition of a junkyard dog. They were both pushing thirty years old. Barry worked at a bookstore, while Reed drifted from garage to garage, getting his sorry self fired for drinking on the job or coming in late. Or not coming in at all.

Reed opened another beer. "There's a new guy at the garage, name of Dylan Gilbert, not more than twenty-two or twenty-three years old, and scrawny as a free-range chicken. He doesn't know shit about American cars, but he's pretty good with Jap imports."

"Fascinating," Barry said as he moved a stack of old gun magazines from a chair and sat down.

"He needs a place to crash, so I told him he could stay here until he finds something."

"And?"

"And he says he was with that group in Colorado until a month ago when he heard a warrant had been issued."

Barry shook his head. "Did he just happen to tell you this when you two went outside for a smoke?"

"Yeah," Reed said grudgingly, "something like that. We was standing next to my pickup, and he took to admiring the modified shotgun on the rack. He was real impressed when I said I'd done the work myself, and then we got to talking about weapons in general. He converted an SKS rifle to an automatic that uses AK-47 magazines. He went on to say he'd had to sell it before he left town, and that's what led to him telling me about the warrant. Seems he sent an early Christmas present to a judge, but a hotshot at the post office called the bomb squad. Somehow or other they traced it back to Dylan."

"I hope you didn't reciprocate by spilling your guts to him," Barry said with a dark look. "He sounds like he's got a big mouth and a propensity for sharing secrets with strangers. The last thing we need is for him to have too many beers and start talking about our operation to anyone who'll listen."

"I didn't say shit about anything to him, but I'm going over to Pitts's house tonight to discuss this guy with him. Since Bradley got thrown in the state prison, Carter Lee upped and disappeared, and Mo got gunned down by thievin' mongrels, we're down to what—four members? The women are useful, but I wouldn't share a fox hole with either of them. A bed, maybe, but you can't trust women in combat. God put 'em on this planet to bear children, which is why they're as useless as tits on a boar hog when the going gets rough." He opened yet another beer and drained half of it, ignoring the dribbles on his chin. "I came home one night and found Bobbi Jo bawling on account of she'd spilled her fingernail polish on the bedspread. Jesus!"

"The manual says the optimum number for a cell is ten. That doesn't mean we ought to stand on the corner and pass out application forms to anyone who walks by."

"Yeah," said Reed, back to staring at the blank screen.

Barry left to find something to eat in one of the dives along Thurber Street. Although usually alert, he failed to notice the figure sitting in a small car parked across the road from the apartment building.

CHAPTER 3

Estelle pranced across the dance floor, her heels clattering like castanets, and fidgeted impatiently on the stool at the end of the bar while Ruby Bee finished filling two mugs from the tap and took them to Jim Bob Buchanon and Roy Stiver.

Ruby Bee was grumbling as she came back behind the bar. "I swear, I don't know how men can talk as much as they do about deer season. You'd think they were out to get a buried treasure instead of a flea-ridden old buck. Those two"—she jerked her thumb at the corner booth—"have been jabbering for more than an hour. If they'd spend half as much time earning a living as they do talking about dogs—"

"I had a real interesting letter this morning," Estelle said, unable to restrain herself. Beaming, she took a folded piece of paper out of her purse. "It's from a lawyer over in Oklahoma."

"Since when do you know any lawyers in Oklahoma?"

"Since I got this letter this morning." She paused while she unfolded it and smoothed it out on the surface of the bar. "His name is Chester W. Corsair, and his office is in Muskogee."

Ruby Bee gazed blandly at her, then shifted her attention to Jim Bob and Roy. "You boys want some pretzels or a couple of pickled eggs?" she called, knowing full well Estelle was close to bubbling over with excitement. However, it was *her* bar and grill, not Estelle's, and she could do as she pleased when it came to earning a living.

Instead of answering, Jim Bob dropped a few dollars on the table, and he and Roy walked out of the bar, still deep in conversation about how many bottles of whiskey and bologna sandwiches they'd need.

When the door closed, Ruby Bee said, "Does this Mr. Corsair want you to go to law school and become his partner, or is somebody suing you for wrongful hair?"

Estelle decided to be magnanimous about this petty display of poor manners. "Do you recall me talking about my Uncle Tooly?"

"I recall a little about him. Didn't he marry a one-eyed widow woman with a lot of money?"

"You'd think one eye would be enough to see he was nothing but a skinny old geezer with more hair poking out of his ears than on his head, but she married him anyway. They lived in her fancy house on Lake Eufaula until she died. Then he bought himself a farm way out in the middle of nowhere and took to experimenting."

"Experimenting in what?" asked Ruby Bee, thinking of Dr. Frankenstein's laboratory with its blinking lights and body parts scattered around the floor. "Why doncha stop telling me his life story and get to the point, Estelle? It's nigh onto three o'clock, and I haven't finished cleaning up the kitchen so I can sit a spell and work on my column. Writing a weekly column ain't like making a grocery list, you know, and I have to turn it in by noon tomorrow if it's gonna appear in the *Shopper* on Saturday."

Estelle folded up the letter. "Why don't I wait until tomorrow evening to tell you the rest of it? I'd feel just awful if I interfered with scrubbing pots and writing about who's been in the hospital. Maybe I'll run by Elsie's for a cup of coffee and a nice visit. She's not as busy as some folks."

"Just tell me."

"Well, the letter says how Uncle Tooly was attacked by sheep in his front yard. He—"

"Sheep?" said Ruby Bee, snickering. "That's the silliest thing I've heard in my entire life. It sounds like one of those yarns Samsonite Buchanon would spin to anyone fool enough to listen. He could have been a regular guest on the *Geraldo* show."

"While Uncle Tooly was trying to get away, he fell and broke his hip. Three days later a neighbor happened to drive by and spot him sprawled in the grass, but it was too late for Uncle Tooly. His mouth was full of fleece. He'd died of dehydration and shock not fifty feet from a telephone."

"I'd sure go into shock if I was attacked by sheep. Was it a flock—or a gang?"

Estelle gave her a reproachful look. "We are talking about my kinfolk, one of whom passed away in a most tragic manner. I'd appreciate it if you could show some respect."

"Sorry," Ruby Bee murmured, reluctantly forgoing a remark about a "drive-by bleating." "Does this letter from the lawyer mean your uncle remembered you in his will?"

"Yes, it does. It doesn't say exactly what Uncle Tooly wanted me to have. He gave all his money to charities, so all I'm expecting is an heirloom of some sort. It's kind of exciting, though."

"What's exciting?" Kayleen asked as she came across the dance floor and joined them at the bar.

Estelle explained about the letter, adding, "I don't recall him having a coin or stamp collection, so it's liable to be a mantel clock or a ship in a bottle or a carton of family albums. The letter said it'll be delivered next week."

"How's the remodeling coming along?" Ruby Bee asked Kayleen, since there wasn't much point in discussing Estelle's inheritance till they found out what it was.

"The walls have been stripped of that cheap paneling and some boards in the floor have been replaced. All the wiring will have to be redone, though, and a lot of pipes are so rusty the water comes out like silt. I have a feeling I'll spend a goodly part of the next six months in the motel out back. That reminds me, Ruby Bee—I need to book a room for Sterling Pitts."

Estelle cocked her head. "I thought he was all gung ho about surviving in the woods. The Flamingo Motel's not much to look at, but it has your standard conveniences like hot water and clean sheets. The parking lot's hardly what you'd call rugged terrain."

"He needs a telephone and a place to set up a computer," Kayleen said. "Most of the time he'll be in the woods, but he likes to stay in communication with his office in case there's an emergency. To be honest, I don't think he's real thrilled about sleeping in a tent in this kind of weather. He's close to sixty and has spells of rheumatism."

Ruby Bee struggled not to sound sarcastic, but she didn't have much luck. "So he sleeps in a nice warm bed while the other fellows freeze their butts up on Cotter's Ridge? What do they think about it?"

"I don't rightly know." Kayleen took a pretzel from a basket and nibbled on it for a moment. "Can I ask y'all something of a different nature? I'm a little curious about Brother Verber. Is he originally from these parts? Do you know anything about his background and his family?"

Estelle and Ruby Bee smirked at each other, then Ruby Bee said, "He's been here for maybe ten years. Before that, I don't know where he was living, but you might ask Mrs. Jim Bob. You can be as sure as a goose goes barefoot that she knows every last detail of his life up to the time he moved into the rectory."

"I ran into her at the supermarket," Kayleen said with a wry smile, "and I have a feeling she won't tell me the time of day. She went right by me with her nose in the air and her lips squeezed tight, then made a production of telling someone in the next aisle that a pawnshop was nothing more than a gathering place for drug dealers and rapists. I can't imagine why she took such a dislike to me right off the bat, but she did. I felt like I had bad breath or oozing sores all over my face and hands."

Estelle decided to help out Ruby Bee, who clearly was having trouble finding a response. "Mrs. Jim Bob takes her role as the mayor's wife real serious, not to mention being president of the Missionary Society.

She thinks everybody should get her permission before they sneeze so she can make sure they have a
clean hankie.''

Ruby Bee nodded. "And she's suspicious of single women because she knows her husband strays with
every hussy in Stump County. If he had a notch in his
belt for every one of them, his trousers would be
around his ankles and he'd be waddlin' like a duck.''

"I prefer men with Christian values," Kayleen
said firmly. "Men who come from solid Anglo-Saxon
stock and are loyal and trustworthy, dedicated to their
beliefs.''

"Like Sterling Pitts?" suggested Ruby Bee. Match-
making was one of her favorite hobbies, and she'd
about given up on Arly.

"Sterling's married, so as far as I'm concerned,
he's ineligible. There's no chance Brother Verber has
a wife stashed away somewhere, is there?''

"I shouldn't think so," said Estelle. She stopped
and thought for a moment, then said, "Unless she's
in an insane asylum or prison. I don't suppose he'd
say anything that might reflect poorly on him as a
man of God.''

Ruby Bee scooted the pretzels out of Estelle's
reach. "That's hornswoggle—and you know it.
Brother Verber may have his faults, but I can't see
him leaving some pathetic woman locked up all these
years. Why, he got all misty at Kevin and Dahlia's wedding, and had to stop and blow his nose at least three
times before he pronounced them man and wife. He
almost single-handedly raised the money to put a bap-
tismal font in the Assembly Hall after one of the ladies
in the choir got chased across a gravel bar by a water
moccasin down at Boone Creek." She racked her

brain for other examples of his worthiness, not because she had all that much respect for him but to impress Kayleen. "He collects discarded clothes and spectacles to send to a mission in Africa, too."

"That ain't all he collects," Estelle inserted.

"Hush, Estelle," Ruby Bee said sharply, possibly because she was still smarting over the comment about the Flamingo Motel not being much to look at. "Tell you what, Kayleen—if I run across Mrs. Jim Bob, I'll tactfully see what I can find out about Brother Verber's past. Are you planning to attend the Sunday morning service?"

"I said I would." Kayleen slid off the stool and waggled her fingers at them. "I'd appreciate it if y'all didn't mention that I was asking questions about Brother Verber. I've lived in enough small towns to know how tongues get to wagging. I need to run along and make some calls." She paused in the middle of the dance floor and looked back at them. "You two are just being so sweet to me. Once I get the house fixed up, I'll have you over for supper so we can get to know each other even better."

Ruby Bee and Estelle smiled brightly until she was gone, then set aside their differences and got down to business discussing how to find out whatall they could about Brother Verber's past. It had never before been of interest, but now it was downright intriguing.

As Eileen Buchanon drove out of the clinic parking lot and headed toward Maggody, she glanced at her daughter-in-law. Dahlia was downcast, but no more than usual these days. Being pregnant was harder on her than it'd been on Eileen, what with the

strict diet and exercise program to control her blood
sugar. They'd had a real scare when Dahlia had allowed a faith healer to convince her the diabetes had
been cured, but his exposure as a quack had brought
her to her senses. What there were of them, anyway.

"What did the doctor say?" Eileen asked as she
slowed down for a chicken truck.

Dahlia sighed so gustily that the windshield
fogged up. "Same as he always sez, I reckon. I got to
keep pricking my finger and writing down the numbers in my notebook. I haft to come back next week
so he can poke my privates. He's still harping about
this test called a sonogram, but I ain't gonna allow it
on account of it turns the baby into a mutant with the
wrong number of arms and legs and eyes. No one's
doin' that to my baby."

"The doctor wouldn't suggest something like
that."

"He brings it up at every visit," she said, her
chins quivering with distress and her placid expression turning fierce. "I signed a paper saying I refused
to do it, and I meant it!"

Eileen finally got around the chicken truck and
pressed the accelerator. "What makes you think this
test would do the terrible things you said?"

"I read about it in the newspaper. Would you
stop at that gas station over there? My bladder's liable
to burst if I don't git to a potty real quick."

Eileen obliged, then glumly watched Dahlia disappear through a doorway on the side of the concrete
block building. Other than the diabetes, which was
under control, Dahlia seemed healthy and had gained
no more weight than the doctor had allowed. Women
had been giving birth for thousands of years without

complicated tests, and a good number of them were doing so these days. It was probably better not to cause Dahlia more distress by pressuring her to have a sonogram or anything else she didn't want. It was hard enough keeping her away from what she *did* want.

Jake "Blitzer" Milliford opened the closet door and squatted down to paw through the shoes on the floor. "Where're my boots?" he shouted at his wife, who was in the kitchen.

"Wherever you dropped them," Judy shouted back, more concerned with the cornbread in the oven and the beans in a pot on the stove. "Did you leave 'em on the back porch?"

He slammed the door and started hunting under the bed. "When's the last time you cleaned under here—Easter?"

She gave the beans a stir, then turned off the burner and came to the doorway. She was small-boned and barely came up to his shoulder, but living with him for twenty-three years had thickened her skin. It had also etched some wrinkles in her pretty face and turned some brown hairs gray, as well as extinguishing a good deal of what had once shone through her eyes. "Maybe you left them in the back of the truck," she suggested, "or in the toolshed."

"Bullshit."

"You ought to look anyway," she said, fully aware the boots were in the hall closet, where she'd put them after he left them on the kitchen table.

Jake got up off the floor and hitched up his worn, greasy jeans. "I ain't got time for a damn scavenger hunt. LaRue is pickin' me up as soon as he gets off work. He bought hisself a new laser sight for his Glock, and he wants to test it over at his brother's place."

"You don't need your boots for that, do you?"

He gave her a disgusted look. "No, I don't need my boots for that. I need 'em next week for the retreat. We'll leave for Maggody on Friday afternoon, soon as I can get away from the salvage yard. Shorty wasn't real happy with me missing work, but he shut up when I pointed out that everybody else'll call in sick all week long on account of deer season. At least I'm givin' him some warning."

"Were you aiming to mention this beforehand or was it supposed to be a surprise?"

He brushed past her and went into the front room to see if LaRue was out in the driveway. "Yeah, I was aiming to mention it beforehand," he muttered under his breath, then raised his voice. "When you find my boots, clean 'em up and set 'em on the back porch. While you're at it, see if the sleeping bags need to be hung out on the clothesline. Last summer I spilled some fish guts on one of them and it's liable to stink worse than a buzzard's roost by now. And check the cooking supplies. I ain't gonna be pleased if I have to drive back to Emmett because you forgot your pancake turner."

"What makes you think I'm going with you next week, Jake? I've got better things to do than sit around all day in a drafty tent and cook over a campfire. Friday evening I have a church bazaar committee meeting. I told Janine that I'd keep the baby on Saturday so she can get her hair cut and do a little shopping. She hasn't been out of the house in six weeks, and that fat lout she married won't even change a diaper."

"He puts groceries on the table, doesn't he? Janine's a whiner, same as you. It's gonna be cold and wet out at the campsite, and we need better than those gawdawful ready-to-eat meals. Janine doesn't have any call to waste her husband's hard-earned money on a hair cut. She can get a pair of scissors and whack it off herself."

Judy thought of something she'd like to whack off with a pair of scissors, but he most likely wouldn't appreciate hearing it. "Who all is going this time?"

"Who all is going?" he said in a falsetto, mocking her. "Do you think Pitts invited the cheerleaders over at the junior high and all the sumbitch politicians down in Little Rock? Same as last year, except for Carter Lee and Bradley. We figure we can dig up ol' Mo and prop him against a tent pole. It's not like we'd be able to tell the difference." He looked out the window, then took his jacket off a hook and made sure the can of Red Man was in the pocket. "LaRue's here. After we test the sight, we'll probably stop by the Dew Drop for a couple of beers. Don't wait up."

After she heard the truck back out of the driveway, Judy took the vodka bottle out from behind the cereal boxes, poured some in a glass and added a splash of orange juice, then returned to the living room to make a call.

She listened to the phone ring, instinctively smoothing her hair as if the person who picked up the receiver could see her. "Jake just now told me that retreat's set for next weekend," she began in a breathless voice.

On Saturday I could hear gunfire in the distance as I finished writing up a report for Harve about a motorcycle wreck out by what the high school kids called "Dead Man's Swerve." The driver hadn't been wearing a helmet, but since he was a Buchanon, landing on his head had done no perceptible damage. I'd had to explain this to the paramedic, who was concerned when the cyclist couldn't say for sure how many fingers the paramedic was holding up.

Deer season had officially started. I put down my gnawed pencil and opened a drawer to ascertain I had enough blank forms to survive the next three weeks. The previous year there'd been two wrecks out by the low-water bridge, a half-dozen DWIs, three instances involving nonfatal shootings, and one fatal shooting. Harve and I had agreed the last was suspicious, since the victim had been dating his companion's ex-wife, but there was no way to prove anything.

Earlier in the day Harve had called with the scoop on Sterling Pitts, which amounted to zilch. No rap sheet, no outstanding warrants, no entanglements with the law more serious than parking violations. A year ago Pitts had complained to the police about a neighbor's dog, and more recently about black teenagers loitering in his parking lot in the afternoons. All in all, he was a law-abiding citizen and a successful businessman, and there wasn't a damn thing I could do to keep him out of Maggody.

I was getting ready to take the accident report to the sheriff's office (and maybe take myself to a matinee) when the door opened and in stalked Raz Buchanon, a successful businessman if not precisely a law-abiding citizen. As always, he was wearing bib overalls stained with tobacco juice and other unidentifiable substances. His whiskers were caked with the remnants of meals from the previous decade, and what remained of his gray hair glistened with grease.

"I got to talk to you," he said as he plopped down in the chair and scratched his chin.

"And how are you today, Raz? Enjoying the last of the autumn foliage?"

"That ain't what I come here to talk about."

I rocked back in my chair, but there was no way short of going out the door to avoid his sour stench. "How's Marjorie these days? Is she snuffling up tasty acorns and hickory nuts?"

Raz let out a wheeze that engulfed me in a toxic haze. "Marjorie ain't doin' well. She's a pedigreed sow, ye know, and has a delicate nature. Lately she's taken to moping around the house, sprawled in the corner instead of in front of the television, turning up her snout at most ever'thing she used to gobble down. Why, yesterday evening she wouldn't take one bite of turnip greens."

"Did you fix them with ham hocks?" I asked.

He gave me a horrified look. "I'd never do something like that! That'd be like her eating kin. No, ma'am, I don't even use lard anymore." He resumed scratching his chin and sighing. "I reckon the problem she's bein' crumpy is on account of that dad-burned cousin of mine. You know about Diesel livin' up on the ridge?"

"Actually, I do."

"Well, used to be Marjorie'd wander around while I was"—he hesitated, obviously not wanting to confess to a felony right there in the PD—"huntin' squirrels or pickin' poke salet, but the other day she must've got too close to Diesel's cave. The next thing I knew, she came trotting as hard as she could into the clearing, her eyes all round and her ears pasted back, and squealing somethin' awful. Afore I could figure out what in tarnation was goin' on, Diesel charged right into me and liked to knock me plumb out of my boots."

I clucked sympathetically. "I don't know what to tell you, Raz. There aren't a lot of veterinarians trained to deal with traumatized sows, pedigreed or otherwise. All I can suggest is that you leave Marjorie at home when you go fiddle with your still."

"Who sez I got a still?" he said, puffing up indignantly.

"Get off it, Raz. Everybody in the damn county knows you have a still up on the ridge. One of these days the revenuers are going to locate it and reduce it to a pile of scrap metal. Moonshining's a federal offense. That means you'll be up in Leavenworth instead of enjoying the company of your relatives at the state pen."

His rheumy eyes met mine. "I ain't got a still and ain't nobody gonna find it. What do you aim to do about Diesel? He's got no call to scare Marjorie like that, or me, fer that matter."

"I'm not going to do anything," I said, shaking my head. "If you don't have business on Cotter's Ridge, stay off it. You and Marjorie shouldn't be there during deer season, anyway. Neither of you resembles a buck, but that doesn't cut any mustard with a bullet fired from a mile away." I stood up in hopes he'd take the hint and leave, but he remained seated, glowering like a jack o' lantern well past its prime. "Something else?" I asked.

"I heard there's gonna be some fellers dressed in soldier clothes crawling all over the ridge."

"There's nothing I can do about that, either. It's going to be crowded up there next week, Raz. Take my advice and stay away."

I held open the door and tried not to grimace as he shuffled past me and climbed into a muddy truck. The thought of Sterling Pitts and his followers had given me the stirrings of a headache; Raz's redolence had escalated it to the quintessence. The report I'd planned to take to Farberville could wait until Monday. In the interim, I was going to crawl into bed, cram a pillow over my head, and imagine what it would be like to be somewhere else.

Anywhere else.

On the far side of Stump County, Sterling sat in his Bronco, drumming his fingers on the steering wheel and watching raindrops slither down the windshield like transparent slugs. He was parked at one of their carefully chosen meeting places, a farm that had been abandoned more than ten years ago. The windows of the house were as vacant as a dead man's eyes, and the rusted screen door groaned as the wind dragged it across the surface of the porch.

Sterling reminded himself he was not the sort to entertain irrational notions about ghosts. He was organized, efficient, decisive, truly a general's general. The fact that his underlings were so ill-disciplined was disturbing; he made a mental note to require them to study their manuals and the additional guidelines he'd typed up and stapled to the back covers. After all, the Second Amendment stressed the need for a "well-regulated" militia as necessary to the security of a free state.

He pulled back his cuff to look at his watch. Red Rooster had agreed to be there at 1700. It was now 1720, and Sterling was growing increasingly peevish. It was cold, damp, and getting dark. His wife was expecting him to come straight home from his office to escort her to some fool dinner party. She had no idea what he did in his free time, but it was getting harder to come up with lies about conventions in other cities and emergency meetings at the office.

Muttering to himself, he switched on the ignition and prepared to leave. Before he could back up, however, a pickup truck came up the weedy driveway and stopped.

Reed climbed out of the driver's side and came around to the car. "So, did you check him out?" he asked loudly.

Sterling could smell the beer on Red Rooster's breath. "I do not care to be kept waiting while you and your friend are drinking beer in a bar somewhere. Were you also shooting off your yaps about our activities? Should I expect a carful of ATF agents to pull up next?"

"Naw, we just stopped off for a quick one on the way out here. Wasn't nobody else in the joint except for a bony hooker, and she was talking the whole time on her cell phone." He put his hand on the roof of the car and blearily smiled down at Sterling. "Did you hear back from Colorado?"

Sterling glanced at the young man in the pickup who was staring at the ramshackle farmhouse. "Yes, I communicated with the second-in-command in their group. He acknowledged that Dylan Gilbert had been with them for eighteen months before getting into trouble with the authorities in Denver. Apparently, he's quite adept with electronic surveillance equipment."

Reed turned and thumped the truck window. "Hey, Dylan, you fucker, you never told me you were a bug-meister."

Dylan rolled down the window, looked coolly at Pitts, and said, "I majored in electrical engineering for two years before I dropped out of college. What's the verdict? If I'm not welcome, I'll find another group someplace where the weather's not so shitty."

"Well?" Reed said to Sterling.

"The procedure," he said through clenched teeth, "is for the cell to interrogate a potential recruit before taking action. I for one have questions about why he came here and chose to make contact with you instead of having his former commander contact me through proper channels. I also need time to verify his credentials. Then, if we are unanimous in our decision to accept him, he will be inducted as soon as possible. Until that time, he can participate in the training, but he will not be present at sessions of a more tactical nature."

Reed grinned at Dylan. "That okay?"

"Exactly what I anticipated," Dylan answered without inflection. He pushed long black hair out of his eyes and stared at Sterling. "I've got some questions of my own, Pops. I don't want to get hooked up with a bunch of guys who are liable to spill secrets to the nearest undercover cop. I've got the FBI searching for me, and not so they can wish me a happy

Thanksgiving. With my juvenile rap sheet and a few minor felonies since then, I'm looking at up to forty years."

Sterling bristled. "You have no fear of indiscretion from this group," he said sternly (if somewhat mendaciously, considering his previous thoughts). "We are highly disciplined and tight-lipped."

"Gotta take a wiz," Reed announced, then stumbled into the darkness.

Dylan waited until Reed was out of sight, then gave Sterling a contemptuous smile. "Then aren't you concerned about the informant in your group, Pops?"

From *The Starley City Star Shopper,* November 8:

What's Cooking in Maggody?
by Rubella Belinda Hanks

This column is going to be short on account of nobody much bothered to share any news with me, even though I'm right here in Ruby Bee's Bar & Grill from morning till midnight, fixing everything from grits and redeye gravy to fried chicken and scalloped potatoes. The food's tasty, and the price is right.

Mrs. Twayblade out at the county old folks' home reports the residents spent a real nice afternoon making turkeys out of pine cones and colored paper to decorate their tables on Thanksgiving. Everybody enjoyed themselves except for Petrol Buchanon, who had to be sent to his room after he pinched a nurse's aide on her fanny.

Estelle Oppers is all excited about an inheritance from her Uncle Tooly, who was killed by sheep. It's supposed to arrive sometime this week. She said to tell everybody that she has a big assortment of fingernail polish and lipsticks at bargain prices, and her ten-percent discount on perms will run until December 24.

There's still no date for the grand opening of Smeltner's Pawn Palace, but Kayleen says she should be in business by the end of the year. Progress is just as slow on her remodeling out on County 102 because all the workmen are off deer hunting instead of showing up like they promised.

Arly Hanks, our chief of police, asked me to remind hunters that not wearing bright orange is against the law, just like hunting on property that's been posted. If you're over in Farberville, stop by the sheriff's department to pick up a free pamphlet with tips on gun safety.

Until next time, God bless.

Garlic Cheese Grits

6   cups water
2   teaspoons salt
1½   cups grits
2   teaspoons (or more) garlic powder
¼   teaspoon cayenne pepper
1   stick butter
3   eggs, beaten
1   pound grated cheddar cheese

Bring the water to a boil, add the salt, and
slowly stir in the grits. Cook according to the
directions on the box. Add the rest of the
ingredients, stir real well until the butter melts,
then pour into a buttered baking dish. Bake
1 hour and 15 minutes, or until the top is
puffy and golden.

CHAPTER 4

"Maybe you should call that Oklahoma lawyer," Ruby Bee said as she tied a scarf on her head and studied the effect in the bathroom mirror. "For all you know, he could be sending some of those killer sheep. You can't just let them run around your living room."

Her only response was a snort from the living room. Estelle had come by to take her to the Sunday morning service at the Assembly Hall, but she'd shown up ten minutes early and was being all persnickety because Ruby Bee hadn't been standing in the parking lot and ready to leap into the station wagon as it rolled by.

Estelle finally relented. "I thought about it, but I don't want to run up my long distance bill. I don't have more than two or three appointments this coming week, one of 'em for nothing but a trim. All I can say is, there are going to be some mighty scruffy folks eating turkey and cranberries this year."

"I suppose it can't hurt to wait," Ruby Bee said as she came into the living room and put on her coat. "There's a lot of that going around. Kayleen's waiting on the plumber, Dahlia and Kevin are waiting on the

stork, customers at the SuperSaver are waiting on
themselves since all the employees are deer hunting,
Antwon Buchanon's waiting on his roof for a chariot
to swing low and carry him home, and Arly's waiting
for the first casualty on Cotter's Ridge. I'm waiting to
find out what the IRS is going to do when they don't
get my fourth quarterly payment."

"Is that what's been bothering you?" asked Estelle, pulling on her gloves.

Ruby Bee opened the door, then recoiled as the
wind snatched at her scarf. "I reckon so. If business
doesn't pick up, I'm not going to have two dimes to
rub together on New Year's Day. It's not like Arly can
loan me enough to tide me over, either. When I told
her that she needed a warmer coat, she just laughed
and said something about saving up for mink. One of
these days . . ."

"She'll leave?"

Ruby Bee waited to answer until they were settled
in Estelle's station wagon and the heater was on. "I'm
surprised she's stayed so long. There aren't but a scattering of people her age, and they're married and
busy with babies. I can't remember when she last mentioned that nice state trooper, or even hinted that she
was seeing somebody on the sly. The light's on in her
apartment most every night. It ain't natural."

They drove to the Assembly Hall, but after some
discussion about not getting caught in traffic after the
service, decided to park across the road in front of
the soon-to-be Pawn Palace.

Estelle gestured at the dark interior. "You spoken
to her lately?"

"No, I haven't laid eyes on her since she was in
the bar and grill the other day when you were talking

about Uncle Tooly's will. I guess she's been out at the Wockermann place, trying to do the carpentry work herself. It burns me up how every male in the county that's over the age of ten sees nothing wrong with forgetting about work in order to go deer hunting. It's a good thing doctors don't feel the same way."

"Or lawyers," added Estelle, wondering if Uncle Tooly might have set aside some stocks and bonds in her name because of the homemade cookies she sent every year at Christmas. Blue chips in exchange for chocolate chips, in a manner of speaking.

Ruby Bee pointed at the front of the Assembly Hall. "Well, look who got himself dragged to church this morning. I'd have thought Jim Bob would be up on the ridge in the trailer that he, Roy, and Larry Joe use as a deer camp. You can tell from the way he's walking that he hasn't worn those dress shoes in a good while, and his collar looks tight enough to choke the cud out of a cow. Do you think Mrs. Jim Bob finally put the fear of God in him?"

"Right now she looks like she could put the fear of God in most anybody, including ol' Satan himself," Estelle replied. "Did you ever get a chance to ask her about Brother Verber's mysterious past?"

"There is nothing mysterious about his past, Estelle. We just don't know anything about it. No, I haven't tried to worm the details out of her as of yet. I saw her in the SuperSaver, but she was being so crabby with the checkout girl that I figured it wasn't a good time."

They joined the stream of souls heading into the foyer and found seats toward the back so they could be the first out the door after the closing "Amen." After nodding to Earl and Eileen and a few other folks, Ruby Bee whispered, "There's Kayleen in the second pew. Brother Verber must have nagged her into coming."

"Or sweet-talked her into it," Estelle whispered back, then resumed speculating about her inheritance. Maybe a deed to a piece of acreage she could sell for a tidy sum, or even a set of china or expensive silverware. Uncle Tooly had once owned a fancy antique car; his one-eyed wife might have given him another one as a wedding present. Or a mantel clock, she reminded herself.

Eula Lemoy pounded out the opening hymn, which was kind of hard to recognize and downright impossible to sing along with. Folks coughed and sneezed through the announcements, the passing of the collection plate, and a solo sung by an atonal teen-aged girl. Brother Verber presided from his folding chair set to one side, alternately smiling at the congregation and wincing at the sour notes. At one point, Ruby Bee thought he winked, but decided it was more likely a gnat got in his eye.

Eventually, the girl ran out of steam, curtsied, and scurried to her seat. Brother Verber stood up, stuck out what chin he had, and walked to the lectern as if he were leading a processional to the guillotine.

"Brothers and sisters," he said, dragging out the words as he made eye contact with as many folks as he could, "I have in my possession some information that is so startling that you may think it came from a tabloid. Some of you will laugh at what I'm gonna share with you this morning. Some of you will sneer. Some of you, like Earl Buchanon and Lewis Ferncliff, will snooze through the sermon same as you do every Sunday morning. But those of you who listen with an open mind are gonna be shocked. That's right, brothers and sisters—*shocked*!''

Uneasiness rippled through the congregation as they prepared themselves for this electrifying revelation. Earl sat up straight so everybody could see he was wide-awake. Lottie Estes settled her reading glasses on the bridge of her nose, then took a pad and pencil from her purse in case she needed to take notes. Dahlia sighed, wondering if Brother Verber was gonna carry on so long she'd wet her pants. Ruby Bee and Estelle wiggled their eyebrows at each other.

Brother Verber cleared his throat and scanned his notes one last time. ''We're gonna begin with a passage from Genesis, chapter twelve, verses one through three: 'Now the Lord had said unto Abraham, Get thee out of thy country, and from thy kindred, and from thy father's house, unto a land that I will shew thee. And I will make of thee a great nation, and I will bless thee, and make thy name great, and thou shalt be a blessing: And I will bless them that bless thee, and curse him that curseth thee: and in thee shall all families of the earth be blessed.' ''

He gave them a moment to stew on that, then smiled and shook his head. ''That ain't all. Now let's take a gander at chapter twenty-two, verses seventeen and eighteen, where the Lord's still talking to Abraham: 'That in blessing I will bless thee, and in multiplying I will multiply thy seed as the stars of the heaven and as the sand which is upon the sea shore, and thy seed shall possess the gate of his enemies. And in thy seed shall all the nations of the earth be blessed; because thou hast obeyed my voice.' ''

''Sounds like Abraham won't need to buy any seeds at the co-op this spring,'' Earl said, then grunted as his wife's elbow caught him in the ribcage.

Brother Verber shot Earl a dirty look. "These have to do with producing children, not soybeans, and the multiplying ain't the two-times-two sort of multiplying. What you just now heard is called the Abrahamic Covenant, and it was made some thirty-eight hundred years ago. Yes, the Lord gave Abraham a thirty-eight-hundred-year warranty on his seed because he obeyed the Lord's voice and commandments. You can bet Abraham was pleased as punch, and his children and grandchildren and their children and so forth were, too."

Suddenly, his expression darkened and his hands gripped the sides of the podium. He waited until everybody stopped squirming and sneaking glances at their watches, then dropped his voice to a throaty whisper. "But then the tables turned. Shalmaneser, the king of Assyria, marched his army into Israel, and took prisoners back to places like"—he consulted his notes—"Halah and Medes. Thirteen years later, the Assyrian army came back for more, and that ain't the end of it. In the year five hundred and ninety-six B.C., Nebuchadnezzar, the king of Babylon, attacked Jerusalem and pretty much captured the last of the Israelites. Now where do you think all these seeds of Abraham ended up?"

Nobody offered a guess. Earl's chin was on his chest and he was snoring softly. Dahlia was trying to determine if she could get out of the pew without stepping on too many toes. Beside her, Kevin was tugging at his collar and wondering if Kevin Junior would have Dahlia's eyes. Lottie Estes was agonizing over the correct spelling of Nebuchadnezzar. Mrs. Jim Bob was perplexed, aware that Brother Verber's religious

training through the mail-order seminary in Las Vegas
had been slanted toward the consequences of sinful
behavior rather than obscure biblical history. Beside
her, Jim Bob was cursing himself for coming home
from the poker game at two in the morning with whiskey on his breath—and discovering his wife sitting in
the kitchen.

Brother Verber went in for the kill. "All these
seeds ended up in the Caucacus mountains or there-
abouts—which is why they became known as Caucasians. Now, they didn't stay there forever, these twelve
tribes of Israel. After maybe a hundred years, they
packed their bags and migrated toward the west.
When they got someplace they liked, they settled
down and took names like Celts, Teutones, Gaels,
Scots, and Scandinavians. After a time, some of them
like the Vikings and Pilgrims sailed across the Atlantic
Ocean to a place called North America. Let's have a
look at Second Samuel, chapter seven, verse ten,
where the Lord says plain as day: 'Moreover I will ap-
point a place for my people Israel, and will plant them
so they may dwell in a place of their own, and move
no more; neither shall the children of wickedness af-
flict them any more, as beforetime.' " He took out a
handkerchief and blotted his forehead, stealing a
peek at Kayleen. She nodded encouragingly at him,
her eyes all dewy with admiration.

"So what this boils down to," he continued, "is
two things. One is that we're Caucasians and therefore the true descendants of the twelve tribes of Israel,
who were assured by the Lord that they were the chosen people. The second is that we are living in the
Promised Land right here and right now!" He
thumped the podium for emphasis, then rocked back

on his heels and waited while everybody considered what he'd said. Everybody but Earl, of course.

Mrs. Jim Bob stood up. "Are you saying that we're Jewish?" she asked.

"Not for a second," he assured her, hoping he had his facts straight. "I'm saying that the Jews are *not* descended from the twelve tribes of Israel, any more than the Africans or the Ethiopians or the Eskimos—because they ain't Caucasians. Only the folks from the western Christian nations qualify."

As Mrs. Jim Bob sank down to sort this out, Eula Lemoy fluttered her hand. "And the United States of America is the Promised Land?"

Brother Verber nodded. "Just like the Lord promised in the Abrahamic Covenant. Let's all bow our heads and offer a prayer of thankfulness for this blessing that has been bestowed on us."

Raz Buchanon spat angrily as a gun was fired somewhere higher up on Cotter's Ridge. "These dad-burned city folk got no call to come here and start shootin' at anything that moves," he muttered to Marjorie, who'd refused to get out of the truck. "And if Diesel values his worthless hide, he'd better stay away from here. I'd sooner blow off his head as look at him!"

Marjorie blinked as sunlight glinted off the copper tubes and empty Mason jars.

"What's more," Raz went on, "I ain't gonna feel any kindlier toward those soldier fellers if they come snoopin' around here. I'll blast the lot of them to Kingdom Come. You jest see if I don't." He spat again, glared so savagely at a squirrel that it liked to fall off a branch, then replenished his chaw and re-

turned his attention to the fine art of making moonshine. Business was always real good during the
holiday season.

Jake Milliford belched as he pushed away from
the kitchen table. "Fine dinner," he forced himself
to say, not being comfortable throwing out compliments but doing it anyway. Short of stuffing Judy in a
gunny sack and putting her in the back of the truck,
there wasn't any way he could force her to go to Maggody for four days. He should have been able to just
lay down the law 'cause she was his wife, but he knew
better than to try it. "I'm gonna go watch the game.
When you get finished with the dishes, come into the
living room."

"I'm not interested in ballgames," she said as she
carried his plate to the sink. "I told Janine I'd come
over this afternoon and help her make curtains for
the nursery. She found a real cute gingham print on
sale—"

"You don't have to sit there all afternoon. I got
something to show you. After that, you can go wherever you please." He left the room before she could
start whining, which, as far as he was concerned, was
about all she ever did. It wasn't like all he ever did
was lie around the house all day or take off two weeks
to go deer hunting. No, he worked eight-hour shifts
five days a week at the salvage yard just to keep them
from having to live in a neighborhood where they'd
be surrounded by lazy half-breeds. He didn't go
around beating up faggots like some of the fellows
did. He took her to church most Sundays, even
though he didn't cotton to all the pious shit about
lovin' thy neighbor and turnin' the other cheek. The

only time he was gonna turn the other cheek was while he was pulling out a gun.

"What do you want?" said Judy, coming to the doorway with her coat over her arm.

He picked up a six-foot aluminum pole. "LaRue gave me this to try. It's called a take-down blowgun, and it's supposed to be accurate up to sixty feet. He said he got himself an eleven-pound turkey."

"So?"

"So I was showing it to you. At halftime, I'm gonna go out back and see if it's as powerful and accurate as LaRue sez. If it is, I'm gonna order one for myself and a shorter one for you."

"What would I do with it? You know I don't like to hunt."

"When the time comes that we have to take to the woods, you may need it for self-defense."

Judy put on her coat. "Well, at least you can't shoot yourself in the foot with it. I'll be back at suppertime. Don't call me over at Janine's. We're going to try to get the curtains done while the baby's napping, and the phone always wakes him up."

"Why would I want to call you?"

"To stop by the store or something. Anyway, don't do it if you want supper on the table tonight. We're determined to finish the curtains in one sitting."

"Okay, okay," he muttered, stroking the polished aluminum of the blowgun. The darts with their colorful plastic tips only cost about ten cents apiece. He might just forget about the game and find out if they were as lethal as LaRue said.

"What's up, Harve?" I asked, having made the tactical error of stopping by the PD for a magazine and feeling obliged to find out who'd left a message on the answering machine. Most of them tend to be from Ruby Bee and therefore on the monotonous side.

"Thought you was gonna have that accident report here yesterday," he said.

"My dog ate it, but I'll write up another one and bring it over tomorrow. It's not exactly the stuff of which bestsellers are made."

He rumbled unhappily. "That ain't the real reason I called, Arly. I need you to do me a favor and go check out a burglary on a county road over past Drippersville. I'm real short-handed on account of all my boys calling in sick. Odd how something always goes around this time of year, ain't it? If I were a suspicious sort—and we both know I'm not—I'd almost wonder if deer season had anything to do with it."

"So what's the deal in Drippersville?"

"It's the fourth damn burglary in the last month. The same MO, too. The houses are in remote areas and the owners are out of town. The perps break a window, collect everything of value, and waltz out the back door and load their vehicles. None of the stolen goods have turned up in the county."

I made the face that Ruby Bee always complains will leave more lines than a road map. "Professionals?"

"Damn straight," Harve said. "They pull out all the trays and serving pieces, then take the silver and leave the cheap stuff on the floor. They don't take jars of pennies or paste jewelry. They didn't bother with a computer that was a couple of years old."

"And nobody's seen them coming or going?"

"Like I said, the houses are in areas without

neighbors. The owners are on vacation, and none of them sees anybody lurking nearby when they put suitcases in the trunk. At the third house, the guy'd rigged up a device to make the lights go on at dusk and off at midnight so it'd look like someone was there, but it didn't do a damn bit of good. In fact, the perps hung around long enough to cook a frozen pizza."

I found a notepad and a pencil. "Okay, I'll go out there and look around. Give me directions to the house."

Reed banged down the telephone receiver, then took a couple of deep breaths to steady himself. "The bitch says she's filing for a divorce first thing in the morning," he told Barry. "She already talked to a lawyer, and he told her she can take half my paycheck for the next fifteen years. Fifteen fucking years! Her brother's coming over toward the end of the week to get the rest of her crap." He made a fist and hit the wall with such fury the plaster cracked. "Goddamn it to hell! I'm not putting up with this shit! I've got half a mind to drive over there and beat her until she gets down on her hands and knees and begs to come back."

Barry quite agreed Reed had half a mind (and not a fraction more). "Then she'll file charges like she did last time, and you'll find yourself doing ninety days at the county jail."

"At least she won't get half of any paychecks," Reed said, examining his knuckles for cuts.

Dylan Gilbert came out of the kitchen, a glass of milk in one hand and a sandwich in the other. "What's going on?"

"Reed was talking to his wife," said Barry. "I would have thought you could hear every word. Are you sure you used to be a college boy?"

"Phi Beta Kappa," he said, then kicked an empty beer can off the couch and sat down. He was wearing jeans and a neatly pressed shirt, and his hair was still damp from the shower. "Sure, I heard, but he calls to yell at her at least three times a day. I was just wondering if there had been any new developments in the drama."

"Hell, no." Reed stomped into the kitchen and returned with a bottle of tequila and a smudged glass. "You know what they call a roomful of lawyers? A target. Maybe we can find out where they hold their annual convention and blow 'em all sky-high."

Barry lifted his eyebrows. "An interesting idea, but a very imprudent one. Let's save our energies and resources for a more significant project. Don't you agree, Dylan?"

"I've never had any use for lawyers, especially the public defenders who want you to plead out so they won't have to waste a day in court. However, I agree that we have better things to do than disrupt a bar association luncheon." He took a bite of the sandwich and washed it down with milk, his eyes never leaving Barry's face. "I've heard Reed's life story, but I don't know much about you."

"And I don't know anything about you," Barry countered.

"There's nothing to know. I grew up in Idaho. When my father lost his ranch to the bloodsuckers at the bank, we moved to a compound where he worked in the machine shop and my mother taught school. I split five years ago, did a couple of years of college, and ended up with the Denver brethren. Now I'm here until something better comes along."

Barry sat back and gave him a bemused look. "Reed said you tried to send a bomb to a federal judge and brought the feds down on you. Did you put a return address on the package or what?"

"Get off it," said Reed. "Nobody's that stupid, fer chrissake." He paused to down a shot of tequila. "Except for that bitch Bobbi Jo and her brother. They've probably been screwing each other since they were in grade school."

Dylan showed small, even teeth. "It seems someone called the FBI and mentioned my name. I don't know what else they had, but they had enough to get the warrant. I didn't stick around to hear the details or to track down the squealer and have a talk with him. One of these days I will, though."

Although Dylan's voice had been unemotional to the point of blandness, Barry felt a twinge of apprehension. Dylan was dangerous, he decided. Reed was too, but in a blustery, see-it-coming sort of way; he was as subtle as a grizzly bear charging through a thicket. Dylan was more of a poisonous snake, silently gliding through the grass, its eyes slitted and its tongue flicking as it approached its prey.

Barry put on his cap and reached for his jacket. "Guess I'm going. I'll see you Friday in Maggody."

Reed ignored him. "Hey, Dylan, you ever re-armed a sixty-six-millimeter light antitank weapon?"

In a much nicer house in a neighborhood populated by white Anglo-Saxon Methodists, Baptists, Presbyterians, and a smattering of Episcopalians, Sterling Pitts sat in his study. The proposal for the group health plan should have occupied his attention, but he was seated in a leather chair, staring sightlessly at the photograph of himself holding up a large, dead fish. An informant in their midst? Members came and went, either voluntarily like Carter Lee or involuntarily like Bradley and Mo. But he, Reed, Barry, and Jake had been involved since they met at a week-long retreat in Missouri. Reed and Barry were fresh out of the army; Reed, in particular, was having a hard time adjusting to civilian life and was ripe to be recruited. Barry had proved himself by setting a fire in a warehouse in Little Rock. Jake was taciturn, but his eyes blazed and he had plenty to say whenever the talk turned to the mongrelization of the white race by civil rights legislation.

Sterling had been unable to recontact his counterpart in Colorado. He'd tried e-mail, but the address had been switched. The only telephone number he knew had been disconnected, which was not surprising since many of those in the movement often moved to ensure their privacy.

He took a pen and wrote down the code names: Silver Fox, Red Rooster, Apocalypse, Blitzer. It was unthinkable that any one of them would betray the cell. Judy Milliford seldom evinced enthusiasm, but she was too mousy to envision in such a role. Kayleen was deeply dedicated; he could hear it in her voice whenever they spoke about the insidiousness of the federal government and the threat posed by the international conspiracy. If she'd not been a woman, she would have easily replaced Mo in the hierarchy.

But Dylan Gilbert swore he'd received the tip from a double agent in Oklahoma. He'd been given no hint about the duration of this despicable infiltration. Sterling looked back down at the code names, imagining faces and recalling fragments of conversation. Had anyone inadvertently slipped up? Had anyone missed a meeting and been unable to supply a satisfactory excuse?

Most important, was there a way to force the informant to expose himself? If so, justice would be served coldly and swiftly. There was no place for mercy if the movement was ultimately to succeed.

CHAPTER 5

On Sunday afternoon I'd obliged Harve and gone to the scene of the burglary in Drippersville, but it had been a bigger waste of time than trying to teach Diesel to read (Buchanons don't get hooked on phonics). The break-in had been discovered by a neighbor who'd stopped by to put bags over the rose bushes to protect them from frost; the owners were on their way back from Florida to make an inventory of the stolen items. A deputy showed up to take fingerprints, but none of the prints from the earlier burglaries had set off bells and whistles in the FBI files. My report had been written Monday morning in less than ten minutes (I left out my poetic musings about the sense of intrusion that lingered like a bad cold).

By Wednesday morning, I'd written a few more reports, most involving trespassing on private land and one in which a 1982 Pontiac Grand Am was mistaken for Bambi's dear old dad. If Raz had run into any wayward hunters, he'd buried the bodies in shallow graves and kept it to himself. Which was fine with me.

I'd just refilled my coffee mug and settled down

to do some serious whittling when Dahlia stormed into the PD.

"You got to look at this," she said, thrusting a much-creased pamphlet at me. "Kevvie tried to hide it underneath his boxers, but I found it anyway. I wanna know what it means."

"How are you feeling?"

She sat down. "I reckon I'm doing fine, excepting I can't sleep for more than fifteen minutes without having to go to the pottie. My finger's a dad-burned pincushion. Kevvie's scared to so much as touch me 'cause he thinks it's not fittin' in front of the baby. I ain't had a Nehi for seven and a half months."

"It'll all be over soon," I said soothingly, "and then you can have a Nehi whenever you want. Have you and Kevin chosen names for the baby?"

"We're gonna name him Kevin Fitzgerald Buchanon, Junior. I think it's kinda long for such a little thing, but Kevvie won't have it any other way. Ma suggested we call him Jerry so's not to confuse the two. I don't know where she came up with that, though."

"Then you're sure it's a boy?" I asked. "Did you have some sort of test at the clinic?"

"I came here 'cause I want you to read that thing and tell me what's going on. There's something about it that stinks like a backed-up septic tank, but I can't rightly put my finger on it."

I picked up the pamphlet. " 'Our nation is in terrible danger,' " I read aloud. " 'No longer can we trust our elected officials to run the country according to the premises laid out by the dedicated and selfless patriots who formulated the Declaration of Independence and the Constitution of the United States.

Many of these patriots lost their families, properties, and lives to make this republic free from oppressive governments and dictatorships, a republic with freedom and liberty, a republic guided by the principles of the one true God.' " Frowning, I turned to the second page.

"So whatall does that mean?" demanded Dahlia. "Is it true that Congress and all the big corporations can do whatever they please without paying any attention to the needs of the ordinary folks like Kevvie and me? That the 'Pledge of Allegiance' we always recited in school should have been called 'The Pledge of Alliance with the International Conspiracy'?" She put her hand on her pendulous bosom in case I couldn't follow her. "You know, 'I pledge allegiance to the flag—' "

"I know," I interrupted, continuing to skim the blurry purple words that had been reproduced on an old-fashioned mimeograph machine. When I was finished, I put it aside and said, "This is crazy stuff, Dahlia. Do you have any idea where Kevin got hold of it?"

"Most likely at the SuperSaver. He don't go anyplace else except there, the Assembly Hall, and his ma and pa's house. He promised to stay real close in case the baby comes early and I got to hightail it to the hospital."

"Was this all you found in the drawer?"

"Oh, I forgot." She dug into a pocket hidden in the folds of her tent dress and pulled out a crumpled slip of paper. "This sez there's a meeting for concerned citizens on Saturday morning at ten o'clock. They can learn how to protect themselves and their families from"—her brow crinkled with exertion as she sounded out the words—"oppression and sub-mission to a foreign army."

I winced. "Does it mention where this is going to be held?"

"It sez to go one mile east on County 102 and look for signs. Shouldn't you be doin' something to stop the country from being invaded by foreigners that want to take away our babies and put us in concentration camps? I don't want someone to snatch my baby right out of my arms, Arly."

"I think we're safe. Maggody's not on the maps, so it's unlikely the foreigners can find us any time soon. May I keep this pamphlet?"

"I 'spose so," she said, sniffling. She wiped her cheeks on her sleeve, then struggled to her feet and trudged out the door. The walls didn't come tumbling down, but the coffee in my mug may have sloshed a couple of times.

I reread the pamphlet more carefully. There were no specifics about the ethnicity of the so-called conspirators, but it wasn't difficult to figure out. A lot of the text was aimed at small farmers, demanding to know why our government ignored their plight in order to bankroll a politically unstable Middle East aggressor state. I doubted the author had North Carolina or Virginia in mind. Affirmative action was another bogeyman under the bed, stealing good jobs from hard-working Christians with families to feed. There were murky references to brainwashing in the public schools, fluoride in the water, and the unlawful imposition of income taxes.

It was one thing for General Pitts and his group to embrace this dogmatic twaddle and act on it by donning olive drab for a weekend. It was another to attempt to recruit locals to their cause. Maggody was hardly a hotbed of resentment leveled at the federal government; the majority of the residents griped more about the weather than they did about taxes. However, we'd had a manifestation of mass hysteria at the end of the summer that rivaled nothing I'd ever seen. Even Estelle and Ruby Bee had been sucked into the madness.

I put the pamphlet in my coat pocket and went out to the car. I'd planned to confront Kayleen, but I decided to grab some lunch first and find out what was on the grapevine. There was a smaller than usual assembly of pickup trucks outside Ruby Bee's, most of them adorned with gun racks and bumper stickers extolling the virtues of the NRA. As I walked across the barroom, I spotted several pamphlets lying beside pitchers and napkin dispensers.

"Where have you been all week, missy?" Ruby Bee asked as I chose a stool near Estelle's roost. "I left three messages on that infernal answering machine on Monday and four yesterday. You better take it to be repaired."

"You're probably right," I said meekly. "Can I have meat loaf and mashed potatoes?"

She folded her arms. "I don't believe you answered my question, and I don't want to hear how you're cooking for yourself in that dingy apartment. There's no way to prepare a well-balanced meal on a stove with only one working burner and an oven that never heats up."

"That's why I'm here for lunch, but if you're not going to serve me, I'll go across the street to the deli in the SuperSaver and get a ham sandwich. Do dill pickles count as vegetables?"

"Keep your tail in the water," she said, conceding defeat as graciously as always, then went into the kitchen.

I glanced over my shoulder at the customers in the booths, wishing I could eavesdrop to discover their collective reaction to the pamphlets. However, the jukebox drowned out whatever was being said, and everybody appeared more interested in beer than inflammatory rhetoric.

Ruby Bee returned with a plate piled high with meat loaf, et cetera, and I had just picked up my fork when Estelle skidded across the dance floor, her hair tilting at a precarious angle.

"Arly! I been looking everywhere for you! I left my engine running so it'll be faster for you to ride with me!"

Ruby Bee's jaw dropped. "Land sakes, Estelle, you sound like your house is on fire. What's wrong? Did Uncle Tooly's lawyer send those sheep?"

Estelle grabbed my arm, and between gasps, said, "Someone broke into Elsie's house! Let's go!"

"Is he still there?" I said as I reluctantly put down the fork.

"We don't know. Lottie went by to feed the cat, and she noticed right away that a window was broken and the back door was open. She wasn't about to run smackdab into a criminal, so she drove home and called the PD. When nobody answered, she called me to ask me what she should do. I said I had a pretty good idea where to find you."

Catching Harve's professional perps might be more satisfying than meat loaf, I told myself as I slid off the stool. "Can you keep the plate warm in the oven?" I asked Ruby Bee.

"Where's your gun?"

"Where it's supposed to be," I said as Estelle dragged me toward the door. "Calm down, for pity's sake. Why did you come all the way over here instead of calling?"

Instead of answering my question, she dove into the driver's seat and slammed the car into reverse. Before I could close my door, we were halfway across the parking lot.

"Slow down, damn it!" I said as she pulled out in front of a truck.

"If we get there quick enough, we can catch 'em in the act," she said. "You'll be a hero and get a reward from Elsie's insurance company. It seems to me giving you a small sum would be a sight cheaper than replacing Elsie's Hummel collection."

I closed my eyes and reminded myself of the necessity of breathing as she squealed around a corner and headed down an unpaved road. The station wagon was bouncing madly, but the grim driver made no concessions to the specter of bent axles and broken oil pans.

She slammed on the brakes at the foot of Elsie's driveway. "I'll watch the front of the house while you go around back. We don't know how many there are of them or if they're armed, so keep your eyes peeled."

"Wait a minute," I said as she opened her door. "For starters, you're going to stay right here until I make sure there's no one, armed or otherwise, in the house. If you don't see me on the porch within five minutes, drive back to the bar and call the sheriff's office. Have them send a backup to the bar, then lead them here."

Estelle hesitated, one foot on the gravel. "Maybe we ought to go to the PD to get your gun. Ruby Bee'd never forgive me if you got yourself killed."

"Neither would I." I left her twitching indecisively and walked up the driveway, fairly sure the burglars were long gone. There had been no mention of a vehicle by the back door, and even if there'd been one, Lottie's arrival and hasty departure would have sent the burglars on their way.

The back door was ajar, and a window next to it was broken. I eased open the door, listening for an indication someone might be in the house ("fairly sure" is not the same thing as "absolutely certain"), and stepped into the kitchen. When nothing much happened, I veered around a muddy path and continued into the living room, then poked my head into the two bedrooms and bathroom. I was tempted to make sure no one was hiding in a closet or under a bed, but I was worried that Estelle might panic and drive away to summon the sheriff, the state police, and the National Guard. The Mounties, too, if she could find their telephone number.

I went out on the porch. "It's okay, Estelle," I yelled, waving at the station wagon. "Go let Ruby Bee know I didn't get myself shot defending the Hummels."

Her face popped up from the far side. "How do I know there ain't someone behind you sticking a gun in your back?"

This was not your typical crime-scene scenario in which the ranking officer on the scene barks out orders that are promptly and unquestioningly obeyed.

"Suit yourself," I yelled, then went back inside, sat down on a settee, and called the sheriff's office.

LaBelle did her best to remind me I'd fallen from grace, but eventually put me through to Harve.

"Another one?" he said after I'd told him where I was. "Goddammit, I feel like I should put bars on all the windows here—the ones that don't already have 'em. Can you tell what was taken?"

I looked around the room. "Probably a TV set, if the cable dangling from the wall is any indication. The Hummel figurines were not deemed worthy. I doubt Elsie had a computer or a silver tea service, but we'll have to wait until she can get back here and determine what's missing. Lottie Estes probably knows how to reach her."

"We've got to put a stop to this, Arly. The election's coming up real soon, and this is making me look bad. If my opponent wasn't dumber than a possum, I'd think he was behind it."

"There has to be a link," I said, feeling slightly dumber than a possum myself. "The houses are too far apart to have the same carrier, but the owners might have notified the post office to hold their mail. Same thing with the area newspapers, although there's no home delivery in Maggody. Even if she could afford it, Elsie wouldn't have a cleaning service. She didn't leave her cat at a kennel." I plucked at a crocheted doily on the armrest as I racked my mind for other feasible links. "Do you want me to interview all the previous victims and see if I can stumble onto something useful?"

"Yeah, I guess so," Harve said with a drawn-out wheeze. "Your phony soldiers caused any problems as of yet?"

I decided not to mention the pamphlet for the moment. "They won't be here for another two days, which gives me some time to work on the burglaries. It'll be more stimulating than trespassers and drunks."

"I'll send Les out to take fingerprints and photos of whatever footprints you find. He can bring copies of the reports, but they don't say anything that's gonna inspire you. Lemme know if you get anywhere."

I froze as I heard a creak in the kitchen. "Stay on the line," I whispered, then put down the receiver and tiptoed to the doorway. The back door was as I'd left it, and the muddy tracks on the linoleum appeared undisturbed. I took one step, then caught movement in the corner of my eye and leapt back just in time to save myself from being smacked on the head with a broom.

"Estelle, damn it," I said shakily, "what do you think you're doing? You came within an inch of giving me a heart attack."

"Is that what I get for risking life and limb to make sure you weren't being held hostage? If that's all the gratitude you can show, I'll take Elsie's cat and be on my way."

"Good idea." I returned to the telephone to assure Harve I hadn't been beset by burglars. He was in a much better mood when we ended the call.

"That was a real pretty sermon on Sunday morning, Brother Verber," Kayleen said as she poured a cup of tea. They were in her motel room, but she'd made sure the drapes were pulled back so there'd be no gossip about her entertaining a gentleman. "Would you like lemon and sugar?"

"Yes, and thank you kindly for your compliment.

I have to admit I was a little nervous about those un-familiar names, but I just told myself nobody'd notice if they came out wrong. I must have spent an hour the night before practicing 'Nebuchadnezzar.' It's a sight harder than Matthew, Mark, Luke, or John.''

She set the cup and saucer on the table beside his chair, then poured a cup for herself. "You sounded like you'd been saying 'Nebuchadnezzar' since you were in grade school. In fact, I can't think when I've heard it said so melodiously.''

He lowered his face to hide its pinkness and tried to keep his hand from shaking as he picked up the dainty porcelain cup. "Mighty fine tea, Sister Kay-leen,'' he said after a tiny slurp. "If I may be so bold, can I ask you why you decided to move to our little community?''

She launched into the story of her ill-fated first marriage, stopping every now and then to wipe her eyes or give him a rueful smile. "So I suppose the reason I'm here is because of that anonymous Good Samaritan. If I could remember his name or where his house was, I'd go over and thank him for bringing me back here.''

"I'm sure he was a member of the Voice of the Almighty Lord congregation on account of what a good Christian he was,'' Brother Verber said, shrewdly doing a little public relations work. "The Methodists down the road are real big on how devout they are, but their teen group had a dance in the basement last spring and they're talking about hold-ing another one before Christmas.'' He tsked sadly. "Dancing in the basement of the church. I wouldn't be surprised to hear they'll be serving alcoholic bev-erages to celebrate Baby Jesus' birthday.''

"Oh, dear," Kayleen murmured. "I'm confident you'd never allow such a thing in the Assembly Hall. How long have you been a pastor?"

"Long enough to make sure there'll be nothing of a sinful nature taking place in our basement." He finished his tea and stood up. "I'm supposed to go by Sister Barbara's house to finalize plans for the Thanksgiving pageant. Will we be seeing you tonight at the prayer meeting and pot luck supper, Sister Kayleen?"

She thought for a moment, then said, "It's possible, but I'm not promising anything. I'm a little disappointed that you have to leave so soon. I was hoping you might be able to help me find that Samaritan so I can give him a big ol' hug. I'm not familiar with the back roads. Perhaps another time when you're not too busy, you could drive me around. I might recognize the house if I saw it again. It would mean so much to me, Brother Verber, and I'd be real grateful."

He glanced at his watch. It was already past the time he was due at Sister Barbara's house, and he knew he'd have some explaining to do as it was. But Sister Kayleen was watching him with pleading eyes, as if he was the only person who could bring joy into her life. And weren't all Christians admonished to follow in the footsteps of the Good Samaritan by rushing to the aid of their fellow travelers?

Kayleen looked down at the avocado shag and said, "I don't want to interfere with your afternoon. You just run along and get prepared for the pageant. I've met so many nice people here in Maggody, and I'm sure one of them will be willing to help me. A gentleman named Lewis Fernclift greeted me real warmly after the service on Sunday and said I should call on him if there was any favor at all he could do for me. And a widower named—"

"Oh, I can take you," he said hastily. "I was just thinking how much gas I have in my car."

"Why, we'll take my car, and you can give me directions. You're generous to a fault, Brother Verber. I do believe I'll say a special little prayer for you tonight before I go to bed."

Trying not to allow his gaze to wander toward the bed, he picked up her coat and held it open for her. "It's my Christian duty," he said. "Maybe while we're driving around, I can convince you to become a permanent member of our congregation."

"Aren't you the sly dog," she said with a grin.

"Did you ever think about how the federal government sends money to other countries but won't take care of its own citizens?" Earl Buchanon asked his wife as she wrestled with the balky ironing board.

"Can't say I have," said Eileen, more concerned with not getting her finger pinched. "Did you oil this like I asked you to last week?"

Earl took a cookie off the plate and dunked it in his buttermilk. "What's more, income tax is voluntary, and none of us can be forced to volunteer. There's not a thing in the world those IRS leeches can do if I up and refuse to hand over my money so that the government can send it to countries that'd like to take us over."

"Ow!" She dropped the ironing board and stuck her finger in her mouth. "That blasted thing! If you want your shirts and trousers ironed, you'd better get busy with the oil. Otherwise, you can walk around town looking like a hobo for all I care."

"Do you know how much I paid in taxes last year? Close to two thousand dollars, that's how much. If I had that money now, I could make a down payment on a decent tractor that I don't have to spend half my time tinkering with."

"Or buy me a one-way ticket."

Earl was so surprised that he dropped the cookie. "Where do you want to go?"

"I don't know," she said, looking out the window at the pasture dotted with withered clumps of weeds. "Nowhere, I guess—or at least no time soon. The baby'll be here in a matter of weeks, and Dahlia is gonna need help with housework and the cooking. I'll most likely stay there all day, so you'll have to fend for yourself at lunchtime."

"She doing okay?"

Eileen picked up the ironing board and headed for the hall closet. "If she's having a problem with her blood sugar, she didn't tell me."

"I guess Kevin's all excited," Earl said when she came back into the kitchen.

"That's real insightful of you, Earl, since they come over for supper two or three times a week and that's all Kevin talks about."

He put on his coat and jammed a John Deere cap on his head. "I think I'll go over to the co-op and pick up a bag of layer grit. When I get back, I'll take a look at the ironing board."

"Sure you will," she said as he went out the back door.

———

Jeremiah McIlhaney came into the dining room, where his wife was chewing on a pencil as she decided who would be honored with Christmas cards and who wouldn't, based mostly on what they'd sent last year. Cousin Queenie had sent a long, rambling, photocopied letter telling how her daughter was a cheerleader and her son won a full scholarship to college and she herself was elected president of the garden club. Millicent drew a line through that name. Eula Lemoy had recycled a card she'd received from somebody else by covering the name with a sticker. Eula was gone with a slash. Aunt Bertha had sent nothing, as usual, but she didn't have any children and was rumored to have a sizable savings account.

Jeremiah hesitated, aware how seriously she took the master list every year. "I was thinking about a sandwich for lunch," he said apologetically, "and a piece of that apple pie we had for supper last night."

Millicent moved to the next name on her list. This was a mite trickier. Cousin Beau's wife had sent a real nice embossed card two years ago, then tried to weasel by this past year with a cheap one. What would she do this year?

Jeremiah licked his lips. "I can see you ain't got time to fix my lunch, so maybe I'll swing by the Dairee Dee-Lishus and get something there. Are you planning to use the truck Saturday morning?"

She banged down the pencil. "I am trying to concentrate on the list, and every time you interrupt me, I forget what I was thinking. Am I planning to use the truck—when?"

"Saturday morning."

"I told Darla Jean I'd take her shopping in Farberville on Saturday, but we didn't set a time. I suppose we can go after lunch. I wish you'd figure out what's wrong with my car and get it fixed. It was bad enough with Darla Jean borrowing it all the time to get to basketball practice or go riding with Heather. Now that all three of us are dependent on the truck, I just want to scream."

"I told you I'm waiting on a part," he said, retreating toward the living room.

Millicent picked up the pencil and resumed gnawing on it. Cousin Beau's wife was wily enough to send another embossed card this year, which would put her in a position to say something catty at the family reunion if she received a cheap card. Then again . . .

"I cain't work Saturday morning," Kevin said as he stood in the middle of Jim Bob's office. He put a piece of paper on the desk and pointed at it with a trembling finger. "It sez on this schedule that I ain't supposed to come in till three in the afternoon to work the second shift."

Jim Bob ripped the schedule into small pieces and let them flutter to the floor. "What schedule?"

"The schedule you posted in the employees' lounge on Monday," he said, gulping. "That one right there on the floor."

"All I see on the floor are scraps of paper, boy. Next time you're allowed a break, have a look at the schedule in the lounge. See for yourself if you're not supposed to be here at seven o'clock Saturday morning to turn up the thermostat, switch on the lights, and clean the toilets in the restrooms. I'll find out if you're late and take pleasure in firing your skinny ass."

Kevin felt his eyes begin to sting, but he squared his shoulders as best he could and said, "I got something else to do Saturday morning. Besides, it's not fair for you to change the schedule any time you want. Employees got rights, too."

"You got the right to get a job someplace else." Jim Bob lit a fat cigar, then entwined his fingers over his belly and regarded Kevin through a cloud of blue smoke. "I was planning to get in some hunting last weekend, but Mrs. Jim Bob changed my mind. Larry Joe's gonna call in sick first thing Friday morning, then him, Roy, and me are leaving for our camp. But I tell you what, asshole—since you'll be acting assistant manager, I'll pay you an extra dollar an hour till I get back."

Kevin opened and closed his mouth several times, then gave up and left the office. "It ain't fair," he said to a woman studying canned tomatoes. She was still staring at him as he went around the end of the aisle.

CHAPTER 6

By late Friday morning I was more stumped than a beauty pageant contestant asked to explain the ramifications of global warming. I'd talked to the victims of four of the burglaries (Elsie wasn't back) and come up without a clue. The houses were in different parts of the county and had different post offices, electric cooperatives, and sanitation services. Two of the retired couples frequented the same square dancing club, but one of the couples swore they'd never discussed their vacation plans with anyone there. Only one couple had left pets at a kennel. None of them went to the same church. Three of them had fancy new houses once filled with expensive electronic toys and heirloom silver. The fourth house was similar to Elsie's, modest but clean.

I hadn't talked to Kayleen about the pamphlets, either, since Ruby Bee had informed me that her sole tenant had gone to Malthus for a few days to deal with some legal matters. I could have tracked down Kevin to ask him who'd given the pamphlet to him, but I wasn't masochistic enough to deliberately initiate a conversation with him.

The burglary reports were fanned out in front of me and I was scrutinizing them for some obscure connection when the telephone rang. Hoping that one of the perps was calling to own up, I answered it.

"We got another one," Harve said brusquely, not bothering with pleasantries, "and it's bad."

"How bad is it?"

"About as bad as it gets. This woman and her daughter over in Mayfly went to visit kin for a week. They'd heard of the rash of burglaries, so they asked one of the daughter's friends to stay in their house while they were gone. They got worried when the house sitter didn't answer the phone for a few days, and called here first thing this morning to request that someone go out to the house and make sure she was okay. The deputy found the girl's body on the living room floor, her head crushed by a blow from a piece of firewood. She was wearing pajamas, so it looks like she heard a noise and got out of bed to see about it."

"Was there a broken window in the back of the house?"

"Yeah," Harve growled, "and the house was set off by itself on a hillside. After killing the girl, the damned clowns went ahead and hauled off two TV sets and a VCR."

"No witnesses spotted a truck or van?" I asked, although it was a perfunctory question at best.

"Hell, no. All we've got is that the coroner estimates she was killed three or four days ago. That fits in with when she stopped answering the phone and showing up for classes at the business college. The mailman noticed the mail was piling up in the box, but he didn't have any reason to go around to the back of the house."

"Did you check him out?"

"He's sixty-three years old and has a heart condition." Harve rumbled for a moment, then added, "I know Mayfly's nowhere near Maggody, but I'm even more short-handed than I was a week ago and the only available deputy started working here two weeks ago. Can you go over and have a look?"

I regretted having offered to tackle the burglaries in the first place, but I'd voluntarily climbed out on that particular limb and I was stuck until it broke— or I fell off it. "Yes, I can leave right now."

"The woman and her daughter should arrive home early this afternoon. I suppose you ought to hang around while they figure out what else is missing and see if they have serial numbers. I don't like the way this is pickin' up so fast, Arly. Folks have homeowner's insurance to replace what's stolen, but that girl wasn't more than twenty years old. Life insurance won't offer much comfort to her family."

I wrote down directions to the house, then calculated my time of arrival and told Harve to warn the deputy at the crime scene. The last thing I needed was to surprise a nervous neophyte with a .38 special in his hand.

Ruby Bee was taking off her apron when Estelle came into the barroom. "I'll be ready to go as soon as I cover the sweet potato pie with aluminum foil," she said. "And remind me to put the 'closed' sign on the door when we leave. Did you hear from that lawyer fellow?"

"No," Estelle said gloomily, "and it's getting harder and harder not to fret about this inheritance.

Last night I dreamed I bought a car twice as big and gaudy as Mrs. Jim Bob's convertible. She let on like she didn't care, but everybody knew she was hoppin' mad."

"I saw her coming out of the supermarket this morning, and she looked like she was fit to be tied. It may have been on account of Jim Bob; early this morning I saw him, Roy, and Larry Joe loading up Jim Bob's truck with cases of beer in front of the supermarket. They probably made it all the way to their deer camp before Mrs. Jim Bob found out their plan. Jim Bob might be wise to stay up there till she thaws out in the spring."

She picked up the pie pan and they went out to the parking lot. As they started to get into Estelle's station wagon, a peculiar-looking vehicle almost as wide as a semi drove up. It had a mean-lookin' grill across the front, like it wanted nothing more than to push over a building.

Sterling Pitts rolled down the window. "Good afternoon, ladies. I went out to the property that Kayleen bought, but she's not there. Do you know if she's in her motel room, Mrs. Hanks?"

"Her car wasn't parked out back a few minutes ago when I set out some trash. She told me she was going to Malthus and return sometime today. She's staying in number three, if you want to leave her a note."

Estelle gave him a sugary smile. "Or you can give us a message and we'll be sure and tell her when she gets back. That way you won't have to hunt for paper and pencil, or worry about the note blowing away in the wind."

"It's awful windy," added Ruby Bee. "What's this thing you're driving?"

Pitts caressed the dashboard. "It's more than three tons of America's toughest vehicle. It has one hundred and ninety horsepower and three hundred pounds of torque. With this baby, I can drive through two feet of water, climb sixty-percent grades, and plow through three-foot snowbanks."

"Why would you want to do all that?" asked Estelle.

He rolled up the window and drove out of the lot in the direction from which he'd come. Estelle drove out of the lot in the same direction, although they had a different destination. "I wonder if we should alert Arly that he's in town," she said.

"I don't know where she is. She didn't show up for lunch, and her car's not at the PD or over behind Roy's store. Of course she couldn't go to the trouble of telling her own mother where she was going or when she'd be back. If I didn't know better, I'd think she was raised in a barn."

"Maybe it was an emergency, like chasing down a bank robber or an escaped convict."

"Even so, she should have had the decency to call me so I wouldn't worry," Ruby Bee said irritably, if irrationally. However, she reminded herself of the importance of their current mission and did her best to simmer down.

Minutes later they were at the door of the rectory. Estelle knocked, then stepped back and said, "Brother Verber must have gone somewhere. His car's not out in front."

"Knock again, Estelle, and do it real hard in case

he's in the bathroom and didn't hear you the first time. This pie's fresh from the oven."

Estelle did as ordered, but nobody opened the door or even hollered that he was coming as fast as he could. "I guess we'll have to try later."

"He's not here?" said Mrs. Jim Bob as she approached them. She was carrying a covered casserole dish, but her expression was not that of an angel on an errand of mercy. "Where is he? How long's he been gone?"

"We don't know," said Ruby Bee. "We just got here ourselves." There wasn't any way to put her pie behind her back, so she forced herself to smile. "I reckon we're here for the same reason, Mrs. Jim Bob. I heard something about Brother Verber having a touch of the flu and I thought it'd be nice to bring him a special treat."

Mrs. Jim Bob pinched her lips together and stared suspiciously at them. "Did you?" she said at last. "Who would have thought you'd worry about Brother Verber, especially since you're not a member of the congregation. Maybe that has something to do with you selling alcohol."

"To folks like your husband," shot back Ruby Bee.

"My husband has been known to stray at times, but whenever he does, I do my best to get him back on the path of righteousness. I presume you do the same with your daughter, even though it doesn't seem to do a smidgen of good." Ignoring Ruby Bee's gasp, she took a key from under the door mat, unlocked the door, and went inside.

"Well, I never!" said Ruby Bee as the door slammed in her face. "The nerve of her!"

Estelle snorted. "One of these days Mrs. High and Mighty'll get what's coming to her, and I hope I'm there to see it. Come on, Ruby Bee, we might as well go have some sweet potato pie."

Ruby Bee was more in the mood to stomp into the rectory and tell Mrs. Jim Bob what she thought of her, but she followed Estelle back to the station wagon.

Jake saw the Hummer parked at the far edge of the pasture and drove toward it, cursing as his tires spun in the mud. "I hope to hell it don't take a tow truck to get out of here on Monday."

Judy pulled her coat more tightly around her. "Then Sterling can pay for it, since he selected the spot. At least over at Bradley's place, there was a gravel road. This is ridiculous. I never should have agreed to put up with this another year."

He glared at her, then concentrated on getting through the shriveled corn stalks that slapped at the front of the truck. As he parked alongside the Hummer, Pitts came out of the woods and called, "You're early. I wasn't expecting to see you all till six or seven."

Jake climbed out of the truck and pulled down the tailgate. "I took off early so we could get here before dark. My boss thinks I'm over in Farberville having a look at junkers at the auto auction lot. How long you been here, Pitts?"

"We're supposed to use code names on retreats! Unless you wish to risk the possibility of a court martial, Blitzer, address me as Silver Fox."

Jake dragged a canvas tent bag out of the bed,

hoisted it onto his shoulder, and said, "Where are we making camp—Silver Fox?"

"I've reconnoitered the area and chosen a clearing with adequate drainage. It's just on the other side of that gully and up about fifty feet. No one can see you from here, but you should be able to see anyone who approaches. I'll show you the way."

Jake looked back at Judy, who was sitting in the cab like she was planted there for all eternity. "Get the sleeping bags and whatever else you can carry," he shouted at her, then slithered down the side of the gully and made his way up the far side.

Sterling waited until Jake reached the top, then turned and continued between thickets of brambles and thin, stunted trees. They arrived at a rocky clearing encircled by scrub pines and more brambles.

Jake dropped the tent. "Where's your crap?"

"I'll set up the communications post in town. I can hardly plug the computer into that tree, can I? I think I hear another vehicle coming across the pasture. I need to make sure it's one of our people instead of some nosy federal agents." He paused to study Jake's face for a telltale flicker of guilt. "I had a communiqué from the outfit over in Oklahoma. It seems they discovered an informant in their midst, a sneaky bastard taking money from the FBI. He'd been in their cell for over two years before they uncovered him."

"Did they hang him by his balls?" Jake asked as he pulled the tent out of the bag and began to unroll it.

"Something like that."

"Sumbitch deserved it."

"My sentiments exactly." Sterling left him to struggle with the tent and returned to the pasture. The truck belonged to Red Rooster. For a moment, he assumed the passenger was Apocalypse, but as the truck got closer, he recognized Dylan Gilbert. It was unfortunate, he told himself as he crossed the gully, that the young man had not drifted elsewhere. Theirs was an enthusiastic group, but hardly as professional as the one in Colorado. Red Rooster had passed along Dylan's remark about the compound in Idaho, too. Sterling knew the brethren there had been ruthless when they'd been under siege by the feds for nearly three weeks. Some of them had been given life sentences despite the fact they were doing nothing more than protecting their families.

Reed cut off the engine and got out of the truck. "How's it going, Pitts?" he said as he began to unload his camping equipment.

"You're supposed to call me Silver Fox."

"Yeah, okay," said Reed. "How're you doing, Judy? Where's Jake?"

Sterling stomped his boot in the mud. "Refer to him as Blitzer, damn it! This is not a Boy Scout Jamboree. We are here for a purpose—and it's not to roast marshmallows and tell ghost stories. Tell your friend to get his gear, and I'll lead you to the encampment. I myself will be staying at a motel in order to remain in communication with the network."

"What's the matter, Pops?" said Dylan as he lazily emerged from the truck. "Getting too old to rough it with the rest of us?"

"My name is Silver Fox! Can't you morons get that through your thick skulls?"

"Look at this, Silver Fox," Reed said, holding out

a blowgun. "Jake—I mean Blitzer—told me to check it out. It's a helluva lot more accurate than a knife. I took down a crow at more than forty feet."

"Interesting," said Sterling.

"You bet it is. I got some paint pellets so I can show everybody how powerful it is. It didn't cost but about thirty dollars." He pointed at a sparrow on a limb across the gully. "Watch this."

He loaded a pellet into the blowgun, leveled it, and took a deep breath. A noise no louder than a mouse's fart accompanied the release of the pellet. The sparrow continued to watch them, its head cocked.

Pitts looked at the orange splotch on the front of his field jacket. "Good work, Red Rooster. I can see how terrified all of our feathered friends will be in the future. Now, would you put that blasted thing away and get your gear?" He looked at Dylan, who was sniggering. "You, too, if you're planning to participate in the retreat. Otherwise, take a hike back to Colorado."

"Yeah, yeah." Dylan balanced a sleeping bag on one shoulder and picked up a duffel bag.

Reed fondled the blowgun. "Hey, I'm real sorry, Sterling. I practiced all day yesterday with this baby, and I was getting to where I could hit something clear across the parking lot behind my apartment. 'Course there were some wild shots while I was learning. This old boy that lives below me liked to have gone crazy when he saw the paint on his car, but I told him next time I'd use a dart and aim for his tires if he didn't stop squawking."

"Just call me Silver Fox," Sterling said in a discouraged voice, then started back across the gully.

"Did you do that on purpose?" asked Judy as Reed walked by.

Reed was torn between not wanting to admit he'd made a bad shot and confessing that he'd purposely assailed their leader, which might amount to treason. "It was one of those things," he muttered. "You aiming to sit there all night?"

"I might."

Dylan joined them. "You're too pretty to spend the next few days wallowing in the mud. Judy, right? I'm Dylan. I think I'm going to like it here more than I thought."

"Hey!" Reed said, thumping Dylan on the back with the blow gun. "You'd better watch that kind of thing. Jake's liable not to like it, and he's one mean fucker when he's riled up. He did six weeks in the county jail for biting off a biker's ear in a brawl."

Judy winked at Dylan, then went back to studying the dusty dashboard. The two men crossed the gully and disappeared into the woods. After a while, Jake emerged and came back to the truck, his eyes hard.

"Thought you was coming to the camp," he said.

"You thought wrong. If Sterling can stay in a motel in town, then I can, too. He can bring me out here to do the cooking and washing up, but there's no reason why I should spend the next three nights in a smelly sleeping bag on the rocks. If you don't like it, I'll find a way to get myself to Emmett in time to babysit tomorrow. Take it or leave it, Jake."

"You planning to sleep alone?"

"Heavens, no. I was planning to ask Silver Fox to crawl into bed with me. He may still have a little life in his old pecker. Or maybe that new fellow named Dylan. I could tell from looking at him that he's a real stud. After all, he's got be a good twenty years younger than you.''

"Damn it,'' Jake said, making a fist but keeping it at his side, "you got no call to talk like that. I 'spose you can stay in town as long as Sterling keeps an eye on you. I want you to promise to stay in your motel room and not go wandering around town. From what I've heard, there are some mighty peculiar folks in Maggody.''

Judy decided not to comment about grown men who snuck around the woods with green and brown makeup on their faces and guns that fired paint pellets. Boy, that'd stop the foreign troops in their tracks. They'd be laughing so hard they could be rounded up effortlessly and deposited in makeshift stockades.

"I promise to stay in the motel room,'' she said.

"Make sure that you do.'' Jake stared at her, then gathered the rest of his gear and headed for the gully.

"This is more like it,'' Jim Bob said as he opened a beer and settled his muddy shoes on the crate that served as a coffee table in the trailer. "Hey, Larry Joe, if you're gonna fix yourself a bologna sandwich, make one for me. I skipped breakfast on account of not wanting to disturb Mrs. Jim Bob when I left the house.''

"What'd she say when you told her we was going hunting?'' asked Larry Joe. "Joyce was mad like she always is, but she said she'd cover for me if the principal at the high school calls to check up on me. It isn't like those little bastards in my shop classes aren't cutting school to go huntin,' too. There were so few of them yesterday that I sent them to the library.''

"To do what?''

"Hell, I don't know. Study or something.'' Larry

Joe opened a cooler and dug around for the package of bologna. "So what'd she say?"

"Some critter must have died in the outhouse," said Roy Stiver, zipping up his fly as he came into the trailer. "It stinks to high heavens."

Jim Bob slapped his brow. "And us without a can of pine-scented air freshener! I knew we'd forget something essential. Put mustard on my sandwich, Larry Joe—unless we forgot that, too. Cut off the crust while you're at it, and put on the tea kettle."

Roy sat down at the kitchen table and shuffled a deck of cards. "I was just making an observation, for chrissake. You want to play poker or sit there like a boil on a preacher's ass?"

"Deal the cards," Jim Bob said, smugly congratulating himself for changing the subject. Mrs. Jim Bob would have figured out by the middle of the morning where he'd gone, but there wasn't anything she could do about it until he got home. That scene was something he didn't want to think about and spoil his weekend, not when they had plenty of beer, whiskey, bologna, and cards.

"I think we forgot the mustard," Larry Joe said with a sigh.

Instead of going straight back to Maggody, I went to Farberville to report in person to Harve and find out if he'd heard anything from the FBI about the prints. The sheriff's department, which housed the county jail as well as offices, a weight room, and more showers than to be found in all of Maggody, was a complete contrast to my two-room, shabby PD. It always depressed me.

LaBelle glanced up at me over the top of her sequined bifocals, sniffed, and resumed talking on the telephone. From what I could tell, the conversation concerned a young relative with head lice. LaBelle's not a Buchanon, but she should be.

"I need to speak to Harve," I said.

She covered the mouthpiece. "He's busy. You'll have to make an appointment for sometime next week."

"I've just come from a murder scene, and I need to speak to Harve. I cannot wait until next week, or even until you stop offering nit-picking advice to your sister or whoever it is."

"Then go on back to his office," she said with a flip of her hand. "Don't blame me if he bites your head off, though. I warned you."

Harve was seated at his desk, gazing dully at a stack of folders. An ashtray contained a veritable mountain of burned matches, and flakes of gray ash decorated most of the nearby surfaces. The potted plant on his desk appeared discouraged, if not yet dead.

"What'd you find?" he asked.

"Not much." I took out my notebook and flipped it open. "The victim's name was Katherine Avenued, twenty-one, lived alone in an apartment on Thurber Street. Her parents moved to Tucson several years ago. She waited tables at a Mexican restaurant and started taking classes at the business college in August. Her only friend seemed to have been Heidi Coben, the homeowner's daughter. Katherine didn't mention anything out of the ordinary when Heidi last talked to her on Monday. We pulled up a lot of prints, but you know as well as I that if these perps are pros, they wear gloves.''

"What else did the Coben women say?''

I tried not to wince as he pulled a splintery cigar butt out of his shirt pocket and reached for a box of matches. "Mrs. Coben received a hefty divorce settlement and could afford nice things. Besides the stuff you already knew about, she's missing a computer, a fax machine, a cordless telephone, a bunch of silver pieces, a pair of antique dueling pistols, a camcorder, and a jewelry box that deserved a spot in Fort Knox. There may be more after she does a thorough search.''

Harve fired up the cigar, eyed the overflowing ashtray, and dropped the match on the floor. "They had all that expensive stuff, lived in the middle of nowhere, and *didn't* have a burglar alarm?''

"Heidi said that Katherine set it off by accident when she first moved in. After that, she refused to turn it on because she was afraid she'd do it again. I guess she figured her presence was enough, but she parked her car in the garage and more than likely turned off the lights when she went to bed.''

"Damn,'' Harve drawled, the cigar bobbling. "Did you ask the women all those questions about who could have known they were away?''

"Not a single concurrence,'' I said as I closed the notebook. "The burglars obviously weren't watching the house, or they would have been aware of Katherine's presence. They weren't worried about the alarm, either.''

"Any of the other houses have alarms?''

"No, all the victims have in common is that they chose to live in rural areas. One couple retired here from Chicago, another from someplace in California. One husband's a history professor, one a minister, one a consulting architect. Elsie gets by on Social Security and what I imagine is a modest savings account." I slapped the notebook on his desk. "This is driving me nuts, Harve!"

"You and me both—and you're not up for reelection."

I glowered at him for a moment, wondering what he'd do if I yanked off my badge and stomped out of his office. Probably not much, since my paycheck came from the town council. I calmed myself down and said, "I may as well go by Sterling Pitts's office and try one last time to talk him into rescheduling his so-called maneuvers. You have the address handy?"

He looked it up in the telephone directory, told me how to find it, and was back to staring at the folders when I left. LaBelle ignored me as I went through the reception area, no doubt disappointed that my head was still firmly attached to my neck. She did not instruct me to have a good day.

The Tri-County Patriots' Insurance office was housed in a shabby little building on an unfamiliar street. On one side was a warehouse, and on the other a dry cleaning establishment. There were no vehicles in the parking lot, but through the window I spotted a young woman seated at a desk.

I went inside and said, "Is Mr. Pitts here?"

"Oh, no," she said, popping her gum earnestly. "He won't be back until Tuesday morning. Is there something I can do for you?"

"I guess not," I said. "Did he tell you where he was going?"

"He didn't tell me, but I heard him on the

phone with his wife, and he said something about a seminar in Kansas City. Do you need to file a claim or something? I can give you the forms.''

"I just wanted to speak to Pitts," I said, then went back to my car and headed for Maggody, where I suspected I'd find him.

CHAPTER 7

I drove past the old Wockermann place, but I didn't see any vehicles in the driveway or indication anyone was in the house. I considered stopping at Estelle's to ask if she'd noticed any activity, but a UPS truck blocked her driveway. Not wanting to be subjected to a private viewing of the latest batch of fingernail polish, I headed for Ruby Bee's.

She scowled as I took a stool. "I don't suppose it occurred to you to inform me before you took off this morning, did it? After all, I'm only your mother."

"Sorry," I said humbly, in that I'd missed lunch and it was well past suppertime. "The sheriff asked me to investigate a crime over in Mayfly. I just now got back to town, and I sure could use a grilled cheese sandwich and a glass of milk."

"I was so worried about you that I got a bad case of heartburn. I had to suffer through happy hour before I could slip away to my unit to take some medicine." She paused so I could appreciate the immensity of my misdemeanor, then said, "General Pitts and a woman named Judy Milliford checked in about an hour ago. They took separate rooms, so I don't guess he's up to any hanky-panky. I put her between me and Kayleen, and him in the building across the parking lot."

I was not impressed with this minor concession to virtue; the locals refer to the Flamingo Motel as the Stork Club—and not because they're ornithologically challenged. "Have you seen any of the others in this group?"

"I reckon they're camping on Kayleen's property. She's back in town, by the way. She stopped by to tell me, in case I was worried about her having car trouble on that narrow highway from Malthus. I think that's real considerate of her. Don't you think so?"

"Oh, yes," I said, still hoping for some supper. "About that sandwich and—"

"Ruby Bee!" shrieked Estelle from the doorway. "I don't know what I'm gonna do! I couldn't believe my eyes!"

I spun around, nearly toppling off the stool. "Was your house burglarized?"

"This is a sight worse than that. Get your coat and come with me, Ruby Bee. You got to help me figure out what to do!"

"Does this have anything to do with the militia?" I asked. "Did somebody fire a gun or launch a grenade in your direction?"

This finally got her attention. "No, missy, I haven't seen hide nor hair of them. My inheritance from Uncle Tooly was delivered half an hour ago. The polite young man helped me get the crate into the living room and even pried the top off. Well, I liked to have died when these big ugly birds hissed at me, and the delivery man bolted out the door to his truck and was almost at the stop sign before I got out to the porch."

"What are they?" demanded Ruby Bee.

"How should I know? Are you coming or not? I can't leave them in the living room. I got two appointments tomorrow, and I can't see Eileen having her hair trimmed while she's being hissed at."

"It's Friday night, Estelle, and I usually get a decent crowd. I can't afford to close the bar just because you've got hissy birds in your living room."

I grinned at Ruby Bee. "Don't worry about that. I'll hold down the fort while you go to Estelle's house, as long as you don't mind if I make myself a sandwich."

Estelle acknowledged my generous gesture with a nod, then said, "So are you coming or not, Ruby Bee? If you were having some terrible crisis, I'd like to think I'd drop everything and come galloping to your rescue. Remember when you ran out of gas at the flea market and I drove all the way out there, even though it meant canceling an appointment? I seem to recollect it was a good twenty miles each way. And what about the time I went with you to Noow Yark City so you wouldn't—"

"If you'll stop jabbering, I'll get my coat," Ruby Bee said in a wintry voice, clearly not pleased at having certain incidents dredged up. "It seems to me you might should call that lawyer and ask him what you're supposed to do with the birds. He's the one who sent them, after all."

"His office is closed by now. I can call him Monday, but I've got to do something right this minute!"

I waited until they were out the door, then went

into the kitchen. I was hunting for the mayo when I heard a voice call, "Hello? Are you open?"

My stomach whimpered as I dutifully returned to the barroom. The voice belonged to a guy approximately my age. He had agreeable features, short brown hair, and a surprised expression as he stared at my badge. To my dismay, he was wearing a camouflage jacket, but he could be nothing more exotic than a hunter stalking a beer instead of a deer. Or so I told myself.

"I'm covering for Ruby Bee while she's out on an errand," I said. "Can I get you something?"

"I stopped for directions. I'm looking for County 102, but I must have missed it in the dark."

I relinquished my hunter conjecture. "Could your destination be Kayleen Smeltner's property?"

"That's right. I guess you heard about us coming, huh? You don't have to concern yourself. We've been doing this for years and never had any problems with the authorities. My name's Barry Kirklin. What's yours?"

"Arly Hanks. The turnoff for County 102 is next to a funny-looking metal structure with a trailer parked in the yard. Kayleen, a woman named Judy something-or-other, and your fearless leader are staying in the motel behind the bar. I don't know which units they're in, but they're the only ones out there."

"Pitts is hardly a contemporary version of Daniel Boone," Barry said with a wry smile. "I'm kind of surprised that Jake would let Judy out of his sight all night, although it's not as if she gives him any reason to distrust her. She's a mousy little housewife, not especially attractive or vivacious. God knows no one would ever accuse her of being sexy."

"The way Kayleen is?" I suggested.

"Kayleen's a potential land mine, but she doesn't seem to realize the impact she has on every man in the room. An interesting mixture of naïveté and sexiness, wouldn't you say?"

Frankly, I didn't think it was the least bit interesting. "Do you want a beer?" I asked him.

"Pitts doesn't permit alcohol on retreats, so I'd better not. I might be in the mood Monday evening —if you'll let me buy you one."

"If you survive the weekend, I'll think about it. As I said, they're out back in the only units liable to have lights on. Surely someone clever enough to unmask an international conspiracy can find them."

"Surely," he said, then turned and left.

Mrs. Jim Bob drove by the rectory, slowing down to peer at the dark windows. Having grilled employees at the SuperSaver, she knew darn well where Jim Bob was, but she had no idea where Brother Verber had been ever since the Wednesday night prayer meeting. She'd been too annoyed to speak to him after the service, due to his failure to appear at her house to discuss the Thanksgiving pageant—which most likely had something to do with a particular person who'd had the nerve to show her painted face again. Maybe he was too kind-hearted to point his finger at the moneylender and order her to slink away in disgrace. Maybe he believed his duty was to welcome sinners into the congregation.

She'd been inside the rectory several times, making sure he hadn't drowned in the bathtub or suffered a stroke in his bed. As a gesture of Christian compassion, she'd even cleaned up his kitchen, run a dust rag over the furniture in the living room, and straightened up the piles of what he assured her was study material (even though it took a lot of willpower to touch the nasty things with names like *Naughty Nipples* and *Whiplash*). Why, she'd gone so far as kneel in the Assembly Hall to pray for the strength to forgive him for his transparently feeble excuse for postponing the pageant meeting.

Surely he'll be grateful, she thought, as she turned around in Lottie's driveway and drove back toward her house on Finger Lane. It wouldn't hurt to keep the rectory more attractive, either. She could have Perkins's eldest clean for him half a day a week, and she herself would bring fresh flowers from her garden in the spring. Although Jim Bob would object, she'd invite Brother Verber to supper several times a week and make a better effort to make him feel appreciated.

Once at home, she sat down at the kitchen table and started on a list of ways the legitimate members of the congregation could keep him occupied in his free time. Lottie might be persuaded to invite him over for coffee, and the Missionary Society could have him attend their weekly meetings to say grace before refreshments. She'd ask him to accompany her to Farberville to select new fabric for the sofa, and afterwards to have lunch at a tea shoppe.

She said a brief prayer of gratitude to the Lord for blessing her with a creative mind, then got back to work.

"I don't see them," Estelle whispered to Ruby Bee, who was standing on her tiptoes next to her while they peeked through the living room window.

"They might be in the crate—or they might be running loose in the house. We need to be real careful. They have sharp beaks and beady orange eyes, and they're ornery enough to peck the freckles right off your arm."

"Did you leave the door open when you left?" whispered Ruby Bee, although she wasn't sure why they were worried that the birds might be listening to them.

"You can see for yourself that it's closed. I guess the only thing to do is go inside and find them. If they're in the crate, you put the lid on and I'll get the hammer and nails. First thing Monday morning they'll be on their merry way back to that lawyer in Oklahoma."

"You said Uncle Tooly took to doing experiments. Do you think the birds are freaks that he created in his laboratory? You might be able to sell them to a carnival show, you know. The one at the county fair last September advertised they had a boy that was raised by wolves, a five-legged calf, and a prehistoric fish."

Estelle bit her lip as she tried to recollect exactly what the hissy birds looked like. They were almost as tall as she was, with gangly necks, scruffy brown feathers, and those demonic eyes. "I wouldn't have any idea how to get in touch with a carnival, but I know for a fact I won't get a wink of sleep until they're out of my house. Are you ready?"

"I guess so," said Ruby Bee. "You go first. I'll be close behind you in case I need to jerk you back to safety."

"It'd be better if you went first so you can get the lid on the crate. The hammer's in a drawer in the kitchen, and I'll have to hunt around for nails. I'd feel a sight safer if you were holding down the lid."

Ruby Bee looked at her. "They're *your* birds, not mine, Estelle. If you're too scared to go in there, you can stay at the Flamingo until you can find someone to get 'em in the crate. You could persuade Diesel to come down from the ridge and bite their heads off. General Pitts might agree to attack the house."

"I wonder why Uncle Tooly said in his will that I was to get them. He was a mite odd, but he always seemed fond of me. I had a parakeet when I was in pigtails. He may have assumed that I was a bird fancier on account of that."

"Piss or get off the pot," snapped Ruby Bee. "It's cold and dark out here. Arly can't handle the Friday night crowd by herself. She went to the police school, but I'll bet they never taught her how to throw a fractious drunk out of a bar. That takes years of practice."

Estelle took a last peek in the window. "I don't see anything. I think I'll go around to the back and look through the kitchen window. You wait here." She disappeared around the corner of the house.

Ruby Bee put her hands in her pockets and tried not to shiver as the wind did its darndest to sneak down her collar. It was crazy to stand here half the night, she thought as she went up on the porch and tried to catch a glimpse of the birds through the glass panes in the door. Surely Estelle was exaggerating. Alfred Hitchcock had made a movie about killer birds, but nobody in real life had ever been attacked like that. Then again, she reminded herself, Uncle Tooly had owned some mighty queer sheep.

A gust of wind liked to push her off the porch. "This is ridiculous," she said, not bothering to whisper. "If you birds are in there, you'd better mind your manners 'cause I'm coming in and I'm not putting up with being hissed at or pecked."

She didn't exactly charge into the house, however, but instead turned the knob and eased open the door a scant inch. Nothing. She tried another inch, then squinted into the room. She was about to throw open the door when something hit her hand. The unexpected burst of pain was so startling that she jumped back, lost her balance, and went tumbling off the porch into a massive forsythia bush.

"Estelle!" she howled, fighting to get free of the brittle branches. One foot was snagged above her head, the other twisted under her in a most undignified position. "Estelle, darn it, get back here!"

"What in tarnation . . . ?" said Estelle as she rounded the corner, not spotting the arms flailing from the middle of the forsythia. "Where are you, Ruby Bee?"

"Here, and I'm stuck, in case you didn't notice. Would you stop gawking and do something?"

"What're you doing?"

"I am trying to get free of this bush. It's got me tangled up like it's got barbed wire for branches." She grunted as she wiggled around to get her hands on the ground.

Estelle pulled back branches as best she could, and after getting swatted in the face and scratched up to her wrists, managed to help Ruby Bee escape. "I still don't understand why you were in the forsythia," she said. "Did you jump in there for a reason?"

"I fell in there," Ruby Bee said, trying to hide her mortification. She went on to relate how she'd opened the front door, then added, "I suppose one of those birds pecked me on the hand. It hurt worse than a pebble from a slingshot. If I hadn't had on gloves, it would have drawn blood."

"I told you they're not the most mannersome critters. You should have—" She broke off with a gurgle of dismay, then grabbed Ruby Bee's arm and hustled her toward the door. "They're over by the station wagon. We'd better get inside before they come after us."

Ruby Bee wasn't inclined to dawdle.

"The public forum is at ten o'clock sharp," Sterling told Barry and Kayleen, who were seated on his bed. The table was burdened with a computer, monitor, and laser printer; a cord slinked from the modem to the telephone across the room. His duffel bag was unpacked and in the closet. A holster hung on the headboard of the bed. On the wall next to a topographical map of the region was a framed picture of wide-eyed kittens in a beribboned basket. Variations of the latter (but not the former) were in all the units.

"I'll put signs along the road first thing in the morning," said Barry. "From what Dylan said when he was out here earlier in the week, we won't get more than a dozen potential recruits. He hit the pool hall, the supermarket, a body shop, and even the launderette, trying to spark some interest in the cause, but he says there's a lot of apathy in this town."

Sterling shook his head. "Apathy is our biggest challenge, and the only way to overcome it is with education and persistence. Kayleen, do you have the printed material to be distributed tomorrow?"

"The boxes are in my trunk," she said. "I gave

Dylan all the remaining brochures, so you'd better order some more.''

"We don't need to order them now that I have a photocopier at my office. I'll write one up on the computer and run off copies in the evenings when that snoopy secretary of mine isn't there. It seems we're set for the moment, so you"—he gestured at Barry—"can leave. Judy has been ordered to be ready to depart for the encampment at 0600 hours. Kayleen, you can transfer the boxes and ride with us to minimalize visibility.''

"In the Hummer?" she said, winking at Barry. "I don't think anybody in this podunk place has ever seen a vehicle like yours. They may ask you to be in the homecoming parade.''

Sterling bristled at the implication he had erred in selecting the Hummer. "When the crisis strikes, transportation will play an important role in survival. A tactical withdrawal may be the only solution. Having a proper vehicle may be the difference between being able to escape from a dangerous situation and being stranded and at the mercy of the enemy.''

"How much did it cost?" asked Barry.

"None of your damn business. Now get out to the encampment and do whatever it takes to keep Red Rooster from having a hangover in the morning.''

Barry gave him a casual salute, smiled at Kayleen, and left the motel room. Instead of continuing to his car out in front of the bar, he pressed his ear against the door.

"—that I haven't received this month's payment," Sterling was saying in a stony voice.

"Moving here left me temporarily short of cash,

what with down payments for the two properties and the initial outlay for the remodeling. Give me some time and I'll get caught up."

"I certainly hope so."

"Are you done with me? I spent the last two days rearranging the storage cubicle, and I'd like to take a hot shower and get to bed early."

"Sit down."

Barry headed for his truck.

The telephone rang at the end of the bar. I swallowed a mouthful of cherry cobbler, took a drink of milk, and sauntered down to answer it.

"Is that you, Arly?" said Ruby Bee.

"Arly's locked in the pantry," I said gruffly. "This here's the convict what's holding all the rednecks hostage on account of the SWAT team outside. Let me tell ya, them cops are mean as their hides will hold."

"This ain't the time for childishness, young lady. Estelle and I are experiencing a small problem at her house. Shoo away all the customers and get your smart-aleck self over here this minute."

Resuming my regular voice, I said, "For starters, there's nobody here except yours truly. A foursome from the trailer park came by for coffee and pie, but they're gone. Some college kids came in, looked at my badge, and scurried out the door. Being a highly trained professional, I concluded they were underage. Who else . . . ? Oh, a guy asking for directions. That about sums it up. Not a very impressive crowd, I'm sorry to say."

"Then lock up and get out here."

"It's only eight-fifteen, and more people might

show up. What if Mrs. Jim Bob comes cruising for truckers and finds the door locked? You wouldn't want to lose her business, would you?'' I was being perverse, true, but it had been pretty darn boring for the last hour. I'd not yet sunk to the level of dancing to some nasal ballad on the juke box. I had, however, checked the titles.

"I've about had it with you, Ariel Hanks. You're not so big that I can't still turn you over my knee and give you a paddling with my hair brush.''

"Yes, I am. You may outweigh me, but I'm a good four inches taller than you, and furthermore, I can outrun you. Want to race sometime?'' I listened to her sputter incoherently for a moment, then added, "Okay, what's the problem?''

"Well, you know how Estelle's uncle was killed by sheep, and—''

"Sheep?'' I said. "You've got to be kidding.''

"It was mentioned in my column last week, so I assumed you knew about it.''

"You write a column?''

"I told you I'd been asked to do a little column every week for *The Starley City Star Shopper.* I never dreamed you of all people wouldn't make an effort to read what your own mother writes. I'm as sure as I live and breathe that Dear Abby's daughter reads her column, and real faithfully, too.''

"You're writing an advice column?'' I said, filling a glass with beer. "You're telling people how to manage their marriages and children? Do you honestly think you're qualified to—''

"It's not an advice column. It's more of a friendly letter to let folks know what's going on in Maggody.

Now, are you done asking questions? I don't aim to spend the night here at Estelle's. She has so much junk in the guest room that I'd have to sleep on the couch. My back's been acting up lately—if I slept on that lumpy old thing, I wouldn't be able to hobble across the room in the morning."

"What's going on?"

"Just get out here—and bring your gun. You most likely won't need more than two bullets, but it wouldn't hurt to have a spare in case you miss."

For an insane moment, I wondered if I was supposed to shoot her and Estelle. "Does this have something to do with the birds?" I asked. "Are they still in the crate?"

"Not exactly," she said, then hung up, leaving me to gape at the neon Coors sign on the wall behind the bar.

Reed tossed a piece of wood on the fire, then took a beer from the cooler and sat down on a log. He stared at the flames, imagining what it'd be like if Bobbi Jo was in the tent, all snuggled up in the sleeping bag and waiting for him, her lips moist and her eyes hungry. It was her own damn fault the marriage had gone down the drain, he told himself sourly. He'd offered to drag her along when he went fishing—not every time, but once in a while—but she always stuck up her nose like she thought she was too good to clean a mess of fish. It wasn't like he'd *had* to invite her.

"Hey, good buddy," said Barry as he came into the clearing and dropped his gear. "Where's everybody else?"

"Dylan took my truck to go back to Farberville to get us a couple of pizzas. Jake muttered something about checking on his wife and stalked off. The others are staying in some dumpy motel."

"Yeah, I know. I stopped there before coming up here. You'd better make sure Sterling doesn't smell pepperoni on your breath in the morning. The old fart'll bore you to tears talking about surviving off the land." Barry got himself a beer and squatted across the fire from Reed. "Do you trust Dylan?" he asked.

"No reason not to. Sterling said he talked to one of the brethren in Colorado that confirmed Dylan's story. What's your beef with him?"

"I thought I saw your truck parked behind some abandoned building that sure as hell wasn't a pizza joint. What time did he leave?"

"Maybe six. So what if it's after nine? It's Friday night and the pizza joints are liable to be crowded."

"Not *that* crowded. I'm beginning to wonder if he's who he says he is. What if he's trying to infiltrate our group so he can tip off the feds?"

"Tip 'em off about what?"

Barry shrugged. "Okay, so we haven't done anything illegal as of yet. He doesn't know that. He may believe we're stockpiling assault weapons and building bombs in Sterling's garage. He could even have us confused with that group that used to be over past Harrison. They had a factory in the compound for making hand grenades and another for manufacturing silencers and shit like that to sell at gun shows. Their survival school cost five hundred dollars, and they could pick and choose—" He clamped down on his lower lip, wishing he hadn't mentioned the sur-

vival school. Reed had damn near exploded when
he'd been rejected. "Anyway, if Dylan's who he says
he is, why's your truck in town?"

Jake came into the clearing. "I saw it, too. If we
got some bastard in our midst, we're gonna make him
real sorry."

From *The Starley City Star Shopper,* November 15:

What's Cooking in Maggody?
by Rubella Belinda Hanks

I hope all my readers are planning a fine feast for Thanksgiving. If you're not gonna spend the day with kinfolk, come out to Ruby Bee's Bar & Grill. The blue-plate special will feature turkey, stuffing, cranberries, and all the fixin's for a special price of $4.95, including sweet potato pie for dessert. I don't want to brag on myself, but it's been said I make the lightest biscuits west of the Mississippi. Come find out for yourself.

Dahlia is getting along just fine. She and Kevin have settled on a name for the baby: Kevin Fitzgerald Buchanon, Junior. If you want to drop by a little present, I'll see that she gets it.

Dontay Buchanon got out of prison last week, and his wife wants him to know that if he so much as sets foot on their farm he'll end up with a load of buckshot in his behind. If you're reading this, Dontay, you'd better take heed.

The County Extension Homemakers meeting has been changed to the first Tuesday of every month, except for December, when it's the first Monday, and January, when it's the third Thursday.

Elsie McMay got home safely, and she reports that all that was taken in the burglary was her television set.

On Wednesday afternoon Kayleen Smeltner and Brother Verber searched all over this part of the county for the fellow who did her a kindness twenty-three years ago. Give me a call here at Ruby Bee's Bar & Grill if she's talking about you.

Until next time, God bless.

Ruby Bee's Sweet Potato Pie

¾   cup butter
¾   cup sugar
⅓   cup milk
1½ cups grated cooked sweet potatoes
¾   teaspoon ginger
2   tablespoons grated orange rind
1   10-inch pie shell

Cream the butter, adding the sugar as you go, until it's all fluffy and light. Take turns adding the milk and sweet potatoes, then toss in the ginger and orange rind and mix real well. Pour into the pie shell and bake at 300 degrees for maybe 45 minutes, until it's golden brown and set. Serve warm with whipped cream.

CHAPTER 8

Sterling looked at his watch, which was guaranteed to depths of three hundred feet below sea level and displayed the phases of the moon. "It's 1000 hours. Where is everybody?"

"I forewarned you about the apathy," Barry said, straining to hear the sound of vehicles coming toward the edge of the pasture where they'd set up a card table to distribute information and application forms.

Kayleen was by the table, rearranging booklets with titles like *The Grisly Truth About Fluoridation* and *Is International Drug Trafficking Masterminded by the British Monarchy?* "You'd think there were a few concerned citizens in this town, though. Brother Verber said a couple of folks asked him questions after his sermon last week. I'm not real sure he could answer them, but he said he tried."

"Where's Dylan?" growled Sterling.

Barry pointed at the farmhouse. "I sent him, Red Rooster, and Blitzer to excavate the old root cellar to utilize as a storeroom and bunker. If we lubricate the weapons and wrap them in plastic, we shouldn't have a problem with corrosion. Red Rooster will price cots and water jugs at the army surplus store."

"Good work, Apocalypse," Sterling said, shading his eyes and peering vainly across the pasture. "I realize no one showed up when we tried this at Bradley's place, but I assumed that was because of the remote location. You'd think the citizens of Maggody could —Look! A pickup truck's coming!"

"And someone's walking this way from the direction of the creek," added Barry. "I guess there are a few patriots left."

Kayleen squinted across the corn stalks. "That's Jeremiah McIlhaney in the truck, and he's got Earl Buchanon with him. Neither of them is overly bright, but they're hard workers. They might do just fine."

"Who's the fellow down that way?" asked Sterling.

"I can't rightly say because of the knit cap pulled down so low and those sun glasses and that mustache. I don't think I've seen a mustache like that in Maggody, but I may not have met everybody as of yet."

Barry moved to Sterling's side, and in a low voice said, "I don't like this. Could he be a foreign agent?"

"He could be, I suppose. They've been known to infiltrate groups such as ours. We'll have to be real cautious with him until I can determine his background."

"You had any more luck contacting Dylan's old group?"

"No, and it's rather odd. The password worked the first time, but I've tried several times since then to access the message board with no success. The phone's been disconnected."

"Could that be Dylan's doing?"

Sterling stopped staring at the figure on foot and turned to Barry. "Why do—what makes you say this?" he sputtered. "Do you know something that you haven't told me?"

"I just don't trust him, especially after last night."

The truck came to a halt beside the Hummer before Sterling could demand an explanation. "Welcome," he called to the two men as they emerged. "It's heartening to meet patriots like yourselves."

"Hey, Earl, Jeremiah," said Kayleen, giving them her friendliest Betty Crocker smile. "How're you boys this morning? Earl, I hear you're going to be a grandpa in a few weeks. You and Eileen must be real tickled."

"Yeah," said Earl. He stuck his hands in his pocket and studied the mud caked on the sides of the truck.

Kayleen winked at Jeremiah. "I saw your daughter the other day at the Dairee Dee-Lishus. She's such a pretty thing. I'll bet the boys hang around her like a litter of lovesick pups."

Jeremiah felt his ears heating up. "Thanks, Kayleen," he mumbled. He noticed the figure walking toward them and elbowed Earl. "What's Kevin been doing down at Boone Creek? Don't he know it's too cold for fishing?"

"I dunno," said Earl, pulling off his cap to scratch his head. "I thought Dahlia said he had to work this morning. Maybe the schedule changed or something."

They stood in silence, watching Kevin as he

slipped and slid toward them. When he came around the front of the Hummer, he froze like an ungainly scarecrow and said, "Uh, Pa, I didn't reckon you'd be here. I was—well, out taking a walk and decided to cut up this way on account of it being a shortcut of sorts, and then I noticed the trucks and—"

"Welcome," Sterling cut in smoothly. "You all already know Kayleen. I'm General Pitts and this is Colonel Kirklin. I'd like you to look over our material and take anything that interests you. All of it should —if you're as concerned as we are about the sorry state of the government these days." Rather than stepping aside to allow them to get to the card table, however, he launched into a rambling lecture about the erosion of constitutional rights and the perils of an invasion by foreign troops.

Twenty minutes later, after having thoroughly bewildered Earl, Jeremiah, and Kevin (who never had a chance), he gestured dramatically at Cotter's Ridge. "This may well be your last line of defense, which is why survival training is so vital. You may be forced to take your families up there and live off the land until militias like ours can drive the foreigners into the sea."

"You'd better drive if you're going to the sea," Earl said. "It's a good six or seven hundred miles to the Gulf of Mexico, and more like two thousand to the Pacific."

Sterling reminded himself of the necessity of recruiting privates and corporals, who would be expendable in battle. "How astute," he said to Earl, who was grinning at Jeremiah. "Please examine the material, and don't hesitate if you have any questions."

Earl looked at Kevin. "What's that piece of black paper doin' taped on your lip, son?"

"Read 'em and weep," said Jim Bob as he spread his poker hand on the table. "Didn't believe I'd picked up that third cowboy, did ya?"

Roy Stiver folded his cards. "I'm surprised you can count that high, Jim Bob. From what I hear at the barber shop, you have a tough time making change at the SuperSaver. Perkins said you tried to stiff his eldest out of ten dollars."

Jim Bob was casting around for a response that would leave Roy feeling as naked as a picked chicken when Larry Joe came into the trailer, a magazine in his hand.

"Did y'all hear something a minute ago?" he asked.

"I heard Jim Bob guffawing at how lucky he is," said Roy. "I didn't hear you flush the toilet 'cause it ain't but a hole in the ground. If it's the same to you, I'd prefer not to hear exactly which bodily functions you performed out there."

"No, I'm serious, so listen up," Larry Joe said with enough earnestness to get their attention. "Just as I was leaving the outhouse, I heard a strange boom, kind of like a bass drum. I looked in that direction and saw this—this thing behind some bushes. I couldn't make it out real good, but it was more'n five feet tall and it was sizing me up like I might make a tasty meal. I liked to jump out of my skin."

"It was Diesel, you near-sighted dolt," Jim Bob said as he poured bourbon into his glass.

Roy nodded. "Yeah, everybody knows he's living up here. Or maybe it was Raz, making sure we weren't fixing to help ourselves to a couple of jars of shine. That stuff strips paint better than any commercial goop, and your skin along with it if you don't watch what you're doing.''

"I don't think it was human," said Larry Joe. "It had eyes like orange marbles and a head no bigger than a baseball.''

Jim Bob began to shuffle the cards. "Jesus H. Christ, Larry Joe, the next thing you'll be doing is telling us you saw a flying saucer, too. Are you gonna stand there like a virgin in a roomful of preachers, or are you gonna play poker?''

"They arrived yesterday," I told Harve, who'd called just as I was heading out the door of the PD. His timing was getting downright uncanny. "Rumor has it that Generalissimo Pitts is driving a Sherman tank, but it may be an exaggeration. Other than that, nobody seems to know or care that they're here. I'm not going to worry about them unless they start firing bazookas at Estelle's Hair Fantasies.''

"We'll blow up that bridge when we come to it. I talked to Katherine Avenued's mother this morning about arranging for the body to be shipped to Tucson. McBeen says there's no reason to do more than a perfunctory autopsy since the cause of death's so obvious. He did run a drug screen to make sure she wasn't an addict likely to have unsavory friends. She was clean.''

"I told Mrs. Coben and Heidi that I'd go over there this afternoon to get an update on what was stolen. Let's hope Heidi has remembered something Katherine might have mentioned in passing.''

"Like the license plate of the truck that followed her all over Farberville the day she was killed?"

"Bingo," I said, unamused.

Harve obviously was, and I had to listen to him snort and snicker for a while before he calmed down and said, "LaBelle said to ask you if Estelle ever got her inheritance."

"She wasn't too thrilled," I said, then went on to describe the previous evening's events. "When I got there, the birds were long gone. From Estelle's hysterical description, I think they're ostriches. Uncle Tooly must have had a twisted sense of humor—or been nursing a grudge against his niece for a long while."

"Maybe so. Anyway, if you find out anything new from the Cobens, lemme know."

"Sure," I said, thinking of the proverbial snowball's chance in hell. Not good, from all accounts.

After I hung up, I took out the reports on the previous burglaries and skimmed them. I had no brilliant insights, however, and I was in the back room turning off the coffee pot when the front door opened. I went to the doorway in time to see Raz slam the door.

"I jest come to tell you," he said, his eyes blazing and saliva dribbling out of the corners of his mouth, "what I'm gonna do if you don't get that goddamn Diesel off the ridge."

"What would that be?"

"He's gonna be right sorry he was ever born, 'cause I'm gonna put so many holes in him that the wind'll whistle 'Dixie' through him."

"Shall I assume you and he had another unpleasant encounter?'' I asked as I went behind the desk and sat down. ''Do you want to file a complaint?''

''I ain't got no use for no complaint. I reckon a twelve-gauge shotgun is what I need.'' He stuffed a wad of chewing tobacco in his cheek, apparently forgetting how much I despise the habit. ''This morning I went squirrel huntin'. I left Marjorie in the truck, but I put down the window so she could git some fresh air. She must've decided to root for acorns and wandered up the ridge. All of a sudden she started squealing something terrible, so I runned up a ways and found her huddled under a ledge. She was so scared she could hardly poddle back to the truck.'' He looked around for a place to spit, caught my glare, and swallowed. ''I've had it with Diesel. Unless'n you make him take his sorry ass to a place so wild the hoot owls holler in the daytime, I'm gonna git him good.''

''How am I supposed to do that, Raz? I don't even know where his cave is. I gather it's near your still, so if you want to tell me where that is, I'll try to find Diesel and talk to him.'' The last bit was a flagrant lie, of course, but I was curious to see how he would react in such a quandary.

He opted for his standard response. ''Ain't got no still.''

''Then there's nothing I can do. Give my regards to Marjorie—and stay off the ridge.''

After he stalked out the door, I put on lipstick, buffed my badge with my cuff, and headed for Mayfly.

Dahlia went into Jim Bob's SuperSaver and looked around for Kevin. He wasn't in sight, but he could be mopping one of the aisles or stacking oranges in the produce department. Not wanting to have to walk all over the store, she approached the checkout girl.

"Hey, Idalupino. Where's Kevvie?"

"He was here when I started work at nine, but then he got sick and had to go home. I hear tell there's some sort of bug going around that makes you retch your guts out something fierce."

Dahlia chewed on this for a moment. It didn't seem likely that Kevin was at home, since she herself had left less than ten minutes ago. He could have gone to his ma and pa's house, she supposed, on account of not wanting to expose her to his bug. Ever since she'd told him she had a bun in the warmer, he'd fretted like she was a dainty flower. In fact, he was gettin' to be a pain in the butt with all his questions about how she felt and how many times the baby'd kicked and could he fetch anything for her or rub her feet.

"Can I use the phone?" she asked Idalupino, who was flipping through a tabloid.

"It's in the employee lounge. Hey, Dahlia, do you think they really found a statue of Liberace on the back side of the moon?"

"I 'spose they could have," she said, then headed for the lounge to find out if her gallant knight was retching his guts out at his ma and pa's.

Ruby Bee waited until Estelle was settled on her stool and had pulled off her scarf and gloves. "I've been waiting on you for more than an hour," she said in the snippety voice that always irritated Estelle. "You said you'd be here at two so we could go to that garage sale in Hasty. There won't be anything left by now."

"I had something more important to do than

look at cracked china and broken fishing rods," Estelle said as she took a piece of paper out of her handbag.

"Another letter from that lawyer?"

She shook her head. "I went over to the high school because I figured Lottie'd be there. Every Saturday she snoops through her students' lockers for incriminating evidence. Once she found a cartoon of her that Darla Jean had drawn—and it wasn't flattering. Another time she found a real steamy note to one of the football players implying the girl—I disremember who—had done some shameless things with him out by Boone Creek."

"So you went to the high school," prompted Ruby Bee, "and Lottie let you inside."

"Yes, and she unlocked the library for me so I could use the encyclopedias. They're on the old side, but I found what I wanted, which was about ostriches. I've got to know what I'm up against if they come back. I still get the heebie-jeebies when I think about 'em."

Ruby Bee caught the hint and poured a glass of sherry. "What all did you find out?"

"It's bad, real bad," she said, checking her notes. "The males can be as tall as eight feet and weigh three hundred and fifty pounds. The females are a mite smaller, but they're nothing to be sneezed at. When they're frightened, they can run forty miles an hour. They can also kick the livin' daylights out of you. What could Uncle Tooly have been thinking to burden me with creatures like that? Why couldn't he have left me tropical fish or a cat?"

"They're gone, Estelle, and I'd be real surprised if you ever see them again." Ruby Bee paused to do some calculating. "They've been gone close to fifteen hours, give or take. If they were going forty miles an hour, that's six hundred miles and they could be in Mexico or Canada by now, depending, of course, on which way they went."

"Or they could be lurking out behind my garage, ready to attack me. First thing this morning I tried to call that blasted lawyer in Oklahoma on the off chance he was working on a Saturday morning, but all I got was his answering machine saying the office was closed on weekends. I called information, and this sassy girl told me his home number was unlisted. I don't think I slept more than ten minutes all night, imagining them scheming to sneak back in my house."

"I don't blame you," said Ruby Bee. "Tell you what—why don't you stay at the Flamingo until you talk to that lawyer on Monday and he tells you what to do? There's plenty of space, even with Kayleen, General Pitts, and that other woman staying there."

"Oh, I wouldn't want to cause any bother," Estelle said with a self-effacing smile. "You've got all those other folks to deal with. I'll just make sure all my doors and windows are locked tight and sit up all night in the living room with a rolling pin."

Ruby Bee knew darn well she was expected to beg. Normally, she wouldn't, but she'd seen how Estelle's hand shook when she picked up her glass. "You won't cause a bit of bother, so stop being silly. I'll even go back to your house with you and keep an eye out for the birds while you pack an overnight bag."

"The bag's in my station wagon."

"Well, then," Ruby Bee said, taking off her apron, "let's go get you fixed up. I was planning to shampoo carpets in two of the units tomorrow if I can find time. Would you mind staying next to General Pitts?''

"As long as he doesn't practice barking out orders like a drill sergeant. My nerves are too frazzled for that.''

They collected Estelle's bag and continued around back to #5. Ruby Bee started to unlock the door, then stopped and frowned.

"That's strange,'' she murmured. "The door's not locked. I know I locked it last week when I was inspecting all the units to see which carpets needed to be shampooed.''

"Maybe it didn't catch,'' said Estelle.

"It caught.'' Ruby Bee opened the door, stuck her head in, then went inside. "Somebody was in here recently. I always vacuum after a guest leaves, and you can see that shag has been squashed where a chair was moved. This somebody tried to put it back where it was, but the marks are off by an inch.'' She sidled around the bed and made sure no one was in the bathroom. "Look at this, Estelle! The toilet seat is up. I always leave it down on account of it looks nicer.''

"The lamp's unplugged,'' called Estelle, who had no desire to evaluate the significance of an upright toilet seat. "Would you have left it that way?''

"Once I had a customer who stole all the light bulbs, including the ones in the ceiling fixture, so I make a point of switching on everything to make sure it works.'' She emerged from the bathroom to count coat hangers (three) and ashtrays (two). "Nothing's missing, as far as I can tell. It doesn't look like anybody sat on the bed. Whoever it was just raised the toilet seat, unplugged the lamp, and moved the chair out from under the table for a spell."

"Or you could have done those things yourself. You're getting to that age when folks start forgetting things like where they parked their car at the super-market. The other day I saw Bur Grapper pushing a shopping cart all over the parking lot. He tried to tell me he was looking at the different models—but I didn't just get off the turnip truck."

Ruby Bee put her hands on her hips. "I am no-where near that age, Estelle Oppers! Bur was old enough to vote by the time I was born. Now are you gonna stay here or not? I need to get some cobblers in the oven."

"I expect I will, but only so that you won't have to worry about me all alone with those hissy birds watching through the windows."

"Don't knock yourself out on my account." Ruby Bee marched out the door, resisting the urge to bang it closed behind her, and headed for the barroom. "Who said I was gonna worry?" she demanded of a starling perched on a garbage can.

"Now whatta we do?" asked Kevin as he squirmed in the muddy leaves, trying to get away from the water dripping off the bluff above him.

Dylan was leaning against a rock at the back of the recess. "Just keep a lookout. We only had a fifteen-minute head start, so the others should be getting close by now. Don't squawk when you see someone coming. Give me a hand signal, okay?"

Kevin clutched the rifle he'd been issued and stared so hard at the line of trees that his eyeballs bulged. It was more exciting than a John Wayne movie, he thought, but scary, too. He and Dylan had been assigned to defend the position while everybody else tried to capture them. His pa and Mr. McIlhaney hadn't looked all that enthusiastic, but they'd accepted weapons and had been listening to General Pitts's orders when he and Dylan had lit out of the campsite. That meant it was seven against two.

"You ever been in a real battle?" he asked Dylan. "You know, with bullets instead of paint pellets and fellows trying to shoot you?"

"Yes."

"Did you shoot anybody?"

"That's the point, isn't it? It wouldn't be much of a battle if nobody shot anybody else. Shut up a minute. I thought I heard something above us. Keep watching the treeline." He crawled out to the ledge and stood up to peer at the bluff.

Kevin reminded himself that this was a make-believe battle. General Pitts had assured them that the paint pellets might sting but would do no damage. It wasn't like they'd be taken prisoner and subjected to torture. The worst that could happen was they'd lose the game. His pa'd laugh at him, but he did that anyway.

"Ow!" yelped Dylan.

"What's the matter?" demanded Kevin as he scrambled to his feet without thinking, and promptly banged his head so hard he went sprawling back into the leaves. He was about to repeat his question when a gun was fired from the woods. Whimpering, he covered his head and wiggled to the back of the recess.

After a moment, he found the courage to lift his

head. Dylan was gone, which was a puzzlement. Had he been taken prisoner without so much as a peep? Or had he abandoned their position? It didn't seem like a comradely thing to do, Kevin thought as he cautiously wiggled back out to the rocky ledge. He couldn't see anybody in the brush on the hillside; he rolled over and looked up, but he didn't see anybody there either.

"This is a fine kettle of fish!" he said peevishly, but softly so's not to tip off the enemy, who had to be around somewhere.

A drop of cold water splashed his nose. He rolled back over and continued wiggling until he reached the edge. Risking life, limb, and a paint pellet to the forehead, he looked down.

Six feet below, Dylan lay flat on the ground, his arms and legs flung out as if he were hanging on to keep from being sucked up by a tornado. On his shoulder was a spreading stain that Kevin realized was not paint. There'd been a gunshot, he reminded himself as he scrambled down to Dylan and poked his arm.

"You okay?" he said, gulping.

Dylan opened his eyes. "Not really, so maybe you'd better get help."

"Yeah, right, that's what I'm gonna do." Kevin took a couple of breaths in case there were more orders. When none were forthcoming, he went galloping downhill. He stopped as he reached the line of trees and waved at Dylan, who was sitting up. "Stay there!" he shouted, then plunged into the brush.

It was slow going. Thorns snagged him with every step, and roots lay in wait to trip him. It hadn't seemed this rough when he and Dylan had come up from the camp, he was thinking as he stepped in the entrance of a burrow and fell on his face.

He was blinking back tears of frustration as he got to his feet, but he was determined to carry on just like the Duke did when he was leading his men through the jungle. Sure, his ankle hurt and his hands were muddy, but he was a soldier. Nothing was gonna prevent him from carrying out the mission. He'd taken one step when the paint pellet hit him in the middle of his chest.

"Bang, you're dead," Reed said cheerfully as he materialized from behind a tree.

Kevin looked down at the orange blotch. "You can't just say 'bang.' You have to fire your gun."

"I used my blowgun." Reed's eyes narrowed and his voice turned ugly. "Did you split and leave Dylan up there by hisself? Are you a deserter?"

" 'Course not. I was coming—"

"Then you must be a spy, and I caught you behind enemy lines. If this was the real thing, we could hang you without bothering with a trial."

Kevin glanced involuntarily at a nearby branch, then remembered why he was there. "Dylan was shot, and not with a paint pellet. His shoulder's all bloody. He was sitting up when I left him, though, so he ain't dead or anything like that."

"Damn!" said Reed. He took a fat pistol out of his pocket and fired into the air. A flare streaked toward the bluff. "That'll bring everybody. You wait here. When Kayleen shows up, tell her to get the medical kit."

Kevin wasn't sure if he was supposed to salute, but he went ahead and did it. "Yes, sir."

CHAPTER 9

Mrs. Jim Bob's timing was as uncanny as Harve's. Thirty seconds after I'd arrived back at the PD after a fruitless trip to Mayfly and was debating whether to do anything about the red light flashing on the answering machine, she burst through the door.

"There you are!" she snapped.

"Well, that's good to know. I've been wondering all week where I was."

Mrs. Jim Bob blinked, then said, "Let's have no more flippant remarks, missy. I want to file a missing person report."

"He's at the deer camp. Ruby Bee saw him loading up cases of beer and supplies yesterday morning."

"I don't believe it," she said as she sank down in the visitor's chair and pursed her lips so tightly veins popped out in her neck. After a long moment of silence, she said, "I don't know why Ruby Bee would say such a thing. She may not have much admiration for him, but she wouldn't stoop so low as to make up a bald-faced lie like that. Doesn't she have any regard for his reputation?"

That was not a topic I wanted to explore. "Why

don't you rent a four-wheel-drive and go roam around
Cotter's Ridge until you find the deer camp? I'm sure
the guys will be delighted to show you around and get
some remodeling hints for the outhouse."

"Are you out of your mind?"

I crossed my eyes. "I might be. I certainly must
be hearing voices, because I distinctly heard someone
imply that Ruby Bee should have regard for Jim Bob's
reputation. I hate to break it to you like this, but—"

"Who said anything about Jim Bob?"

"Then who's missing?" I said, surprised.

"Brother Verber. He hasn't been seen since the
Wednesday evening prayer service. I want you to fill
out a missing person report and issue a countywide
alert. It's possible he had an accident and is bleeding
to death in a ditch somewhere."

I leaned back in the chair and settled my feet on
the corner of the desk. "He's only been gone for
three days. Don't you think it's premature to start
planning his funeral?"

Mrs. Jim Bob took out a hankie to dab at her
nose. "I just know that something terrible has happened to him. How can I live with myself if I don't
do everything possible to save him? I realize you don't
believe in the power of prayer, being an atheist and
all, but I have prayed for his return and begged the
Lord to watch over him and keep him out of the arms
of the wretched trollop."

"Wretched trollop?" I said.

"That pawn store woman," she said with a shud-
der. "Brother Verber was riding in her car Wednesday
afternoon when he was supposed to be discussing the
Thanksgiving pageant. Four hours later he vanished
like a puff of smoke. I find that suspicious, and you

should, too.'' She wadded up the hankie in her fist and leaned forward to stare at me. ''What if he agreed to go with her after the service, and she took him to an abandoned house where devil worshipers meet and they sacrificed him to Satan?''

''Isn't it more likely that he heard about a sale on plastic poinsettias and dashed off to buy some to decorate the Assembly Hall next month?''

''He would have told me,'' Mrs. Jim Bob said firmly. ''We have a close spiritual bond based on the strength of our faith in the Lord. While we're on the subject, you could use a healthy dose of that, couldn't you? If you'd bother to read the Book of Revelations, you'd be a sight more worried about eternity.''

''It feels as if this conversation has been going on for an eternity,'' I said as I stood up. ''If Brother Verber's not back tomorrow for the morning service, I'll ask the sheriff to have his deputies keep an eye out for him. I don't think we can call in the FBI until you get a ransom note.''

''Will you question that woman?''

''When I get a chance. Now, if you'll excuse me, I have work to do. You wouldn't want me to get behind on all this fascinating paperwork and disgrace the badge bestowed on me by Hizzoner himself, would you?''

Mrs. Jim Bob tilted her head so she could look down her nose at me. ''These days there's little doubt in most folks' minds that this is *not* a suitable job for a woman.''

On that note, she swept out the door. I waited a moment in case she reappeared with another parting shot, then hit the button on the answering machine. The first two messages were from Ruby Bee and had something to do with upright toilet seats and shag carpet. The third was from LaBelle.

"Get yourself over to where the make-believe soldiers are camping," she said. "Sheriff Dorfer will meet you there. Ten-four."

Sometimes LaBelle goes through a phase of watching cop shows on television, so I figured she wasn't telling me the time of the message. I put on my coat while I listened to the last message, which again had to do with a toilet seat, then drove out to the old Wockermann place.

As soon as I'd passed the farmhouse, I saw half a dozen vehicles at the far side of the pasture. I followed a path of flattened corn stalks and parked between an ambulance and a monstrosity that could probably drive up a tree. Earl Buchanon and Jeremiah McIlhaney were sitting in one of the pickups, passing a whiskey bottle back and forth. Neither looked particularly pleased when I approached them.

"What's going on?" I asked. "Where's everybody?"

Earl pointed a stubby finger at the ridge. "Way the hell up there, but I don't rightly know where. The camp's not too far on the other side of the gully. The sheriff said to tell you a deputy would be waiting there for you."

"What are you and Jeremiah doing, Earl?"

"Drinkin' whiskey so we won't freeze our butts off. The sheriff wants to talk to us after they bring down the body."

"Whose body?" I asked, wishing he was a tad more communicative.

Jeremiah bent forward to look at me. "A young

fellow name of Dylan Gilbert. It sounds like he caught a bullet from a hunter.''

Earl took a drink of whiskey and wiped his mouth with his hand. ''I wish to hell we hadn't showed up in the first place. Eileen ain't gonna like it, especially when she finds out Kevin was here, too.''

''Millicent's gonna be hotter than a peppermill that I didn't get the truck back so her and Darla Jean could go shoppin' in Farberville,'' Jeremiah said. ''I'll hear about this till Christmas.''

''I'll hear about it till Easter.''

''Well, I'll hear about it till the Fourth of July.''

I left them to discuss the impending repercussions and went across the gully. Les was leaning against a tree at the campsite, which consisted of four small tents, several coolers and cartons, and the smoldering remains of a campfire. ''You made it, huh?'' he said.

''It looks like it. What's going on?''

He gave me an abbreviated version of the scenario as we walked uphill. ''What I don't understand,'' he added, ''is why a bunch of grown men want to play 'Rambo on the Ridge' when it's the middle of deer season. A couple of years back a woman was shot in her own backyard. She thought she was safe on account of posting her land, but she didn't realize how far a bullet travels. That's likely to be what happened here. Somewhere on the ridge is a guy that's cussing up a storm 'cause he missed a buck. He'll never know what he really hit.''

I was too busy battling the brush to respond. Five minutes later we came into an open area. Harve was puffing on a cigar butt as he watched the paramedics zip up a black body bag. At his feet were strange-looking pistols, each with a tag. Standing in a group were Pitts, Kayleen, the guy who'd introduced himself the previous evening at Ruby Bee's, and two guys I'd never seen before. All of them wore olive drab and boots, although Kayleen still looked quite stylish. Kevin was sitting on a stump, his bony shoulders hunched, his face puckered, and his Adam's apple rippling as if he were trying to swallow a ping pong ball.

"Hey, Harve," I said as I joined him. "Les told me what happened. Are you really satisfied it was an accident?"

"I reckon so. Les and I checked these morons' pistols, and the only thing they can fire are paint pellets. We'll have ballistics check 'em out just to be sure."

The paramedics picked up the stretcher. "We're out of here," one of them said. "You shouldn't hang around, either. It's not the safest place I've been lately."

Harve waited until the paramedics reached the line of trees. "Okay, everybody down to pasture. We've got some talking to do before you pack your gear and get the hell out of here. Those of you who live elsewhere had better not come back, either."

Sterling harrumped like an ancient bullfrog. "The First Amendment guarantees the right of the people to assemble peaceably. That is precisely what we were doing, and will do so again if we so choose. You are a public servant."

"Don't expect me to wash your windows," Harve said, then stomped on the cigar butt and took off down the hill. Everybody else followed him, except for Kevin, who was surreptitiously wiping his eyes.

"Come on," I said to him. "Like the guy said, this is not the safest place."

"This is all my fault. It was my first mission, and I failed. Dylan told me how we was supposed to watch out for each other. He said that's what they do in a platoon, and we shook hands on it. He even said I was gonna make a real fine WASP."

"As in White Anglo-Saxon Protestant?" I said, confused as usual when trying to follow Kevin's thought process. "That's what you already are."

"No, it stands for White Aryan Superior . . . something or other. Patriot, mebbe. I'd start out as a private, but Dylan said I'd be promoted in no time."

I grabbed his arm and hauled him to his feet. "You can tell me what happened while we walk. Dylan had participated in this kind of thing before, right?"

"Yeah, and he was in a real battle, too. He dint look old enough to have been in Desert Storm. Have there been any wars since then?"

"There've been some military interventions," I said as I ducked under a branch. "Did you see anything at the moment the rifle was fired?"

"Not so's I recollect."

"What exactly do you recollect?"

Kevin stopped and sucked on his lip. "When we first got there, Dylan told me to watch down the hill. If I saw anybody, I was 'sposed to give him a hand signal. He dint say what kind of signal, but I figured I'd kinda wave like this." He flopped his wrist a couple of times. "But I dint see anybody. Then all of a sudden Dylan said he heard something up over us, so he came out and tried to see what it was. That's when he got shot."

"But you never saw anything in the woods?" I asked, shoving him back into motion.

"I saw a li'l squirrel in a tree."

I struggled not to sigh, but I was asking too much of myself. "What's that splotch on your jacket, Kevin?"

"Aw, one of the guys got me with a paint pellet. I told him I dint think it was fair the way he did it, but he just grinned like a mule with a mouthful of thistles."

"Isn't that the point of this nonsense?"

"Real soldiers aren't so dadburned sneaky," he said sullenly.

Rather than examine the goals of guerrilla warfare, I told him to follow me. We went through the campsite and crossed the gully. As I came up to the pasture, a raindrop nailed me on the back of my neck.

"I do not understand why we need to give statements," Sterling was saying to Harve. Their faces were equally mottled, and their noses were inches apart.

Having seen similar behavior in schoolyards, I hurried over to them and said, "Calm down, boys. Harve, why don't you use the PD? It'll be crowded, but noticeably warmer and drier."

"You have no more right to detain us," said Sterling, "than you do to confiscate our weapons. Aren't you up for re-election soon, Sheriff? If your flagrant disregard for individual rights is made public, you'd best start interviewing for jobs in the private sector. I am a member of the Rotary and Kiwanis clubs, a church deacon, and the vice-president of the county insurance agents' association. Furthermore, I am on a first-name basis with the lieutenant governor—"

"Shuddup," Harve snarled, then looked at me. "Actually, I got a small problem. The county prosecutor's holding a press conference about the burglaries, and he wants me there to field questions. It starts in an hour. Since this was an accident and the statements are nothing more than a formality, I was hoping you'd handle them. Les'll hang around in case you need help. I know I've been asking a lot of favors from you, Arly, and I'll make it up to you after the election."

"How are you planning to do that, Harve? Get me my own team of bloodhounds?"

He thought about it for a moment. "Tell ya what—the next time we have to extradite somebody in New Orleans, I'll assign it to you. If you go a few days early, we can cover expenses and it'll be between the two of us."

"Squandering the taxpayers' money?" inserted Sterling with the same supercilious smile I was beginning to know too well.

Kayleen put her hand on his arm. "Honey, you're making things worse. Why don't we go sit in the Hummer?"

I grimaced at Harve. "It shouldn't take long, so I'll do it. As for New Orleans, I'd rather have those bloodhounds."

Ruby Bee used her passkey to let herself into General Pitts's unit. She hung fresh towels in the bathroom, gathered up the damp ones, and went back into the room. Despite the clutter of electronic equipment, everything was tidy and the bed made with surgical precision. She eyed the computer with all its cables, wondering if her electric bill was gonna be sky-high, then ran a feather duster over everything and locked the door behind her.

Estelle opened her door. "Snooping?"

"I'm cleaning the units same as I always do," Ruby Bee said as she headed for Kayleen's unit.

"I'll give you a hand," Estelle said, trotting after her. "Lemme carry those towels."

"I've been doing this by myself for thirty years, and I can manage just fine."

She unlocked the door of #3 and, with Estelle on her heels, went inside. She already knew Kayleen wasn't real orderly, so she wasn't surprised that the bed wasn't made and several articles of clothing were draped over the back of a chair. A small saucepan rested on the hot plate; Kayleen had asked permission, and since she was gonna be there for months, it seemed reasonable. "You can make the bed," she said to Estelle, then went on into the bathroom to exchange towels and clean the tub.

"Kayleen sure does look pretty in this photograph," said Estelle. "This must be her and her husband on their honeymoon at some fancy island resort. I didn't realize he was so much older than her. He reminds me of my grandpappy, who was ninety-seven when he passed away."

"Now who's snooping?" called Ruby Bee as she wiped out the sink.

"I was only making an observation. It's none of my business who she marries. I couldn't care less if she marries Raz Buchanon, although I can't see her sitting beside Marjorie on the sofa."

Ruby Bee came out of the bathroom, mutely made the bed, and went out the door.

Estelle caught up with her as she knocked on Judy Milliford's door. "Isn't she up on the ridge with everybody else?"

"No, I saw her come walking back here less than an hour ago. I invited her to have some coffee in the bar, but she said she needed to take a hot shower and get into some dry clothes. She doesn't sound as gung ho as—" She stopped as the door opened. "I brought you some clean towels."

Judy was dressed in a robe and her face was flushed. "Thanks, Ruby Bee," she said with a small smile. "I was going to take you up on that coffee, but I'm afraid I may have caught a cold. I think I'll just curl up in bed and watch television until I have to go back to the camp and fix supper."

"I thought they were going to live off the land," Ruby Bee said.

Judy's smile faded. "Jake says that's malarkey, that when we take to the mountains, we'll have plenty of supplies with us. If we run low, he can break into the enemy's supply depot and get more. We'll always have fresh fish and game, too."

"That must be a comforting thought," murmured Ruby Bee, "if you have cornmeal, anyway. You go lie down and have a nice nap, Judy. If I can bring you something from the bar, give me a call."

"Thanks," Judy said as she closed the door.

They were walking toward the back door of the bar when Mrs. Jim Bob came into the parking lot in her pink Cadillac. She drove right past them and pulled in beside the brown Mercedes, leapt out of the car, and began pounding on the door of #3.

"I know you're in there!" she shrieked. "I demand to know what you did with him, you wicked, wicked hussy! Don't think you can cower in there until I go away. I'm going to stay right here till you open this door!"

Estelle arched her carefully drawn eyebrows. "Think we should tell her that Kayleen's not there?"

"After what she said to me the other day?" replied Ruby Bee. She watched Mrs. Jim Bob's fist going up and down like a jackhammer for a moment, then went through the back door.

Once we all arrived at the PD, I realized there was no way to cram that many bodies in the back room. Counting myself, we were one shy of a football team—and the preponderance of olive drab made the situation feel even more claustrophobic.

"You two," I said, pointing at Sterling and Kayleen, "can go over to your units at the Flamingo and I'll take your statements there. Jeremiah and Earl, you all go on home and wait for me. Don't tell anybody what happened on the ridge. The last thing I need is a gaggle of sightseers getting themselves shot."

"What about me?" squeaked Kevin.

"You go home, too," I said, already dreading the necessity of taking his statement, even though he was the closest thing we had to an eyewitness. As they left, I heard Earl bawling out Kevin for missing work and Sterling sputtering at Kayleen about his constitutional rights. Now we were down to the size of a basketball team, and the room felt larger (although not the size of a regulation court).

"I reckon I'll go over to the motel," said one of the men I didn't recognize. "My wife's staying there."

When I merely looked at him, he added through clenched teeth, "I'm Jake Milliford from Emmett. I didn't see nothing, so you're wasting your time if you think I got anything to say to you."

I could tell from his surly tone that he wasn't accustomed to taking orders from a female. It was tempting to make him squirm, but I flicked a finger at the door. "Stay in her room until I get around to you."

"I'll stay where I damn well please."

I looked at Les. "Would you escort Mr. Milliford to the Flamingo, then remain in the parking lot and keep an eye on all of them? I should be there in an hour or so."

Les escorted his charge out the door, leaving only three of us. Barry smiled at me and said, "Any chance for coffee?"

"If you make it," I said, then sat down behind my desk and pulled out a legal pad. "Name?" I asked the other unfamiliar man.

He didn't look any happier than Jake Milliford, but he sat down and said, "Reed Rondly."

"Rank?" I asked brightly. "Serial number? This is supposed to be a military outfit, isn't it? Or are you all just a bunch of bumbling idiots who like to act out your anal-retentive impulses in the woods?"

Reed licked his lips. "What's your problem, honey? You having your period?"

"Cool it," Barry called from the back room. "Just tell her what you know so we can leave, okay?"

"Okay," he muttered, glaring at me. "We all got here yesterday evening at different times. Dylan rode with me, and Sterling and Jake were at the campsite when we got there at maybe five. Barry showed up later. This morning Sterling, Kayleen, and Judy came just before sunrise, and later on, the three local fellows. Sterling told Dylan to take the kid and pick a position on the bluff. We waited fifteen minutes, then split up so we could come at 'em from different directions. I was trying to figure out what to do about that clear patch when the kid came stumbling by. He told me what happened and I fired a flare to bring everybody. By the time I got to Dylan, Kayleen was giving him mouth-to-mouth, but he died anyway. That's about it."

I finished scribbling all that and said, "Did you hear a shot right before you encountered Kevin?"

"Yeah, but way off from where I was." He leaned back, clearly proud of his recitation. "Bring me some coffee, Barry. Three sugars, no milk."

I sketched a crude map of the area and pushed it toward him. "Make a mark where you were when you heard the shot," I said.

He sneered at my effort, then took the pencil and drew an X indicating he'd been just inside the woods. "Here, I guess. Hell, I wasn't worried where I was. I was more concerned about where Dylan and the kid were and how I was going to get off a decent shot."

Barry came back into the room, handed a mug to Reed, and put one down on my desk. "You can probably use this, too," he said to me.

"Thanks." I looked over what I'd written, then glanced up at Reed. "And at any time did you have a weapon with live ammo?"

He shrugged. "I got my rifle and some thirty-caliber bullets in the truck in case I decide to do some huntin' after the retreat. I got fired on Thursday, so it ain't like I have anything better to do. Let that dumb-ass process server come find me out here.''

"Process server?" I said.

Barry rolled his eyes at me. "Reed's experiencing marital difficulties, and some guy has been chasing him all over Farberville. He stayed away from work because of that, which is why he's currently unemployed.''

"Damn that Bobbi Jo," said Reed between noisy slurps of coffee. "It's her own damn fault. If she hadn't bitched at me for coming home drunk, I wouldn't have had to teach her a lesson about who wears the pants and who wears the panties." He leered at me. "What about you, baby? You got black silk panties on that firm little ass of yours?''

I considered getting out my gun, but I didn't want to squander one of my precious bullets on him. "Give me your address and phone number, then get out of here," I said levelly. "Someone at the sheriff's department will type this up and bring it to you to be signed in a couple of days.''

He rattled off the information, then added, "I'll be over at that dumpy bar, Barry. I guess we need to find out what Sterling wants to do.''

I waited until he left before I dared reach for the mug. After a couple of sips, I said, "Your comrade's a real jerk, isn't he?''

Barry took the vacated chair. "He's under a lot of stress because of the divorce. Usually he's a real sweetheart.''

"Sure he is," I said dryly. "You have anything to add to what he said about arrival times?''

"No, as far as I know, that was pretty much it. I

had to work Friday, so I was the last one to show up."

I gave him the map. "Where were you when you heard the single shot?"

He studied it for a long while, as if the scattering of lines held some mystical significance. "I guess I was over that way," he said as he drew an X. "I wanted to work my way below the ledge, but I had the same problem Reed did with the open area. I heard the shot, and maybe three or four minutes later, I saw the flare that meant something was wrong."

"You couldn't see the ledge where Dylan was standing when he was shot?" I asked, retrieving my masterpiece to compare Reed's and Barry's marks. One was large and lopsided, the other small and precise.

"No, the bluff juts out and I was coming around from the far side. I couldn't even see the clearing at that point."

"What can you tell me about Dylan? How long has he been a member of your group?"

Barry gave this question as much consideration as he had the map. "He drifted into town about two weeks ago, got a job at the garage, and ended up crashing at Reed's apartment. He claimed he'd been living in Denver."

"Claimed? Did you doubt him?"

"I had some misgivings. I don't know how to say this without making us sound like a gang of desperados. We've never done anything illegal, but groups like ours are often under investigation by certain federal agencies. It's not uncommon for agents to attempt to pose as disciples in order to infiltrate."

My pseudo-professional veneer evaporated. "Are you saying the victim was a federal agent?"

"It occurred to me," he said, shrugging. "It was

almost as though he knew ahead of time that Reed was the one to approach, since the rest of us are quite a bit more reticent when discussing . . . our activities." He put the mug on the floor and held up his hands. "Which are legal, as I said a minute ago. You may not agree with our philosophy, but you have to admit we have the constitutional right to embrace it."

"Which amendments cover racism and paranoia?" I asked sweetly.

"You'll have to ask Sterling. He's our specialist in matters of law." He set the mug on the corner of my desk. "I suppose I won't be buying you a beer on Monday, right?"

"That's very perceptive of you." I stood up so he couldn't look down at me. "I suggest you and your comrades go find some other place to make fools of yourselves. If I have to, I'll declare the entire acreage from the county road to the bluff a crime scene. It'll take a lot of yellow tape to make it off-limits, but I have plenty of free time. That means if you all return, you'll be trespassing, and also that Kayleen can't proceed with the remodeling. I have a feeling that won't sit well with her."

"Probably not. I'll tell Sterling what you said, unless you prefer to tell him yourself."

"Go ahead and tell him whatever you wish. After all, the Constitution guarantees freedom of speech, doesn't it?" I wrote down his address and telephone number, then told him to leave. I still had six more statements to take, but I'd already heard most of Kevin's story and I figured Earl Buchanon and Jeremiah McIlhaney would have little to contribute. For that matter, none of them would if the shooting had been an accident, as Harve believed.

But if Dylan Gilbert had been exposed as a federal agent, it might be a whole 'nuther ballgame, I
thought as I reread the notes I'd taken while interviewing Barry. The logical agencies were the FBI and
the ATF, but I wasn't at all sure I could call Washington and politely ask them to confirm the identity of
an undercover agent.

I gave up worrying about it, and was halfway to
my car when Dahlia came pounding up the road, her
massive arms flopping like prehensile wings. "It's Kevvie!" she yelled at me. "He's disappeared!"

"No, he hasn't," I said calmly. "He was out at
that gathering on County 102 and then at the PD, but
I sent him home half an hour ago."

She huffed and puffed until she caught her
breath. "I was over at his parents' house when his pa
got there. He told us what happened and said that
Kevvie had gone back to the SuperSaver for what was
left of his shift. I went right over there to chew him
out, but Idalupino said he never showed up. He ain't
at home, neither. What if it's time for the baby and I
cain't find him? What am I gonna do . . . ?"

I didn't have an answer.

CHAPTER 10

I drove Dahlia back to her in-laws' house. After she'd been settled on the sofa with a quilt and a diet soda, I asked Eileen to drive to Kevin's house and make sure he wasn't hiding under the porch. Then, without enthusiasm, I asked Earl to join me in the kitchen.

"Okay," I began, speaking quietly so Dahlia couldn't overhear us, "what the hell were you, Kevin, and Jeremiah doing out there this morning? Do you honestly believe this country is going to be invaded by a bunch of Swiss paratroopers armed with pocket-knives?"

He hung his head. "Jeremiah and I went because we were curious. There was this pamphlet being handed out all over town that said we didn't have to pay taxes, and I sure could use a new tractor."

"No, Earl, you *don't* have to pay taxes. It's entirely your decision whether to send a check to the IRS or go to prison. Just bear in mind that tax evasion's a federal offense, so you might end up sharing a cell with Raz and having Sunday afternoon visits from Marjorie." I flipped the pad to a clean page and poised my pencil. "Tell me what happened from the time you arrived at the Wockermann place."

"We got there at ten, listened to Pitts carry on about something or other, and then agreed to participate in this military exercise around eleven. I dunno why we said we would, except I used to love to hear my pa talk about being in France during the war. I would've signed on to go to Vietnam, but our troops pulled out before I turned eighteen."

"I get the picture," I said. "Tell me about this morning."

"Fifteen minutes after Dylan and Kevin went up the hill, Pitts told us to scatter on our own. Jeremiah and I weren't sure about that, so we stayed together."

"And?" I said, perhaps a shade impatiently.

"We got to thinking that we should wait near the gully in case they doubled back to sneak behind our line. We were gonna find a place to sit by the tents, but we heard somebody coming, so we went to Jeremiah's truck."

"Where it was dry," I said. "Did you see anybody after that?"

Earl nodded, although it'd be a stretch to say he did so thoughtfully. "Pitts scrambled across the gully and used a phone in that tank of his. I guess he called for an ambulance, 'cause it and the sheriff turned up within half an hour. You came pretty soon after that."

I didn't bother with notes. "Did you and Jeremiah hear any shots?"

This time he shook his head. "We had the windows rolled up and were listening to the radio. Don't go telling Millicent, but Jeremiah has the hots for this little blond-headed country singer with enormous tits, and he wanted me to hear her new song."

Eileen hurried in through the back door. "Kevin's not at home," she said grimly, "and neither is the car. I stopped at the supermarket, and no one's seen hide nor hair of him since nine this morning."

Earl scratched his head. "Jeremiah and me dropped him off in back of the store less than an hour ago. He was mumbling to hisself, but he was almost to the door when we drove away."

"I can't imagine where he is," said Eileen. "He may be a few dips short of a sundae, but he couldn't get lost between the dumpster and the door."

I had reservations about that, but I kept them to myself and said, "He may have decided to go to the Flamingo to beg forgiveness for his self-perceived dereliction of duty. If I spot him, I'll send him home with his tail between his legs. Is there anything else you should tell me, Earl?"

"Not really," he said, "unless it was that figure I saw come out of the woods way up by the fence at the back of the Assembly Hall. All I caught was a glimpse, and Jeremiah swore I was seeing things."

"Was this before or after Pitts made his call?" I asked.

"Oh, I'd say about fifteen minutes before. I wasn't paying much attention on account of Jeremiah's favorite song coming on. It was something about knockers and knickers, and I told Jeremiah it didn't make a lick of sense, but he said—"

"Let me know if you hear from Kevin," I said. I tiptoed past Dahlia, who was snoring, and let myself out the front door. I suppose I should have been more concerned about Kevin, but he was capable of almost anything, including driving into Farberville to enlist in the army (as if they'd take him).

It was doubtful Jeremiah would have anything to add to Earl's account, so I left him for later, swung by Kevin's house on the off-chance he'd popped up like a fever blister, and then went to the motel behind Ruby Bee's Bar & Grill. Only three more statements, I told myself as I parked, and I'd be rid of the militia once and for all. Kayleen would still be around, but my threat to tie a yellow ribbon around her property was probably adequate to send everybody else away, including the insufferable Reed Rondly. It was kind of a shame about Barry Kirklin, though. I wasn't in the market for a steady beau, much less a husband, but it might have been nice to have a beer and a conversation.

Les got out of his car. "Nobody's so much as poked a toe outside," he reported. "I take that back. Estelle Oppers came out of her room and asked me if I was here because of the toilet seat."

I had a pretty good idea why Estelle was holed up at the Flamingo, although I was getting tired of cryptic messages regarding this nefarious toilet seat. "I don't know what she meant, Les. Maybe plumbers are in such demand these days that they're running around with badges and sidearms. Has Kevin been here?" He shook his head. "Which units are whose?"

Once he'd told me, I decided to give myself a break and start with Kayleen, and then beg a couple of antacid tablets from Ruby Bee before tackling Sterling Pitts and Jake Milliford.

Kayleen must have seen me coming, because she opened the door as I approached. She'd changed into a cashmere sweater and slacks, but her face, devoid of makeup, was sallow. "I know, I know," she said as I went into her room. "You tried to tell me and I wouldn't listen. I've gone deer hunting most every year since I was twelve, and nothing like this ever happened, but—"

"This time it happened." I sat down on the bed and opened my pad. "You didn't go to the campsite until this morning, right?"

"That's right. We got there shortly after six. Judy made breakfast while the rest of us unloaded some things from Sterling's Hummer and prepared for a gathering to share our beliefs with the local citizens. The turnout was disappointing, particularly to Sterling, but he went ahead and gave his talk, then invited them to participate in an exercise."

"Were Dylan and Kevin supposed to be the insidious foreigners or the heroic defenders of truth, justice, and the American way?"

"Oh, I don't think roles were defined," Kayleen said as she sat down on the opposite side of the bed. "We synchronized our watches, waited for fifteen minutes, and then headed out on our own. I thought I'd try to get above their position, but I ended up where it was as steep as the side of a barn."

I handed her my increasingly wrinkled map. "Show me where you were when you heard the first shot."

"Whose marks are these?" she asked.

"Why does it matter?"

She made a vague gesture with her free hand. "It doesn't. Let me see if I can figure out what these lines mean. Is this a tree?"

I pointed out all the relevant landmarks, then watched her as she ran a manicured fingertip up the page.

"I came this way," she murmured. "I spotted

Reed ahead of me and shifted over this way. Then I made my way over this way and ended up behind a thicket about here." She drew an X on the opposite side of the map from Barry's. "I guess that's about right, although I wouldn't testify to it in court."

"Did you see anybody besides Reed?"

"Not a soul, and I couldn't see the ledge, either. I didn't know what to think when I heard the first shot, but then I saw the flare and came out from behind the thicket. I reached Dylan's body first, and I could tell he was in big trouble. When Reed got there, I sent him back to camp to get the first aid kit." She made a little noise that was not quite a groan. "Dylan died within minutes. It brought back raw memories of the night Maurice was killed, and I was hunkered there with my arms around my knees when Jake arrived a couple of minutes later."

"Which direction did he come from?"

Kayleen looked down at the map. "I wasn't paying any attention."

"What about Sterling?"

"He said he ran into Reed and learned what had happened. He went to the pasture to use his car phone to call an ambulance, then came back up to the clearing. There was nothing more to do but wait for the paramedics." She went into the bathroom to blow her nose, and returned with a tremulous attempt at a smile. "I feel so silly about getting all upset like this. Here I am, presenting myself as a hardy, self-reliant woman who can take care of herself, and then an accident happens and I go to pieces. I've bought and sold more guns than most folks see in a lifetime, and what's more, I know how violence has pervaded every segment of our society."

"What did you think of Dylan Gilbert?" I asked.

"Nothing, really," she said as she sank back down. "This morning was the first time I met him. We sat together at breakfast on a log down by the gully, and I did my best to be real friendly. He was young, not more than twenty-five, and like most kids that age, full of himself. Not poor Kevin Buchanon, of course. He's about as forceful as a newborn kitten. After the accident, he was mewling like one, too."

"Let's keep talking about Dylan," I said. "Did you have any reason to think there was anything peculiar about him? Was he telling the truth about his past?"

She studied me for a long while, then sighed and said, "You've been listening to Barry, haven't you? I don't know why Barry was making all those dark comments about Dylan, unless it was because he was jealous, like an older child when a baby's brought home from the hospital. Until Dylan came along, Barry was the smart one. After he got out of the army, he found a job at a bookstore and worked his way up to department manager. Dylan had gone to college for a couple of years and studied engineering."

"So you think Barry was jealous?"

"I don't know any other reason why he was whispering behind Dylan's back. I hate to say this, but the federal agencies would hardly bother with the likes of us. There are groups that stockpile weapons and build explosive devices, and some have resorted to violence. We're all hot air and bravado, like I told you when you first objected to the retreat. None of us would ever find the nerve to do something illegal, much less dangerous."

"Dylan found it dangerous," I said, staring at her.

She looked away. "But that was an accident, and it didn't have anything to do with us."

I told her she'd be asked to sign the statement later in the week, then went out into the lot and steeled myself for the final two interviews. Before I'd talked myself into actually knocking on a door, Les emerged from his car.

"Sheriff Dorfer wants you to call him as soon as you can," he said. "It's real important."

"Did he say why?"

"I asked," he admitted, "but that's all LaBelle would tell me. She's in a real snit these days, isn't she?"

"No kidding," I said as I headed for the PD.

"All I kin say," Kevin said through a mouthful of tamale, "is it ain't fair for whoever shot Dylan to get away with it. Everybody keeps actin' like it was just one of those things. Why, I'd be mighty surprised if Arly bothers with the statements and I sure cain't see the sheriff reading 'em."

His remarks were directed only at the hillside below the ledge. Not even the cute li'l squirrel was anywhere to be seen, having retreated to a leafy nest to escape the cold drizzle.

Kevin finished the tamale he'd had the foresight to pick up at the Dairee Dee-Lishus, crammed the wrapper in his pocket, and discovered that for some crazy reason, he had a cassette in his pocket. Dahlia's relaxation tape, he decided, wondering how he'd ended up with it.

He stood up, this time mindful of his head.

"No," he said, continuing to talk out loud because it was kind of creepy out here by his lonesome, "if Arly's gonna sweep this under the carpet, then it's up to Kevin Fitzgerald Buchanon to find the guilty hunter and see that he goes to jail. I owe that much to Dylan."

Over the treetops he could see the roof of the old Wockermann farmhouse, and beyond that the chimney of Estelle's house across the county road. That was about it, but it was comforting to know he wasn't lost. All he needed now, he thought with a sigh, was some sort of plan.

It wasn't likely the hunter had been between the ledge and the campsite, since that was where the make-believe soldiers had been. He shifted his attention to the woods off to his right. They rose steeply, but they didn't look as thick and gnarly, so he decided to go that way and see if maybe he'd find a deer camp.

He climbed down to the spot where Dylan had fallen, although he kept his eyes averted in case there might be bloodstains on the rocks. Robin Buchanon's old shack was somewhere in that direction, and it occurred to him that it might not be bad to get out of the drizzle before he was soaked to the skin. He could even try to scrounge up some dry firewood and build a fire in the rusty pot-bellied stove. Once he was warm, he'd come up with a real good plan that'd have made Dylan proud of him.

The going was easier for the most part, but there were plenty of thorns and treacherous holes covered with leaves. The birds had retreated, too, except for a crow making a racket from an invisible branch. Kevin made his way around the bluff and continued upward, saving his breath for gasping and panting.

The mountainside grew rockier as he climbed, and he was obliged to slow his pace on account of patches of mud as slippery as wet linoleum.

Several times he thought he was in spittin' distance of the shack, only to discover outcroppings of slick, silvery limestone or desolate logging trails. The mud was so sticky he had to stop every few minutes and scrape his boots.

Maybe he was confused about the shack, he told himself as he stumbled over a log and came within a hair's breadth of landing on his butt in the soggy leaves. Cotter's Ridge was like one of those mazes where you have to find your way to the middle without crossing any lines. Kevin hadn't had much luck with 'em, even with the ones in the kiddie magazines at the supermarket. Jim Bob had pitched a fit when a customer brought one back claiming it was marked up.

Thinking about Jim Bob made him more forlorn than he already was. There wasn't any way Jim Bob wouldn't find out that his temporary assistant manager had gone AWOL, and on the busiest day of the week, too. But Kevin had figured he owed it to his beloved wife and son to learn how to defend them when the country was overrun with foreign soldiers.

He was close to giving up when he finally caught sight of a sagging roof. He hurried up the road, went up on the porch, and dragged open the door. Inside it was still cold and daylight sliced through cracks and knotholes, but it was better'n outside. Dirt was everywhere, along with twigs, dried leaves, tufts of hair, and droppings that indicated animals had taken refuge over the years.

Hoping he wouldn't run into a bear or a wildcat,

Kevin pulled off his cap and eyed the stove. He was trying to remember if he had any matches when a hand clamped down on his shoulder. John Wayne might have whirled around and thrown a punch, but Kevin Fitzgerald Buchanon fainted.

I went into the barroom and looked around for Reed Rondly and Barry Kirklin. They were in the back booth, conversing intently over a pitcher of beer. Before I could reach them, however, Ruby Bee came out of the kitchen and said, "I need to have a word with you, and I need to have it right now."

Reed and Barry glanced up at me. "Stay there," I said to them, then went over to the bar. "What's the matter? Do you need a recipe for ostrich and dumplings?"

Ruby Bee gestured at a good ol' boy slumped at the bar, who appeared to have been crying in his beer for a long while, then moved down to the end and waited for me with a decidedly unfriendly expression. "I have been trying to get in touch with you all day long," she said as I sat on a stool. "You'd better throw that answering machine into the trash and get yourself a new one. What's more, you'd better test it in the store before you pay good money."

I wasn't sure why she'd sidled away from the good ol' boy, then spoken loudly enough to be heard over the roar of the washing machines at the Suds of Fun launderette across the road. "I am not a handyman," I said levelly, "and I don't do toilet seats. If you'll excuse me, I have a sticky situation that requires my professional attention."

"Well, pardon me for daring to interrupt you, Miss Eliot Ness. I'm sure as God made little green apples that someone broke into one of the units out back, but I'll just get in line until you can get around to me. All I can do is pray there's not a rapist hanging around the Flamingo Motel and waiting for his chance to attack me real late at night.''

"All right," I said. "Tell me why you think someone broke into a unit."

"The door was unlocked, but that might have been an oversight on my part. However, there's no way getting around the toilet seat, the shag, and the lamp," she said, ticking them off on her fingers. "If there was only one clue, I might wonder if I was imagining things, but the three together prove I'm not."

I tried to keep a straight face. "I can see someone stealing a toilet seat and a lamp, but the carpet? It can't be easy to move the furniture in order to pull out the tacks, roll up the carpet, and carry it out to—"

"Nothing was stolen. The toilet seat was raised, the lamp was unplugged, and the carpet showed signs that the chair had been moved. If that's not evidence of a break-in, then I don't know what is." She put her hands on her hips and waited for me to reel with shock or race out the door to fingerprint the toilet seat.

I opted for a mildly concerned wince. "That's really fine evidence, and I'm sure it'll come in handy at the trial. It may be enough to secure the death penalty. As much as I'd like to drop this other thing and devote all my energy to catching this rapist, I'm afraid it will have to wait. Maybe you and Estelle can train the ostriches to attack on command."

I turned around and went to the back booth.

Reed stuck his nose in his stein, but Barry smiled and said, "Change your mind about a beer?"

"No," I said. "I just spoke to the sheriff, who had a call from the county coroner. The coroner said that the gunshot wound did not cause Dylan's death. It probably hurt like hell, but it didn't hit an artery or any organs. It didn't cause any significant internal bleeding, either."

Reed lifted his face. "So what killed him?"

"We won't know until the coroner does a more thorough autopsy," I said, "and that won't happen for a couple of days."

Barry was no longer smiling. "Could he have had a heart condition? Maybe the trauma of getting shot set off a fatal heart attack. Aneurysms can burst, too. Most people don't know they have one until it's written on the death certificate."

"Wait a minute," Reed said in a strangled voice. "Are you saying anybody could have this—this thing and not know it? Somebody shouts 'Boo!' and you fall over dead?"

Barry snapped his fingers. "Just like that."

I intervened before we lapsed into a medical school seminar. "We won't know until after the autopsy, so there's no point in speculation."

"What about a snake bite?" said Reed.

"After the autopsy," I said, wishing I'd had the words printed on filing cards. "Until then, we're treating Dylan's death as a possible homicide, so I'll have to get more detailed statements from all of you before you leave town. Ruby Bee has three empty units if you want to stay out there tonight."

"I knew a guy once who got stung by a honey

bee," continued Reed, who clearly had some vestige of shared ancestry with the Buchanons. "He was deader'n a doornail twenty minutes later. We might should've taken him to the emergency room like he begged, but we thought he was being a sissy."

Barry stood up. "I guess we'll go back to the camp and collect our gear, then stay at the motel. We'll get Jake's and Dylan's gear while we're at it. Come on, Reed."

Reed downed the last inch of beer, belched, and got unsteadily to his feet. "You know, I was kinda curious about Dylan kicking off like that. The kid told me Dylan sat up and was gonna be okay. Five minutes later—"

"Come on," Barry said, clutching Reed's sleeve and aiming him toward the door. "The sooner we go, the sooner we can get back for a hot shower and some decent food. Who knows? Maybe the chief of police will join us at the end of her shift."

"Why don't I line you up with a hot little local number named Marjorie?" I said. "She's on the quiet side, but I've been told she squeals when she's excited."

"Cool," said Reed as he was dragged out the door.

I left before Ruby Bee could delay me with a harangue about my shoddy investigative techniques. Les gave me a thumbs-up sign as I went to Sterling's room. He opened the door within seconds. Unlike Kayleen, he was still wearing fatigues, but his feet were encased in slippers.

"It's about time, Chief Hanks," he said. "I intend to file a civil suit citing you and that boorish sheriff. You have no right to detain us against our wishes. In that I have entered into a contract with the owner of this motel room, I am the legal tenant of record. The Fourth Amendment specifically addresses the right of the people to be secure in their houses against unreasonable searches and seizures. You may not enter this room unless you have a proper warrant."

"You're absolutely right," I said. "Since I don't have a warrant, I'll escort you to the sheriff's department in Farberville. He should be finished with his press conference by the time we get there, but if not, we can join him on the steps. You might even get a chance to share your outrage with the media. They'll go wild over your uniform and those medals you most likely bought at an army surplus store."

He gave me a cold look, then opened the door more widely and gestured at me to enter. "My time is too essential to waste in such a manner. Giving a statement is a waste of time, too, but I will cooperate simply in order to be allowed to leave this festering cold sore of a town."

"And we were thinking about asking you to run for mayor," I said as I opened my pad. "Describe your actions after your band of commandos split up."

"If you've studied military history, you would know that it's rare for a commanding officer to join his men in combat. My responsibility has always been to provide leadership and a careful analysis of the obstacles to our joint success. Therefore, I decided to make myself available at the campsite should anyone require further guidance."

"No one else mentioned this," I said, pretending to be puzzled by my notes. "They all seemed to think you started uphill when they did."

Sterling stepped in front of the mirror above the dresser and regarded his reflection for a long moment. I was on the verge of prompting him when he cleared his throat and said, "Although I am reasonably robust for my age, I am aware of my physical limitations. I felt it was in the best interest of morale that my subordinates have complete confidence in me, so I implied I would participate in the exercise alongside them." He turned around to give me a self-deprecatory smile. "I didn't want to admit that I lacked the stamina to climb a hill. I'm nearly seventy years old, Chief Hanks. There are many things I can no longer do, and my contributions to the cause must be of a less demanding nature."

He seemed to be fishing for sympathy from me, but the pool was dry. Instead of patting him on the back, I said, "Like sending them out into the woods when it's deer season? Did you lack the stamina—or the courage?"

"I'm not sure," he said, his words almost inaudible.

I gave him time to brood while I thought about the earlier statements. "You didn't stay at the campsite, though. Two of your so-called subordinates decided to guard the rear line, and they were there when they heard someone coming. If they heard you, you must have been returning from someplace else."

"When I selected the campsite yesterday afternoon, I noticed a spot partway up the ridge that was protected from the elements by an overhang. Dividing my ascent would allow me to catch my breath, so I went there to wait until I heard some indication that the maneuver was over. You must be feeling a great deal of contempt for me."

"Because you're nothing more than a blustery hypocrite? That would seem to constitute a reason, wouldn't it?" I gave him my map. "Show me where you hid."

His hand was trembling as he pointed to a spot halfway between the campsite and the place where Dylan had been shot. "Somewhere in here, Chief Hanks. If we were to return to the area, I could show you the precise location, but I don't see why it matters. The young man was the victim of a tragic accident."

"That's what the sheriff thought," I said vaguely. "What do you know about Dylan Gilbert's past?"

"Very little," Sterling said, his eyes narrowing as he glanced at the blank computer monitor on a table in the corner. "He said he was born and raised in Idaho, attended college, and lived in Denver before moving here."

I poised my pencil. "Where in Idaho and which college?"

"I don't believe anyone thought to ask him, although he might have said something to Reed."

I lowered the pencil and sighed. "Was he a federal agent?"

"We had no proof, but he may well have been. For one thing, when he first appeared, he gave me some cockamamie story about there being a traitor in our midst. After some consideration, I concluded that he did so in an attempt to divert any suspicion away from himself. When I tried to do a background check on him, I ran into some communication problems. Barry was convinced that Dylan was responsible for them. Then again, my computer may be state of the art, but I myself am not, and I've had difficulties learning how to coerce it into doing what I want. I've certainly seen the 'access denied' message more than once."

"Who did you contact to do this background check?" I asked.

Sterling hesitated, then said, "I don't see why it matters anymore. Dylan said he was a member of a group in Denver that has similar goals. I queried one of them on a private electronic bulletin board and received a response that confirmed this. When I attempted to make further inquiries, the password had been changed."

"What's the name of the contact in Denver?"

"We use code names, and it would be a breach of security if I were to tell you his. If it came out, our group would be forever banished from the movement. We're on probation as it is. Reed and Barry displayed gross incompetence at a retreat in Oklahoma and were ordered to leave. Reed became drunk and insisted on loading his weapon with live ammunition. When Barry tried to wrestle the weapon away from him, it went off and shattered the windshield of a car manned by police officers observing the activities. It was embarrassing for me to have my men behave like that."

"It'll be a helluva lot more embarrassing if it turns out one of your men shot Dylan Gilbert in the back."

He gave me a bewildered look. "But . . . they were using paint pellets."

"Thirty-caliber paint pellets?" I said as I headed for the door.

CHAPTER 11

Jake and Judy Milliford were occupying #2. As I approached, I could hear angry voices from inside, but I couldn't make out the words. I knocked and moved to a prudent distance in case whoever opened the door was foaming at the mouth. I've always hated saliva on my shirt.

Jake yanked open the door. He wasn't foaming, but he was far from a genial host. "Whatta ya want?"

"I want to wake up and discover this was all a bad dream," I said truthfully. "However, until that lovely moment arrives, I'm obliged to maintain the pretense by taking your statement. I'll need to speak to your wife, too."

"She don't know nuthin' about this," he said, blocking the doorway like a brawny nightclub bouncer.

"We can do this now, or we can do it later at the sheriff's department. The interrogation rooms are not luxurious, but they have a certain charm. I'm thinking about redoing my apartment in the same pea green and puke color scheme."

"Let her in," said a woman's voice.

Jake moved out of the doorway. "Get on with it," he growled.

Judy was seated on the bed. We sized each other up for a moment, then she said, "Why don't you take the chair, Chief Hanks? That way you'll have the table to write on."

"Thanks," I said as I sat down and pulled out the map. Thus far I had six Xs, four drawn by the parties and the two I'd drawn to indicate Kevin and Dylan. I offered the map to Jake. "Show me where you were when you heard the first shot."

He kept his thumbs hooked over his belt. "What difference does it make where I was?"

"Probably none," I admitted, "but this is an official investigation. If you refuse to cooperate, you should get a lawyer as soon as possible. In fact, you'd better use the phone on the nightstand."

Judy's eyes widened. "But Jake told me it was an accident . . ."

"We're still obliged to investigate," I said.

Jake snatched the map out of my hand and scowled at it. "This ain't nothing but a bunch of scratches. How the hell am I supposed to make any sense out of it?" He studied it for a minute, his forehead creased, and finally tapped it with a greasy finger. "I was over this way."

"Did you see Barry?"

He dropped the map on the rumpled bed and crossed his arms. "All I saw was that kid's goofy face peeking over the ledge. Then Dylan stood up and turned around like he thought there was somebody above them. For some fool reason, the kid jumped up like a snake had bit him on his ass, and then went back down. A shot was fired, and Dylan fell off the ledge. I was climbing down the rocks to see what the hell was going on when I saw the flare. It took me another four or five minutes to get there.''

"And Kayleen was already there?''

"Yeah,'' he muttered, "and she said he was dead. After that, we just sat there, her sniveling and me worrying about a bullet in *my* back.''

I drew an X over the trace of grease he'd left. "You should have been able to see Barry, or at least hear him in the brush.''

"Well, I didn't, and he didn't hear me, neither. I was being real quiet on account of the kid. I dunno if he could've got me, but I had a feeling Dylan was a damn good shot.''

"What did you think about the rumor that he was a federal agent?'' I asked.

"I didn't have any trouble buying it after what happened last night.'' He took a can of tobacco out of his pocket and stuck a wad in his cheek. "Damn sumbitch shouldn't have come spying on us. If I'd had my rifle, I'd have shot him myself. As it was, Reed, Barry, and me decided to have ourselves a little interrogation session after everybody else left for the night. I learned a thing or two from the gooks in 'Nam.''

"Jake!'' said Judy. "Are you really stupid enough to say things like that in front of a police officer who's investigating a death?''

He gave her a puzzled look. "It ain't like we had a chance to go through with it. He's dead, ain't he?''

"That doesn't mean you're not stupid,'' she said sharply.

I held up my hand. "Why don't you discuss this later? Jake, you said something took place last night that made you suspect Dylan. What was it?''

He went into the bathroom to spit in the sink (and wouldn't Ruby Bee love that?), then came back out and said, "We were running low on beer, so Dylan offered to go get some, and a couple of pizzas while he was at it. He borrowed Reed's truck and left around six. When he finally showed up four hours later, he said the truck broke down halfway to Farberville and he spent the whole time messin' with it. Thing is, Barry and me both saw the truck parked on a side road here in town."

"Did you tell him that?" I asked.

"It was gonna be discussed tonight. Damn, I was really looking forward to that."

I did not allow myself to imagine what might have happened. "Where exactly was the truck parked?"

"On some road," he said, shrugging.

"Could he have been in it?"

"Not unless he was lying down on the seat. I'd have seen him if he was sitting up."

I made a note to myself to have a word with Barry and Reed about their recalcitrance. "What were you doing in town?"

Jake tugged at his collar while stealing a peek at his wife. He might have gotten away with it if she and I both hadn't been staring at him. "I was thinking to go by the supermarket and get an extra can of Redman. When I was almost there, I remembered I'd left my wallet at the camp. I drove on out to the edge of town, turned around, and took my time on the way back."

And I'd been named after a Shakespearean sprite instead of a photograph of Ruby Bee's Bar & Grill taken from an airplane. "What time did you get back?" I asked.

"Ten-thirty or so, about the time Barry showed up." He suddenly found the need to retreat to the bathroom, this time closing the door and running water in the sink.

I wanted to ask Judy if he had a legitimate reason to spy on her, but her back was rigid and her expression laden with warning. "Tell me what you did today," I said.

"I went to the camp with Sterling and Kayleen to cook breakfast. Afterwards, I hauled the skillet and dishes down to the creek and washed them, and checked my supplies to make sure I had what I needed for supper. I sat in Jake's tent for a good while, listening to their nonsense, and when it got to be too much for me, I walked back here."

"What time would that have been?"

"I don't know for sure, but Sterling was telling everybody what to do like he always does. I waited until they all left, then came here to take a shower, get into dry clothes, and work on a needlepoint sampler for my grandchild's bedroom. I don't believe in this international conspiracy or any of their other wild ideas. Jake wasn't like this when we got married. He was . . . normal back then."

"And now?" I asked gently.

"He's so full of hate sometimes I think he's going to explode. When we're in the truck, he points out people on the street—ordinary people going about their business—and says how they're responsible for all the problems in this country. He gets things in the mail that make me sick. Most of the time I put them in the trash without even telling him."

The water was still running in the sink, but I knew we only had a few minutes to talk before Mr.

Congeniality came out of the bathroom. "Did you have any conversations with Dylan Gilbert that led you to believe he was an agent?"

"We didn't say much to each other. Jake stuck to me like a thistle seed whenever Dylan came near me, and I didn't want to make it worse for Dylan by being friendly to him. I wanted to ask him if Colorado is as pretty as people say, but I never got a chance."

I heard the toilet flush. I leaned forward and said, "Do you have any idea why Jake was in town last night?"

She shook her head.

I collected my pad and map, nodded at her, and left the room. I waved at Les, then headed for the PD to make some long distance calls that would send the town council into paroxysms of outrage when they got the bill. Did I care?

Larry Joe wiped the window with a damp paper towel, but the grime was invincible. "I don't see him, but he's still out there. I can feel him watching me."

"You'd better lay off the whiskey," Jim Bob said, sniggering. "I went outside this morning and I sure as hell didn't see anything. Maybe this alien of yours has a crush on you, Larry Joe. Could make for some interesting sex, huh?"

"You ain't as funny as you think," Larry Joe said, his nose pressed against the windowpane.

Roy came into the trailer. "I went down to where you said you saw something. There were odd marks in the mud, but that doesn't mean much. They could be black bear tracks that some other animal has trampled on."

Larry Joe looked at Jim Bob, who was cleaning

his fingernails with a fork. "I told you there was something there last night. If you're so all-fired sure there wasn't, why don't you go have a look for yourself?"

"Why should I get wet just because you and Roy are crazier than Jekel Buchanon? 'Member how he used to parade around town in high heels and his ma's flannel nightgown, farting so much everybody in the barbershop liked to pass out?"

"I saw something," insisted Larry Joe, "and it wasn't any bear, black or pink or green with yellow polkadots. You know what I think, Jim Bob? I think you're too much of a coward to go out there."

Jim Bob banged down the fork. "Don't go calling me a coward. I ain't afraid of anything—including you and your goddamn alien!"

"Then prove it. Go down to where Roy found the tracks and see for yourself."

"I'll point out the place," volunteered Roy.

Jim Bob shook a cigar out of the package and slowly pulled off the cellophane, then stuck it in the corner of his mouth and grinned at Larry Joe. "I thought we came here to drink whiskey and play poker. Let's not waste time bickering over what you thought you saw. You want me to make some sandwiches before we start?"

"We should have waited until dark," Estelle grumbled as she and Ruby Bee strolled toward the rectory. Both of them were doing their level best to look nonchalant instead of bent on committing a crime. "What if somebody sees us?"

"Since when is there something suspicious about paying a neighborly call?" said Ruby Bee. She stopped to smile and wave as Lottie Estes chugged by in her boxy little car. "See? Nobody's paying us any mind. Besides, if we wait until it's dark, we won't be able to see anything unless we turn on the lights."

They arrived at the door without further debate. Ruby Bee, having appointed herself master criminal, knocked loudly and called, "Brother Verber? Are you in there?" She did this a couple more times, then dropped her purse on the mat and bent over to pick it up, adroitly collecting the key in the process. Estelle shielded her as she unlocked the door, eased it open, and replaced the key.

"Yoohoo, Brother Verber," she said. "It's Ruby Bee and Estelle. Are you home?"

Estelle shoved her inside. "We can't stand here all afternoon. Sooner or later someone like Mrs. Jim Bob'll drive by, and we'll end up in the poky. You know how bad-tempered Arly can be about this sort of thing."

"Then stop yakking and start searching," Ruby Bee said absently as she eyed the spic-and-span kitchenette and the perfectly aligned magazines on the coffee table. It was most likely Mrs. Jim Bob's doing, she thought as she tried to decide where to find Brother Verber's personal effects. "Come on, Estelle, it's already four o'clock and I need to be back at the bar before five. Let's try the bedroom."

Even though they were assuming no one else was in the trailer, they tiptoed down the short hallway, stopping to peer into the bathroom before arriving in the bedroom. It was as orderly as the living room and kitchenette, with no clothes or shoes scattered on the floor. Ruby Bee was a little surprised at the number of cologne and hair tonic bottles on the dresser, having always believed preachers disdained that sort of vanity. Maybe it had to do with him courting Kayleen, she thought with a tiny smirk.

"You take the dresser drawers and I'll take the closet," she told Estelle. "Remember, we're looking for photographs, letters—"

"I know what we're looking for," said Estelle, who wasn't overly fond of being bossed around. However, Ruby Bee had come to her aid when Uncle Tooly's bequest had arrived, and she'd flatout refused to take money for the motel room. Not that the rate was much, Estelle reminded herself, or that the room wasn't empty anyway.

Ruby Bee opened the closet door. "It looks like a tornado came through here. Mrs. Jim Bob must have gathered up all the dirty clothes and just thrown 'em in here. There are some boxes on the shelf, but I can't reach them. See if you can, Estelle."

Estelle was about to get hold of a promising shoe box when the door opened in the living room. "Someone's here," she whispered. "Now what do we do?"

Ruby Bee felt her blood run cold. "Don't panic," she whispered back. "We can come up with a way to explain this to him."

"Brother Verber?" cooed Mrs. Jim Bob. "I just came by to see how you're doing."

"Get in here," Ruby Bee said, thoroughly panicked. She and Estelle jammed themselves into the closet and managed to pull the door closed just as they heard footsteps in the hallway. The air was stuffy and reeked of sweat and stale cologne. Shirts and coats hanging above them brushed their heads like ghostly caresses. The only light came from underneath the door.

"I don't understand," Mrs. Jim Bob said in a thin, quivery voice. "How could you disappear like this without telling me? I am the guiding beacon of the congregation, as well as the president of the Missionary Society. Don't I invite you over for supper every week?" She continued in that vein, her voice fading but still audible as she left the bedroom.

"Who's she talking to?" whispered Estelle.

"Herself, I suppose." Ruby Bee wiggled around, trying to avoid something sharp poking her in the fanny. "Lordy, it's hard to breathe. It seems to me she might have laundered these clothes before putting them in here. What's more, Brother Verber could use a stronger deodorant. Whatever he—"

"I don't understand," wailed Mrs. Jim Bob from the living room. "What about all those times we knelt to pray in the Assembly Hall or on this very sofa? You said you could hear the Good Lord admiring us for our humility and trust. I thought I could trust you . . ."

"Do you have any more bright ideas?" said Estelle.

Ruby Bee crossed her fingers. "She'll leave before too long, and then we can, too. How long can she sit in there and talk to herself?"

The response came not from Estelle, but from the living room. "I am going to stay right here," Mrs. Jim Bob vowed, "until you come back. It may take all night, but I will be here when you walk through the door—and you'd better have a good explanation for tormenting me like this. What's more, after you've begged my forgiveness, you're gonna get down on your knees and do some serious apologizing to the Lord."

Ruby Bee and Estelle did what they could to get comfortable on the closet floor.

When I finally replaced the receiver, I'd learned several things about the FBI and the ATF. One was that their offices were open during the weekends, which was good to know if Swiss paratroopers came marching down the road. Another, however, was that they were boorish and uncooperative when it came to discussing their undercover agents. I'd explained the situation, blithely assuming they'd take a deep interest in the possible homicide of one of their own. I might as well have tried to convince them that Jimmy Hoffa was eating supper at Ruby Bee's Bar & Grill.

I decided I'd better make sure he wasn't, and perhaps have a piece of pie while I was at it. When I got there, I was startled to find a dozen or so guys standing around in the parking lot. "What's wrong?" I asked as I got out of the car. "Is Ruby Bee holding a fire drill?"

"It's closed," said a red-faced man in a denim jacket. "It's nigh on to happy hour, but Ruby Bee ain't nowhere to be found. Ollie and me was going to have us a beer."

I frowned at the "closed" sign on the door. "The bar was open earlier this afternoon. Do any of you know how long the sign's been there?"

A few of them admitted they didn't, while the rest scuffled their feet and bobbled their heads like a flock of lethargic turkeys. I suggested they find another bar, then got back in my car and tried to think where Ruby Bee would have gone at such a crucial time. As far as I knew, Dylan Gilbert's death had not been broadcast around town, so she couldn't have appointed herself my deputy, as she and Estelle had done so often in the past, and gone charging off to crack the case.

I remembered her dour remarks about the possibility of someone lurking in one of the units. Les wasn't renowned for taking the initiative, but surely he would have informed me if a rapist had accosted her in the parking lot and carried her off on his shoulder.

I went around back and found him sitting in his car. "Any more messages from LaBelle?" I asked him.

"Nothing since the first one. Hey, could you take over for a few minutes? It's been a long time since I answered a call of nature."

"Sure," I said, "but let me ask you something. Did Ruby Bee come back here this afternoon?"

"I didn't see her, and Estelle hasn't returned." His ears turned pink as he gave me a strained smile. "About that break?"

"Go on, Les. When you get back, contact LaBelle and tell her we're going to need someone here the rest of the night. I'm going to have to take more detailed statements from all these people, but I've got some other things to do first."

He babbled his thanks and peeled out of the parking lot, pelting me with gravel. I noticed that Ruby Bee's car was parked in front of #1, but Estelle's station wagon was gone, indicating that they were off together. Telling myself they were probably on an ostrich hunt, I sat down on the hood of my car and glumly watched a formation of geese fly by on their way to a more congenial climate. The best I could do was get back in my car and turn on the heater. Florida, it was not.

I took out my pad and studied the various state-

ments. Earl had said something that began to puzzle
me as I tried to get everything straight in my admittedly muddled mind. Judy had said she left the campsite shortly after the troops had dispersed at 11:15 or
so. Earl and Jeremiah had backtracked minutes later,
then retreated to the pickup when they heard someone coming. Sterling had claimed to have taken
refuge under an overhang; Barry, Reed, Jake, and
Kayleen had embraced the exercise and gone creep-
ing up the hill.

So whom had Earl and Jeremiah heard? And
whom had Earl seen shortly before Sterling called for
an ambulance?

The clouds did not part to allow a ray of sunlight
to enlighten me. I could come up with no reason for
Brother Verber to be on the ridge, unless he'd heard
rumors of naked devil worshipers and gone to check
it out. But according to Mrs. Jim Bob, he'd disappeared by Thursday morning. Even his obsession with
writhing female bodies would not have kept him in
the woods for more than forty-eight hours.

My three least favorite stooges, Jim Bob, Larry
Joe, and Roy, were up there somewhere, but their version of deer hunting involved playing poker and staying drunk. Deer could graze beside the trailer in
perfect safety. Raz was too wily to risk being spotted,
and Diesel would hardly seek out camaraderie.

I wrote myself a note to call Mrs. Twayblade at
the county home and find out if she was missing any
of her white-haired charges. She'd misplaced a couple
of them in the past, but she'd tightened up security
since then.

Whoever it was had not approached the campsite
from the gully. It was possible Earl and Jeremiah had

heard Judy as she was leaving. I had no idea when
they'd begun passing the bottle back and forth; they
certainly could have been smashed enough to misin-
terpret the sounds. I drew a box around Jeremiah's
name to remind myself to ask him.

Even if my theory was right, it did nothing to
explain who'd cut across the back of the Assembly
Hall lawn. It could have been an uninvolved person,
such as a kid buying hooch from Raz or a ditzy
birdwatcher.

I'd gotten nowhere when Reed drove into the lot.
I climbed out of my car and said, "Where's Barry?"

"He's coming." He took a backpack and a cooler
out of the back of the truck, which was littered with
tools, beer cans, greasy blankets, and unidentifiable
auto parts. "Which room is mine?"

I gestured at #6. "You and Barry can share that
one, but you'll have to get the key from Ruby Bee
when she reopens the bar."

"When's that gonna be?"

"Beats me," I said. "Why didn't you tell me that
you, Jake, and Barry were convinced Dylan was an undercover agent?"

"We weren't, that's why. We decided to have a
serious talk with him later this evening. I guess it's a
little late for that." He, like Jake, sounded disappointed at the lost opportunity to engage in brutality.

"But you suspected he was," I prompted.

"Barry and Jake said so, but they didn't know
him as well as I did. He sounded okay to me."

"He was staying at your apartment, wasn't he?"

"Till he found someplace he could afford. Look,
lady, I don't aim to stand here all night. Why don't

you trot your sweet ass into the bar and get the room key?''

"Why don't you hand over your apartment key so I can go through Dylan's things? Then you can trot your sweet ass to someone else's room until Ruby Bee gets back and has you sign the register."

"You got a search warrant?"

I waited a beat, then said, "I can hold you as a material witness until I get one. As investigating officer, I have the right to examine the victim's personal possessions in order to locate his next of kin, as well as any incriminatory items that may suggest a motive for his murder." Or I thought I did, anyway.

He dug a key out of his pocket and slapped it in my outstretched palm. "Don't go grubbing through my stuff, or you'll be real sorry. One of the amendments, I think the third, protects against illegal search and seizure."

"The fourth," I said, then told him which was Sterling's room. He was already inside when Les returned, his demeanor a good deal calmer. I told him what to tell Barry when he arrived, then drove out of the motel parking lot. The "closed" sign still hung on the bar's door, to the consternation of two good ol' boys who seemed to be struggling with the concept. I glanced at the PD's three parking spaces, and then at the empty area in front of the soon-to-be pawnshop. Mrs. Jim Bob's Cadillac was parked in front of the Assembly Hall, and lights were on in Brother Verber's trailer. At least one stray was back in the fold, I told myself as I drove down County 102 to see if Estelle's station wagon was there. It wasn't, so I went on to Farberville to see what I could learn about Dylan Gilbert.

The Airport Arms was cleverly situated across from the airport. In the unpaved parking lot were a Harley-Davidson, a battered white car with Missouri plates, another with no plates, and an overflowing Dumpster. It was likely to be the most disreputable apartment building in Farberville, if not Stump County.

Reed's apartment was on the second floor, with a view of the runway across the highway. The staircase creaked and shifted as I went up it, and the railing was too splintery to touch. I let myself inside the apartment. My stomach lurched as the odor of beer and decaying food hit me, but I turned on a light and ordered myself to pick my way through pizza boxes, catalogs, unopened bills, and several crusty car batteries. It was definitely not *Playboy* magazine's prototype of a bachelor pad.

The bedroom floor was covered with mildewed towels, discarded underwear and jeans, and plates coated with blue and gray fuzz. I tried to open a window, but it was either nailed closed or impossibly warped. I saw a duffel bag in one corner beside a limp, dingy pillow and a blanket. Assuming this was Dylan's allotted area, I knelt down and dumped out the contents of the bag. I wasn't anticipating anything more illuminating than socks and boxers, so I was surprised when I found a small spiral-bound notebook.

My elation faded as I flipped through it, finding one blank page after another. I was about to toss it in the bag when I came upon a notation that read: "Ingram MAC 10, #78264." After pondering this for a moment, I checked to see if there was anything else in the notebook, and then set it aside.

I made sure the duffel bag was empty, then sat back and once again read the cryptic notation. I was still in what Ruby Bee would condemn as an undignified posture when I heard the front door open.

I hate it when that happens.

CHAPTER 12

Before I could scramble to my feet, a man appeared in the doorway. Technically, I'd have to say he *loomed,* since he was husky enough to fill the space, but he wasn't snarling or even frowning. He wore a navy blue suit, a white dress shirt, a serious tie, and shiny black shoes. I continued my inventory: dark eyes, mahogany complexion, straight nose, slightly weak chin, and when he smiled, white teeth with a boyish gap in the front. I doubted he was one of Reed's neighbors.

"What are you doing?" he asked.

I began stuffing socks and shirts back into the duffel bag. "Packing," I said. "How about you?"

"I was in the neighborhood, so I thought I'd stop by."

"Give me a break, buddy. Nobody stops by the Airport Arms Apartments unless his arm is twisted so tightly behind his back that he can pat himself on the top of his head." I stopped, my hand in midair, and stared up at him. "You're the process server, aren't you? Reed Rondly's not here, but I can tell you where he is if you'd like to slap him with a summons. It may not make his day, but it'll certainly make mine."

"Where would that be?"

"In Maggody, a little town about twenty miles east of here. Reed's at the Flamingo Motel. Watch for a sign with a mottled pink bird on the verge of blinking its last." I put the rest of Dylan's clothes in the duffel bag, then stood up and brushed cracker crumbs off my knees. "Good luck catching up with him."

He pointed at the notebook on the floor. "You missed something."

"So I did." I scooped up the notebook and tucked it in my pocket. "I didn't see you when I got here. Were you watching the apartment?"

He nodded. "Before I took my present job, I worked in a private investigator's office, mostly doing surveillance work."

I picked up the duffel bag. "I guess I'm ready to go. If you decide to drop by the motel and surprise Reed, be prepared to duck. He's a racist pig with the temperament to match."

The man stepped back to allow me to go past him. "I'll keep that in mind."

He followed me into the living room. I'd planned to do a quick search of the kitchen and bathroom, but I couldn't come up with a credible explanation. We continued out to the balcony, and he waited while I locked the door. As we walked down the staircase, I said, "Are you heading for Maggody?"

"Not just yet," he said, "but you'll most likely see me again, Chief Hanks."

"How do you know my name?" I said, almost dropping the duffel bag.

"You're wearing a badge." On that note, he went around the corner of the apartment building.

I stood by the car for a moment, wondering if I'd just interacted with a spy from a John LeCarré novel. He'd told me virtually nothing except that he'd once worked for a private investigator. My badge identified me as the chief of police, but I'd refused from day one of the "unsuitable job" to wear a name tag. If he'd gotten his information from something in my car, he would have addressed me as "Chief Taco Bell."

I gave up worrying about him and drove to the sheriff's department. LaBelle was on the phone, this time talking about her bladder infection. She eyed me coldly, then pointed toward Harve's office and resumed reciting her symptoms. She sounded especially proud of her urinary tract.

"Any update from McBeen?" I asked Harve as I came through the doorway.

"Not yet." He held up a plastic bag. "This here's the slug from the boy's shoulder. It could have been fired from any hunting rifle from here to the North Pole." He slumped back and sighed. "McBeen said he'd have a better chance at finding the cause of death if he had the boy's medical records. We went through his wallet, but all we found was two hundred and thirty-seven dollars. That plastic doohickey where most folks keep their driver's license and credit cards was empty."

"He worked at the same garage as Reed. Aren't they supposed to have his Social Security number?"

"Supposed to, yeah. The guy that owns the place said the kid kept stalling, and then quit on Thursday. They settled up out of the cash register."

I told Harve what little I'd learned about Dylan, most of it based on the befuddled speculation of the militia. "Frankly," I admitted, "I'm not sure if any of it's true, including the truck being parked in town. It is peculiar that he didn't have any identification with him, though. You'd think the FBI or the ATF could have produced fake documents for an undercover agent." I took the notebook out of my pocket, opened it to the single entry, and tossed it on the desk. "I found this in Dylan's bag. See what you make of it."

Harve whistled softly. "An Ingram MAC ten is a right serious automatic pistol, and the rest of it looks like the serial number. I'll follow up on it."

"I wish you'd follow up on getting information from the feds," I muttered. "There's an FBI office here, but all I got was a recorded message telling me to call during regular business hours. A guy at the Little Rock office gave me a number in DC. The guy there was as helpful as a chunk of asphalt. I had the same reaction from the ATF. It's possible you or the county prosecutor can get something out of them."

"I know ol' Tinker Tonnato, the local FBI agent. I guess he figures the terrorists are gonna have to twiddle their thumbs while he gets in some weekend hunting. I'll call him first thing Monday morning."

"Even if Dylan had a medical condition, whoever fired the rifle is still looking at a charge of first degree murder." I picked up the plastic bag and studied the misshapen lump of steel. "You sure you and Les got all their weapons?"

"Yeah," Harve said as he reached for a cigar. "All the fellows staying at the camp had handguns and the Rondly boy had a rifle, but they kept them locked in their vehicles. Earl Buchanon told me that Pitts was the only one to come back to the pasture, and that was to use the phone in that ridiculous-

looking tank of his. The only other weapon any of
them had in their possession was the flare gun that
Rondly used to signal there was an emergency.''

Noxious smoke was drifting toward me, so I put
down the plastic bag and stood up. "How did the
press conference go? Did you win any votes?''

"I told 'em we're doing everything we can short
of assigning a deputy to every house set off by itself.
A couple of the reporters had the same idea you did.
At least I could tell them we'd already eliminated
anything the homeowners might have had in common. My best guess is the perps are watching the
houses somehow.''

"From the woods?'' I said dryly. "They sit in trees
and train binoculars on the back door on the chance
the owners are going to come out carrying luggage?
What are the odds they'd get lucky six times in the
last month? And think about Mayfly, Harve. They
waited two or three days before they broke in, which
means they were pretty damn confident that Mrs.
Coben and her daughter would be gone for more
than a day.''

"Did either of them tell anybody?''

"Mrs. Coben said she mentioned their trip to a
couple of people who live out that way. Heidi had
broken up with her boyfriend a couple of weeks earlier, and she was holed up at home, sulking and re-
fusing to talk to anybody. Katherine Avenued may
have told people, but Heidi described her as being so
shy she rarely smiled or spoke to anybody. Katherine's
neighbors at the apartment house had never done
more than say hello to her on the sidewalk, and her
classmates and co-workers said the same thing. Be-

sides, Mayfly is at least twenty miles away from the other houses that were burglarized.''

"I know," Harve said, "but there has to be something, damn it! We can't blame it on a full moon, since that doesn't happen six times a month.''

I told Harve I'd keep him posted, then drove back to Maggody, hoping I'd be in time to see Reed Rondly's reaction when the process server knocked on the door.

Not much had changed in my absence. Mrs. Jim Bob's Cadillac was still parked in front of the Assembly Hall, and Ruby Bee's Bar & Grill was still closed. Les had been relieved by an unfamiliar deputy who introduced himself as Corporal Batson and assured me that although there'd been some movement between units, no one had left the motel parking lot. A car, presumably Barry Kirklin's, was parked next to Reed's truck. Estelle's station wagon was still gone. I was warning Batson about the process server when Sterling came out of #5.

"I have been waiting for you for more than two hours," he said. "That lame-brained deputy refuses to allow us to do something about dinner. Kayleen called the barroom, but no one answered. Prisoners of war are treated better than this, Chief Hanks. The Fifth Amendment clearly prohibits the deprivation of liberty without due process of law.''

"Are you suggesting that I arrest you? It's okay with me.''

"On Monday morning I shall place a call to the lieutenant governor to make a formal complaint. Now, what do you propose to do in order that we receive a decent meal?''

"I'll send the lame-brained deputy over to the supermarket to get some roots and berries. If you all promise to behave, you can have a picnic out here in your tank. Half the town could probably squeeze into the back seat. How much did this thing cost?"

"That's none of your business," he said, then closed his door.

I asked Batson to go across the road to purchase sandwiches and soft drinks, then sat on the hood of my car and tried to envision what had taken place on Cotter's Ridge earlier in the day. None of the current residents of the Flamingo seemed to have an adequate motive to take a shot at Dylan. Sterling, Barry, and Jake suspected Dylan had been a federal agent, but they weren't firmly convinced. Reed and Kayleen were skeptical, at best. And none of them had been carrying a rifle.

Perhaps Harve's first assessment was right, I told myself, and the incident had been nothing more than a coincidence of cosmic dimensions. The burglaries could be that, too, although it was hard to ignore the parallels in all six of them. My eyes drifted to the window of #3 as I remembered what Kayleen had said about Maurice's murder. They'd been awakened by the sound of breaking glass.

I slid off the hood and walked across the lot to knock on her door. When she opened it, I said, "May I come in? I need to ask you something."

Barry and Reed had taken refuge in her room until they could get into their unit. Reed was stretched out on the bed, muddy boots and all, with a beer balanced on his belly. Barry was seated by a table, where it looked as though he and Kayleen were in the midst of a card game.

"Did you find out what killed Dylan?" asked Kayleen. "Was it a heart attack?"

"We don't know yet," I said, "and most likely won't for a day or two. I realize this is a sensitive subject, but I want to ask you about the night Maurice was killed."

"Poor old Mo," drawled Reed, lifting his head to take a gulp of beer.

Kayleen sat down at the table. "Why, Arly? It couldn't possibly have anything to do with what happened today."

Barry leaned forward to squeeze her hand. "I don't see how it could, but it won't hurt to answer a few questions."

"I suppose not," she said unhappily.

Feeling a bit like an employee of the Spanish Inquisition, I said, "I'm sure you're aware that Elsie Buchanon's house was burglarized last week. There have been some other burglaries, too, and I'm trying to find a link."

"Like what?"

"For starters, were you and Maurice supposed to have been away on a trip when the break-in took place?"

She thought for a long moment. "Maurice had suggested going to a gun show somewhere—Kansas City, I think—but we didn't like the looks of the weather." She swallowed several times and her eyes filled with tears. "If we'd decided to go, Maurice would still be alive, wouldn't he? It was my doing, since I was the one who was afraid the roads might turn icy."

Reed belched. "That don't mean Mo'd be around these days. He was old as the hills, and so gimpy he could barely get around. Every meeting we had, all he'd do is complain about his damn prostrate or whatever it was."

"Shut up!" snapped Barry.

I touched Kayleen's shoulder. "Did you or your husband tell anyone that you were going to Kansas City? A neighbor, maybe, or a storekeeper?"

"I didn't," she said, "and I don't think Maurice did, although I can't be sure. He did a lot of business over the telephone. If someone had wanted to make an appointment, he might have mentioned the possibility of a trip. Do you think the burglars broke in because they believed the house was empty?"

I nodded. "That's the only thing we've come up with thus far. I guess I'd better call the sheriff's department over in Chowden County. We might be able to exchange some information and figure out if the same perps simply moved their operation to Stump County."

Barry began to gather up the cards. "Any idea when we can get in our room?"

"Did any of your training include a course in picking locks?" I asked. "Or were you too busy learning how to survive on pizza and beer?"

He gave me a level look. "Anyone with a credit card could get past these locks. Want me to demonstrate?"

Before I could answer, there was a knock on the door. I admitted Corporal Batson, who was carrying several sacks from the SuperSaver.

"Hope ham 'n cheese is okay with everybody," he said apologetically. He handed me a bill. "I said you'd drop by and settle up. You can probably get the sheriff to reimburse you. It may take a while, though. Our budget's so tight we can't afford to fix the microwave in the break room."

I told Barry that he and Reed could move into #6, and Kayleen was distributing sandwiches to her guests as the deputy and I left the room. In #5, I could see Sterling hunched in front of a computer screen, his expression indicative that he wasn't having much luck in his endeavor. Wondering if he was trying to make contact with the Colorado group, I took a sandwich and soda out of one of the sacks and went back across the lot.

He jerked open the door before I could knock. "It's about time, Chief Hanks. I'm beginning to feel light-headed from lack of food. Proper nutrition is vital to maintaining mental acuity."

"Is that protected by the Constitution, too?" I said as I handed him the sandwich. "Does one of the amendments guarantee three square meals a day?"

"The Constitution should be treated with reverence, not derision. It's our only defense against the federal government and its illegitimate manipulation of individual rights."

I fluttered my eyelashes. "Hope ham 'n cheese is okay, General Pitts."

"Yeah, yeah, I heard it," Jim Bob said, flipping over his cards and pushing back his chair. "More than likely Diesel's playin' Injun and taken to beating a tom-tom, or maybe those screwy militia boys are firing cannons at the low-water bridge."

Larry Joe peeked at his hole card to see if it had transformed itself into an ace, then gestured at Roy to rake the pot. "That don't explain what I saw—and I know I saw something straight out of one of Brother Verber's hell-and-damnation sermons. It was evil."

"I heard it, too," inserted Roy as he arranged the chips into tidy stacks.

"So what?" said Jim Bob. "That doesn't prove it's a friggin' demon here to punish us for taking a few days off to relax. Now if I was at the delectable Cherri Lucinda's love nest, I might be worried that Mrs. Jim Bob had struck a deal with Satan. I wouldn't put it past her to sell my soul for a new Cadillac. In fact, I can see her writing up the contract, with Brother Verber there at her side to notarize it."

Larry Joe went to the window to peer out at the utter darkness. "This ain't anything to joke about, Jim Bob. Roy saw the tracks in the mud, and you yourself heard that noise."

Jim Bob grunted. "I heard a noise, not a demonic screech. I reckon I need to make a trip to the outhouse. Will my rifle be enough protection, or should I take a submachine gun and a bible?"

He grabbed a flashlight and went out the door, mumbling to himself about nervous Nellies. The weeds had been trampled into a serviceable path that led around the corner of the trailer and fifty feet down the hillside to an outhouse fashioned of irregular scraps of plywood and a warped sheet of siding. The corrugated tin roof provided minimal protection from rain and gusts of wind.

After he'd finished his business, he came back out and pointed the flashlight at the tangle of vines that Larry Joe kept harping about. He saw exactly what he expected to see, which was nothing more than whatever Mother Nature had planted. Larry Joe had been teaching school too long, Jim Bob decided as he let the beam of the flashlight bobble on the runty trees. Maybe being surrounded by all those hormones had addled his mind.

Jim Bob decided to have himself a little fun. He positioned himself behind the rusty carcass of an old truck, switched off the flashlight, and threw a pebble at the kitchen window. The resulting clink was sharp and loud. Within seconds, Larry Joe's face appeared in the window, and Roy's just behind him. Their expressions were so bumfuzzled that it was all Jim Bob could do not to start laughing.

Eventually they moved away from the window. Jim Bob gave them a couple of minutes to persuade each other that a bird had crashed into the window, then threw another pebble. This time Roy reached the window first, with Larry Joe a close second. Their jaws were wagging something fierce, and Jim Bob could see the whites of their eyes.

He found a third pebble and was leaning back to scare the holy shit out of them when he heard a crackle directly behind him. He spun around. What he saw was enough to make him drop the flashlight and bolt for the trailer.

Despite her in-laws' objections, Dahlia had insisted on being taken home so she could be there if Kevvie turned up. Now she kinda wished she hadn't, what with the wind rattling the loose shingles and rustling the leaves alongside the house.

She turned on the television for company, and was heading for the kitchen when another of those dadburned contractions stopped her in her tracks. The doctor had called them by some fancy name and told her she'd be getting them as the due date got closer, but that wasn't much comfort when her innards were being squeezed like someone was wringing out wet laundry. To top it off, Kevin Junior kicked so hard that a warm dribble ran down her leg.

Once the contraction eased, she went on into the kitchen for a diet soda and a handful of carrot sticks, then sat down across from the television. The silly sitcom did nothing to keep her from brooding. Kevvie had no business going off like this, she thought as she chomped away like a leaf shredder. Here she was, within weeks of havin' the baby, and she was all alone, tormented by the contractions, poking her finger all the time, visiting the potty every ten minutes, and reduced to carrot and celery sticks whenever her stomach rumbled.

"I hope you don't turn out like your pa," she said to Kevin Junior. "He's about as useless as a one-horned cow. What's more, he's liable to git his sorry self fired on account of missing work. Jim Bob's kin, but he ain't gonna be thinking of that when he kicks your pa out the door. We'll all end up at one of those homeless shelters."

The very idea set her lower lip to quivering, and tears to sliding down her cheeks. Her granny had grown up during the Depression, and her stories about scrimping for food were scarier than any tales told around the campfire during church camp— shoes with cardboard soles, clothes from charity stores, watery soup and stale bread.

Dahlia was reduced to snuffling when the telephone rang. She lunged for the receiver. "Kevvie?"

"No, this is Idalupino down at the SuperSaver. Listen, I just heard something peculiar. My second cousin Canon Buchanon was just here, and he said he saw Kevin's car parked by the low-water bridge. Nobody was in the car. He didn't see a body floating in the creek or lying on the gravel bar, but it was right dark and he was leery of going into the woods after what happened this morning. Anyways, I thought you'd want to know about the car."

"Thanks," Dahlia said numbly. She replaced the receiver and slumped back, doing her best to come up with some sort of explanation for what she'd heard. It had to do with that militia game, she figured, since Kevvie's pa had told them about all those grown folks pretending to be soldiers. Eileen had been real scornful, but Dahlia had been a little proud that Kevvie had been chosen for such an important role. She wasn't clear about why they were told they were gorillas, unless they were pretending that Cotter's Ridge was a jungle.

A contraction interrupted her laborious thought process. She grimaced and moaned her way through it, then went into the bedroom and searched the dresser drawers for another pamphlet that might tell about an evening meeting. Finding nothing of significance, she checked under his pillow and on his shelf in the medicine cabinet in the bathroom.

She trudged back into the living room and dialed her in-laws' number. The line was busy. What if, she asked herself, Kevvie was lost on Cotter's Ridge, all cold and scared and hungry? Or even worse, if he'd been shot like that other fellow and was bleeding like a stuck pig while she sat at home eating carrot sticks?

The line was busy at the PD, and nobody answered at Ruby Bee's Bar & Grill. Canon Buchanon was living in his car these days, so there wasn't any way to call him to find out if he'd heard any gunshots while he was down by the low-water bridge. She tried her in-laws' again, but Eileen was still on the line, probably talking to Millicent McIlhaney.

Frustrated, Dahlia ate the last carrot stick and finished the soda. On the television screen, a man with big teeth was begging her to buy a contraption that cut potatoes into fancy slices, but she couldn't bear to listen while Kevvie was in terrible danger. She turned off the set, put on her coat and gloves, went outside, and started down the road. It was a good two miles to the low-water bridge, even if she cut through the schoolyard and the pasture behind the old Emporium. It would take nearly an hour, she realized, and when she got there, all she could do was holler Kevvie's name and pray he answered.

She slowed down as she approached Raz's shack. A light was on in the front room and smoke curled out of the chimney. More important, his truck was parked in the yard. She reminded herself that even though he was an ornery cuss, he was a neighbor and a Buchanon just like Kevvie.

Still, it took her a few minutes to find the courage to go up to his porch and knock on the door. "Raz?" she called. "Lemme in before I turn blue."

The door opened far enough for him to glare at her through the crack. "I don't much cotton to uninvited company. Whatta ya want?"

Dahlia glared right back, hoping her knees weren't knockin' so loud he could hear them. "I want you to drive me to the low-water bridge and help me find Kevvie up on the ridge."

"Cain't do it. Me and Marjorie are watching a

movie about a talking mule. It's the first one all week that's caught her fancy."

"You listen to me, Raz Buchanon, and you listen good. I haft to go find Kevvie, and I don't have time to walk all that way. If you won't help me, I'll break down your door and wring your neck. Then I'll git the key to the truck and drive myself." She held up a ham-sized fist. "I don't aim to raise a child on my own. What's it gonna be, Raz?"

He scratched his chin. "Tell ya what, we'll take you there, but we ain't about to go up on the ridge. Marjorie's still crumpy from the last time we wuz there."

"Leave her here," Dahlia said coldly.

"By herself? Why, I couldn't do that. She's a pedigreed sow, ye know, and has a delicate nature."

"All right, then git her and let's go. I gotta rescue Kevvie before the end of the month when I have the baby."

Within minutes, Raz, Marjorie, and Dahlia were headed for County 102. Raz was making his displeasure known by hitting every pothole. Marjorie sat in the middle, her eyes closed. On the passenger's side, Dahlia stared out the window, battling nausea from the stench in the truck, wishing she'd used the potty before she left the house, and wondering what she was gonna do when Raz left her at the bridge and drove away. The first thing would be to find a bush and relieve herself, of course, but after that . . . she just didn't have a clue.

CHAPTER 13

A very bored dispatcher informed me that the Chowden County sheriff would be in his office first thing in the morning, and no one else knew anything about the case. I replaced the receiver and rocked back, trying to sort out the profusion of problems that had popped up like crab grass in the last week. They came in all sizes and degrees of magnitude, from the brutal murder in Mayfly to the disappearances of local residents. At the moment Kevin, Ruby Bee, and Estelle were out of pocket, as well as two unnamed ostriches. At least Brother Verber had reappeared from his unauthorized outing.

There wasn't anything I could do about Dylan's death until the autopsy was final, nor could I make any progress with the burglaries until I talked to the sheriff. I could clear up one minor issue, however, so I locked the PD and drove to the rectory to ask Brother Verber if he was the person whom Earl had seen coming down from the ridge at noon.

Mrs. Jim Bob's Cadillac hadn't moved. I was reluctant to question Brother Verber in front of her, but I didn't want to put it off until the following afternoon after church. As I walked up the gravel path, the door swung open.

"It's high time, I must say!" Mrs. Jim Bob began, then stopped and took a harder look at me. "I thought you were somebody else."

"There are days I wish I was."

"Have you finally decided to do the job you were hired to do?"

"I saw the lights and assumed Brother Verber was back," I said as I went into the trailer. "What are you doing here, looking for photographs to paste on milk cartons?"

She appeared rather unkempt, even by my admittedly lackadaisical standards. Her hair was mussed, and her skirt and blouse were so wrinkled she might have slept in them. To add to the overall effect, one of her pumps was blue, the other brown. She stared at me, most likely trying to come up with a withering response, then abruptly sat down on the edge of the sofa.

"I'm worried about him," she said in a low voice. "He's not as worldly as some would have you think. No matter how hard I've tried to convince him otherwise, he thinks drinking is fine as long as it's sacramental wine. The Good Lord may think differently, and so may the state police." She looked up at me with a piteous expression. "Would you have heard if he was arrested?"

"I'm sure I would have," I said. I was dangerously close to offering sympathy when I saw Ruby Bee at the end of the hallway, a finger pressed to her lips. Gulping, I made myself look at Mrs. Jim Bob. "How long have you been here?"

"I don't know. A couple of hours, maybe. I got

to where I couldn't stand wandering around my house. He *has* to come back soon so he can prepare tomorrow's sermon. I want to see for myself that he's safe and sound."

"I, ah, don't think you should stay here," I said lamely.

"Why not?" Mrs. Jim Bob countered, regaining a bit of her more typical vinegary spirit. "It's not like I broke down the door to come inside. Brother Verber himself mentioned that he keeps a key under the mat. He wouldn't have done that if he minded me using it. Besides, this place was a real mess, and I took it upon myself to clean it up and stock the refrigerator with a few casseroles and a pot of chicken soup. I'm sure he'll be thrilled to find me here."

I caught a glimpse of Estelle behind Ruby Bee, both of them frantically signaling me not to acknowledge their presence. "Well, sure he would be, but . . . but I think I ought to call in a missing person report to the sheriff's department so they can start searching for him."

"I made that clear this morning."

"I've changed my mind. Why don't you come with me to the PD so you can answer any questions that may arise?"

Mrs. Jim Bob crossed her arms. "I've already told you everything I know. He was seen in the hussy's car Wednesday afternoon, and he had the audacity to wink at her several times during the prayer meeting that same evening. He sat next to her at the potluck, smirking like a dead hog in the sunshine, and she was so syrupy that I kept expecting her to crawl into his lap. She's nothing but a common tramp who's set her sights on him. What if she talked him into eloping?"

"And forgot to go along?" I opened the door and gestured at her to stand up. "Why don't you come with me so you can tell your theories to Sheriff Dorfer? He'll be fascinated."

She switched off the light as she went out the door, but I figured Ruby Bee and Estelle could find their way in the dark. When we arrived at our respective cars, Mrs. Jim Bob said, "You can tell Sheriff Dorfer to call me at home if he wants to. All this worrying has taken its toll on me. I need to lie down."

After she'd driven away, I leaned against my car and waited for the miscreants to come out of the rectory. They could probably see me in the diffused glow from the streetlight, but I doubted they had the nerve to linger inside the rectory until I left. Mrs. Jim Bob was more than capable of returning to continue her vigil.

Eventually the door opened and two shadowy figures scurried toward the old hardware store. I caught up with them at the edge of the road and said, "Would you care to explain what you were doing?"

Ruby Bee put her hands on her hips. "We weren't doing anything that concerns you, missy."

"That's right," added Estelle.

"I want an explanation," I said in a stony voice Ruby Bee had used when I'd missed my curfew in high school.

"Well," Ruby Bee began, "we thought it'd be nice to take Brother Verber a plate of supper so when he got back, he'd have something filling to eat. I had pot roast left over from lunch, along with carrots, potatoes, black-eyed peas, and a piece of apple pie."

"And a clover-leaf roll," said Estelle. "It was cold, of course, but all he had to do was heat it in the oven for—"

"Stop it," I interrupted. "If that's all you were doing—and don't think for a minute that I believe you—then why were you cowering in the hallway? Couldn't you have told Mrs. Jim Bob this same story?"

Ruby Bee moistened her lips. "She's been acting right peculiar these last few weeks, and I'm not one to spit in the devil's teeth. It seemed better to wait until she left. We had no way of knowing she was gonna plunk herself down and start mouthing off. She sounded so crazy we were too scared to come out of the bedroom. For all we knew, she'd taken a knife out of a drawer or brought one of Jim Bob's shotguns with her."

"And if Brother Verber returned?" I asked.

Estelle took over. "We figured she'd grab his ear and haul him over to the Assembly Hall to pray for forgiveness. That was one of the things she kept saying over and over again. The rest of it doesn't bear repeating, although I must say some of it didn't sound very charitable coming from someone who goes around telling everybody what a good Christian she is."

"I should say not," said Ruby Bee. "I'd better get back to the bar in case some customers show up. Come on, Estelle."

They went behind the building, where I presumed Estelle's station wagon was parked. I had no idea what they'd been up to, but I wasn't sure I wanted to know.

I went back to my car and drove to the PD. The red light was blinking on the answering machine. Ruby Bee hadn't dawdled in Brother Verber's trailer long enough to call me before they emerged, and

Mrs. Jim Bob couldn't have made it home yet. I hit the button and heard McBeen's raspy voice:

"I got some preliminary results for you. The boy died of respiratory failure, probably after a few convulsions. Could have been he was allergic to bee venom and was stung, but we haven't found any welts. Nothing in his stomach indicates oral ingestion of anything more lethal than eggs and biscuits. All I can do is overnight some blood and tissue samples to the state lab in Little Rock, where they're equipped to run sophisticated tox screens. I'll try to bully them into getting back to me tomorrow afternoon."

The second message was even more perplexing. It was from Harve, who'd received an amazingly quick response to his query about the Ingram MAC 10. It seemed the weapon had been seized in a raid on a compound in central Missouri and was implicated in the cold-blooded killing of a local radio personality who'd been both revered and reviled for scoffing at the militia movement. A month before the shooting, the weapon had been reported stolen from a dealer in Arkansas. The dealer's name was Maurice W. Smeltner.

Harve hadn't caught the significance of the name, but I did. It now seemed likely that Dylan had been a federal agent who'd infiltrated this particular militia not because he thought they were capable of violence, but because he was tracing the Ingram MAC 10 back to its original source. Since Maurice was no longer available, he'd ended up with Kayleen.

I had an urge to leap to my feet and in a single bound be pounding on the door of #3 and demanding answers. However, I didn't have any questions, and it had been a grueling day. Sunday's agenda was beginning to swell up faster than Boone Creek in the spring. I suppose I should have gone to Ruby Bee's to insist that she and Estelle tell me the truth, or called Dahlia to find out if Kevin had returned, or filed a missing person report concerning Brother Verber, or fingerprinted the toilet seat in #4.

Maybe I *should* have done at least one of those, but I locked up the PD and went across the road to my apartment for a can of chicken noodle soup and an undemanding late-night movie. Considering the way things were going, the only thing on was apt to be *Village of the Damned*.

It's never been one of my favorites.

"You won't believe your ears," Ruby Bee said to Estelle, who'd arrived at the barroom for breakfast the next morning. "I found out what that tight-lipped deputy was doing parked in the lot all night long. You'd have thought that since I own the motel I deserved an explanation right then and there. Anyway, a while ago I took trays to everybody, and Kayleen explained why all the militia folks are staying out back. One of them, a boy from Colorado, was shot while they were playing their war game on Cotter's Ridge."

"Shouldn't he be staying in a hospital?" said Estelle as she poured herself a cup of coffee.

"He's in the morgue—and nobody knows what killed him."

"You just said he was shot. Can I have some cream for this? It's strong enough to bubble the paint off aluminum siding."

Ruby Bee didn't much care for the aspersion, but

she slid the ceramic pitcher down the bar before she got back to the more important affair of repeating gossip. "At first, Arly and the sheriff agreed it was an ordinary hunting accident, but then they found out the bullet wound wasn't all that serious." She leaned forward and lowered her voice. "What's more, Earl and Kevin were there, as well as Jeremiah McIlhaney. I'd liked to have been a fly on the wall when those three told their wives."

Estelle wasn't ready for conversation, so she busied herself calculating the precise amount of cream needed to make the coffee palatable. Ruby Bee went into the kitchen to check on the ham in the oven, then returned just as Eileen came into the barroom and said, "Where's Arly?"

Ruby Bee shrugged. "She hasn't been here this morning."

"She's not at the police department or her apartment. It's real important that I talk to her!"

Estelle patted the stool beside her. "You'd better sit down, Eileen. You're white as a slab of cream cheese. Ruby Bee, why don't you get Eileen a cup of coffee?"

"I've got to find Arly!" said Eileen, remaining where she was. "Yesterday Kevin went off somewhere, and now Dahlia's gone, too. I called their house this morning, then went over there. Nobody was home. I thought maybe Kevin had rushed her to the hospital, but according to the reception desk, they're not there. The clinic hasn't heard from them either, and they were supposed to call before they left for the hospital."

Ruby Bee went ahead and filled a cup with coffee. "Could they have gone to a different hospital?"

"I don't see why they would. The clinic gave them instructions to go to the one in Farberville, and they've already filled out the admission forms and made sure they know which door to go in. Kevin came close to passing out when he heard how much the delivery will cost, but the hospital agreed to monthly payments." Eileen took a swallow of coffee, grimaced, and put down the cup. "I'm beside myself with worry. Earl thinks Kevin came home real late, and by way of apology, took Dahlia for a drive this morning. He says Dahlia forgot her promise to call us when he showed up."

"He could be right," said Estelle.

It was obvious that Eileen was on the verge of bawling, so Ruby Bee hurried around the bar and gave her a hug. "It's gonna turn out fine," she said, "but when Arly shows up, I'll have her call you just to be on the safe side." She waited until Eileen trudged out of the bar, then looked at Estelle. "I don't know what Arly can do, though. The way folks are coming and going these days, you'd think there was a revolving door at both ends of town. It's a dad-burned shame those militia folks pushed their way through it."

"The fellow that got shot would be the first to agree with you. I think I'm gonna go out to my house later this morning to collect yesterday's mail and make sure Elsie's burglars didn't drop by."

"What about the birds?"

"It's broad daylight and there's no way they could be inside," Estelle said coolly, ignoring the sudden flutters in her stomach. "Anyway, all we have to fear is fear itself."

"I don't recollect Winston Churchill being pecked so hard he fell off a porch."

"He didn't say it. It was Franklin Delano Roosevelt."

Ruby Bee gaped at her. "It most certainly was not. It was Churchill trying to calm everybody down when the Nazis started bombing England."

"I beg your pardon. I distinctly remember from my high school history class that it was President Roosevelt."

"Are you sure you didn't *hear* him say it?" Ruby Bee said sweetly. "I've always wondered how much gray hair you're covering up."

Estelle clamped down on her magenta-colored lip until she could trust herself. "I learned about it in school, and my memory's a sight better than yours, Mrs. Walking Amnesia. Why don't we just settle this by calling Lottie? She's a teacher, so she might know."

Ruby Bee was already regretting taking such a firm stance, but she wasn't about to let it show. She opened the cash register, took out a dime, and slapped it down on the bar. "Go right ahead and call anybody you like."

"We'll just see, won't we?" Estelle marched down to the pay phone and dialed Lottie's number. As soon as she heard Lottie's voice, she posed the question and waited for a response. Rather than chortling with self-congratulation, her eyes grew round as silver dollars and her jaw began to waggle. Minutes later, she staggered back to her stool.

"Well?" said Ruby Bee. "Which one was it?"

"I don't think Lottie ever said, because she was hellbent on telling me something else. After I left the high school library, she remembered having flipped through a magazine—*Farmer's Digest,* I think she said —that had ostriches on the cover. She hunted it up and read an article about how breeding them is big business these days. The eggs are worth a thousand dollars, chicks about three thousand, and a mature pair is"—she put her hand on her mouth to hold back the makings of a whimper, but it came out anyway—"between forty-five and sixty thousand dollars. Those hissy birds that Uncle Tooly gave me are worth a fortune, and you let them run off into the woods like nothing more valuable than scruffy little guinea hens."

Ruby Bee didn't recollect letting them do anything except come close to scaring her to death. However, there was no point in saying as much—or mentioning that Estelle had been the one too cowardly to open the door. "Maybe we can get them back. For all we know, they're in your yard. If they're not, they're likely to be on the ridge. We'd have heard if they were wandering around town, alarming folks."

"What'll we do if we find 'em? Ask 'em real politely to follow us back to the house and climb into the crate?"

This was indeed a problem. After tossing back and forth suggestions that ranged from the ludicrous, like roping them cowboy style, to the outright insane, like jumping on their backs, they came up with a plan of sorts that involved being able to get close enough to throw bed sheets over their heads. Estelle finished her coffee while Ruby Bee collected sheets from #1, then they climbed into the station wagon and headed for Cotter's Ridge.

I arrived in Malthus at eight, found the sheriff's department, identified myself, and was ushered into his office one minute later (his version of LaBelle was a nervous youngster with acne and a stammer).

Sheriff Flatchett was almost a carbon copy of Harve in terms of bulk and age, but there was something unsavory about him, something that implied he might be persuaded to look the other way in exchange for an envelope stuffed with money. Rumor has it there are no chickens in the chicken houses of Chowden County, but instead grow lights and irrigation systems. Rumor also has it that Sheriff Flatchett spends his vacations in Europe.

"I've heard of you," he said, not bothering to stand up or feign a smile. "Over in Maggody, right?"

"That's right," I said. I waited a moment to be invited to sit down, then did it anyway. "I'm here because of a string of burglaries in Stump County. One of them included a homicide."

"Is that so?" he said without interest.

I reminded myself that I needed his cooperation, if not his undying devotion. "Yes, and I understand you had one here about a year ago. Maurice Smeltner was the victim."

"Yeah, ol' Mo took three slugs to his abdomen and was dead as a lizard before we got there. They lived way the hell out at the end of an unpaved road. Decent house, though, with one of those above-ground pools. According to his widow, swimming was about the only exercise Mo could handle after hip-replacement surgery. He met her while he was recuperating in a nursing home, and I guess he figured he could get looked after for free if he married her.

Mo preferred to keep his wallet in his pocket. Odds
are he never had a Girl Scout cookie in his life."

"Kayleen Smeltner told me that they were awakened by the sound of breaking glass, and her husband
went down to investigate. When she heard shots, she
called for help and reached the top of the stairs just
as three men ran out the door."

Flatchett nodded. "To the best of my recollec-
tion, that's what she said. She didn't hear an engine
start up, so we assumed they parked someplace else
and came on foot. We rounded up the usual suspects,
as they say in Hollywood. Nobody admitted partici-
pating in it, and none of our snitches heard anything
in the bars and poolrooms."

All the cases in Stump County had involved a vehicle, but I wasn't ready to give up. "Did they get away
with any of Smeltner's weapons?"

"Yeah, I seem to think they did. Hold on and I'll
pull the file. You want some coffee?"

"Yes, please," I said, then waited impatiently as
he left the office, bellowed at the dispatcher to fetch
two cups of coffee, and eventually returned with a
stained manila folder.

He read in silence until the youngster brought
the coffee and darted away. "By the time Mo got
downstairs, they'd pried open the case in his office.
They took a thirty-thirty rifle, a forty-four Magnum,
and an Ingram MAC ten. I reckon once they shot him,
they decided it might be wise to leave with what they
already had."

I took out my notebook and read off the serial
number I'd discovered in Dylan's duffel bag. "That
match?"

"Sure does," said Flatchett, closing the folder

and giving me a sharp look. "The FBI asked me that very same question a while back. You think that this case, the cases over in your county, and that murder in Missouri are all the responsibility of one group?"

"I don't know what I think," I said morosely. "Were there other burglaries around the same time?"

"Some tools were taken from a shed not too far from the Smeltner place. A widow reported a peeping Tom, but over the years she's reported everything from a caravan of drunken gypsies to a platoon of Nazis in the woods behind her house." He reopened the folder and scanned the pages. "Oh, and another guy on the same road claimed that someone had left footprints in his wife's flowerbed alongside the house. I guess all of them out that way were a might edgy. After the murder, most of them moved into town."

"What about burglaries elsewhere in Chowden County?"

Flatchett began to doodle on the folder. "Nothing out of the ordinary. It used to be you were safe living in a small town, where your neighbors could keep an eye on things while you were gone. Nowadays, we got crime just like the city folks. I've enjoyed talking to you, but the reason I'm not hunting this weekend is that I'm supposed to attend a prayer breakfast over at the Methodist church—and elections are coming up soon."

I wasn't sure if he'd been as candid as possible, but I doubted he was going to toss out anything more. "Thanks for your time, Sheriff Flatchett. Harve Dorfer and I'd appreciate it if you could let us have copies of the reports from those burglaries."

"I'll fax 'em to his office tomorrow or the next day," he said, pulling back his cuff to look at his watch. "You might want to talk to Mo's daughter. Miss Lila's a spinster and lives here in Malthus. I don't know her address right off hand, but she's in the directory."

I thanked him more profusely and left to find Miss Lila Smeltner.

Dahlia had found out in no time flat that Kevvie'd had enough sense to lock the car before going off into the wilderness. She'd walked back up County 102, planning to stop at Estelle's and call Eileen, but the house was dark and locked up tighter than a tick. Walking all the way home would have been impossible, what with the contractions so strong she had to sit down at the edge of the road and ride 'em out.

Having decided it was too darn cold to spend the night crouched in ditches, she'd found an unlocked door at the old Wockermann place and spent the night under a tarp, shivering, groaning, and making trips outside to squat on the remains of the patio and pray some critter didn't nip her on the butt. At dawn, she'd explored the house and found a half-full bottle of soda pop, and somewhat later, a lunch box with some stale crusts of bread and a withered apple that bore a remarkable resemblance to her granny.

Now, the contractions had stopped for the most part. She felt a little light-headed, which is what the doctor had said would happen if she didn't eat properly. The soda pop would fix that, she told herself as she went into the front room to look at Estelle's house.

The station wagon wasn't there, and it didn't look like any lights were on inside. She went through the kitchen and out to the patio to study the ridge. Kevvie had been the only eyewitness to the shooting, she thought as she sucked on her cheeks, and it was possible he'd seen something real important that he'd forgotten to tell anyone. Or maybe he had to investigate it for hisself, because it might put her and Kevin Junior in danger.

Dahlia realized she was feeling more perky than she had in the last three months. The soda pop must have given her a sugar buzz, she decided with a contented smile, just like before she got in the family way and could eat a whole package of vanilla sandwich cookies at one time. She patted her belly. "I sure do hope you have a sweet tooth, too," she said to Kevin Junior as she set off across the pasture, following tire tracks and humming the theme song from *Gilligan's Island.*

Jim Bob looked around real carefully as he opened the door of the trailer and pissed on the concrete block that served as a step.

"See anything?" asked Larry Joe.

"Yeah," he said as he closed the door. "I saw trees and wet leaves and a squirrel on a stump next to my four-wheel. I'm shakin' like a molded salad."

"You were shaking last night when you came stumbling inside, slobbering something awful. It made me think of Durasell Buchanon after he accidentally flushed his dentures down the toilet. I never could figure out why he went around telling everybody about it."

Jim Bob took a beer out of the cooler. "Where's Roy?"

"He got up early and went outside to look for

more tracks in the mud. That was more than an hour ago. I've been watching out the window for him, but I haven't seen so much as a branch twitch. Do you think we should go search for him?''

"Fuck that," said Jim Bob. "If he wants to be that goddamn stupid, he can take care of himself. Want to play some gin, dollar a point?''

Larry Joe stayed by the window. "Joyce liked to skin me alive that last time I played gin with you and lost thirty-eight dollars. What's more, I had to babysit all weekend while she visited her sister in Paris.''

"Jesus H. Christ, Larry Joe! You let her go all the way to Paris over thirty-eight dollars? You're stupider than Roy. Where would you have let her go if you'd lost a hundred dollars—the moon?''

"It ain't all that far," protested Larry Joe.

"Of course it's all that far, you pinhead. I don't know how you ever got certified to teach, unless you paid someone to go in your place—or you were such a pain in the ass that they gave you the certificate just to get rid of you." Jim Bob banged down the beer can so hard that foam splashed onto the table. "Jesus H. Christ!''

"There ain't no reason to say those things, Jim Bob. I got my certificate because I passed all the re- quired classes. I may not have been class valedictorian, but I do know that Paris is only about seventy-five miles from here down in Logan County. You got a problem with that?''

"Oh, I was just yanking your cord. If you want, we can play for a dime a point," Jim Bob said, picking up the cards.

———

Lila Smeltner was dressed in church clothes when she opened the door, but her gray hair was wrapped so tightly around pink foam rollers that my scalp tingled. She was at least sixty years old, which made me wonder how she'd felt about having a stepmother who was twenty years younger, twenty pounds heavier, and a foot taller.

"Yes?" she said suspiciously. "If you're one of those missionaries, you can turn right around and go find someone else to pester. I've been a member of the First Baptist Church since I was baptized fifty-one years ago. If the Lord won't take me as I am, I'll negotiate with Satan for long-term accommodations."

I opened my coat to show her my badge. "I'm Arly Hanks from Maggody, Miss Lila. Sheriff Flatchett gave me your name. If I'm not catching you at a bad time, I'd like to ask you a few questions."

"About what?"

"Your father's murder," I said. "There's been a similar case in Stump County, and I'm trying to determine if it was committed by the same men."

Miss Lila hesitated for a long moment, then opened the screen door. "You can ask your questions, but I don't know anything more than what Kayleen and the sheriff told me. When Papa got remarried, I bought this little house. Three's a crowd, you know, and Kayleen appeared to be taking good care of him. Besides, we couldn't get cable out there."

The living room was sparsely furnished but meticulously clean. The only thing on the white walls was a photograph of a sour-looking couple dressed in somber clothing. I moved aside a throw pillow and sat down on a love seat that must have been purchased in a fit of girlish optimism. "So you and Kayleen got along okay?"

"Why wouldn't we? Papa could be very demanding and impossible to please, and I wasn't looking forward to his arrival back home after his hip surgery. To be blunt, Miss Hanks, he was a crotchety old coot. Until I retired from the county clerk's office, I'd have to get up at five every morning to fix breakfast, spend all day bent over ledgers, and then go home to fix supper, clean house, do laundry, make sure he'd remembered to take all his pills, and answer his correspondence. Many a time I regretted not running off with Snicker Dobson on the night we graduated from high school. He enlisted in the army the next day and was sent to Korea."

"Was he killed?" I asked gently.

"Hell no," she said. "He came back four years later and married Marigold Murt. Everybody knew there was so much incest in her family that half a dozen of them made for a full-blown family reunion."

I managed a smile of sorts. "So you were more than willing to step aside and allow Kayleen to take care of your father. Were you concerned about the disparity in their ages?"

"What difference did it make to me?"

I tried to choose my words carefully. "Well, if you thought perhaps Kayleen married your father for reasons other than . . ."

"You mean did I think she was a gold digger? That vein wore out years ago. Papa owned the house outright, but I couldn't even get fifteen thousand dollars for it when I sold it last spring. Medical bills ate up what little savings he had, and he was having to

sell his gun collection to stay out of the county nursing home. Kayleen knew all that before she married
him. She may have been crazy, but she wasn't a gold
digger."

"I guess not," I said, thinking over what she'd
said. "You inherited the family home and she got the
gun collection—right?"

"What remained of it," said Miss Lila. "Once a
month or so she'd get him to hobble out to the car
and they'd go to a gun show to sell what they could.
At one time the collection had been insured for
twenty thousand dollars, but I'd be surprised if he had
a quarter of it when he was killed by those burglars."

She was keeping an eye on a clock on the mantel,
which warned me that my allotted time was about up.
"I have one last question," I said. "Can you tell me
anything about a militia group that your father and
Kayleen might have joined?"

"I don't know much about it, mostly because I
thought it was ridiculous and told Papa so right to his
face. A few years back he met some fellow at a gun
show, and came home all excited because he thought
he'd found a way to avoid paying taxes. It wasn't like
he was paying more than a pittance, but he would
have walked into town to save gas if it hadn't been so
far. I never had a store-bought dress until I got my
job at the county clerk's office. Anyway, Papa started
going to meetings and writing letters to the IRS, and
it took me six months to make him understand that
he could lose his property and be sent to prison if he
didn't pay taxes."

"I'll let you get ready for church," I said as I
stood up. "You've been very helpful, Miss Lila."

"No, I haven't," she said, "but that's your problem, not mine. Am I right in thinking Kayleen's living in your town?"

I nodded. "She's planning to open a pawnshop."

"I'm not surprised. I always thought she was more interested in Papa's collection than he was, but of course he was having all those health problems toward the end. Give her my regards when you see her."

"I'll be sure and do that. May I ask one more question?"

She went to the door and opened it. "One more, Miss Hanks. My Sunday school class is composed of teenagers. The last time I was late I found two of them grappling behind the piano."

"The man who encouraged your father not to pay taxes—was his name Sterling Pitts?"

"I believe so," she said as she closed the door.

I swung by a fast-food joint for a sausage biscuit and orange juice, then drove back toward Maggody at a leisurely speed. My mind, on the other hand, was going a hundred miles an hour—or more.

CHAPTER 14

Dahlia was making turtlish headway up the ridge since she had to sit and catch her breath every few minutes. It didn't help that the contractions had started up again, or that black clouds were rolling into the valley, accompanied by fierce wind and the murmur of thunder in the distance.

She could kinda make out where folks had stomped around and left footprints in the mud, and after a spell she arrived at a clearing that fit with what Kevvie's pa had said about the shooting the previous day. Not that he'd been there, of course, since he and Mr. McIlhaney had been too yellow-bellied to try to sneak up on Kevvie and the other fellow.

Kevvie hadn't been afraid, though. He'd been as brave as a real soldier like Rambo. Dahlia sat down on a log and marveled at his courage while she ate the last crust. After a few minutes, she started feeling restless again, so she heaved herself to her feet.

She was trying to guess which way to go when she spotted a wad of paper under a bush. Her heart pounded as she unfolded it, but it proved to be nothing but a greasy wrapper from the Dairee Dee-Lishus.

Still, it was a clue, so she put it in her pocket and began to climb once more.

She'd given up wearing a wristwatch when it became impossible to find one that didn't cut into her flesh. Now was the first time she wished she had one, since it felt like the contractions were coming more and more quickly and the doctor had said how important it was to time 'em. 'Course she was supposed to call, which was a might difficult at the moment.

"Kevvie!" she bellowed into the woods. When she didn't get an answer, she found a log and sat down to figure out what to do. It was a long way back to County 102, and then a longer way back to town if Estelle hadn't come home so Dahlia could use the telephone. On the other hand, Kevvie could be most anywhere on Cotter's Ridge.

She took out the wrapper and stared at it as if it might change itself into something helpful—like a map. It wasn't all bedraggled like it'd be if it'd been under the bush for years, she decided. It was wet, but not real muddy or faded. The militia fellows that'd camped out were supposed to find their food in the woods, so they wouldn't have been eating something from the Dairee Dee-Lishus. Kevvie would have, though, and nobody seemed to know where he went after he'd been let out at the SuperSaver.

This meant she was going in the right direction. She panted through a contraction, then resumed pushing her way through the brush. Pretty soon she fell into a regular routine of panting, peeing, and plaintively calling Kevvie's name. It worked out real good.

Estelle stopped the station wagon and uncurled her bloodless fingers from the steering wheel. "I'm surprised we've made it this far," she said, nervously eyeing the thick, dark woods on either side of the narrow road. "Every time we go around a bend I expect to run into a tree trunk or bog down in a patch of mud."

"So turn around," said Ruby Bee. "We're chasing after your inheritance, not mine. It makes no matter to me if you want to give up and go back to town. Being closed all those hours yesterday evening didn't exactly remedy my money problems, you know."

Estelle pressed down on the gas pedal. The back tires spun for a heart-stopping moment, then caught and the station wagon lurched forward. "That was your idea, and it didn't have anything to do with fetching the ostriches. You just wanted to poke through Brother Verber's shoe boxes. Instead, we got to sit on his boxers for more than three hours, listening to Mrs. Jim Bob carry on about him having lust in his heart for Kayleen. I don't think it's fitting for a married woman to concern herself with anybody else's lust but her husband's. Surely Jim Bob's got enough of that to keep her occupied."

"Hush!" said Ruby Bee. "I heard something."

"You heard the muffler scraping on a rock."

"No, it was something else." Ruby Bee rolled down the window and stared at the impenetrable growth. After a minute, she rolled up the window and shook her head. "I don't know what I heard, on account of you jabbering like a magpie, but it wasn't like anything I've ever heard before."

Estelle wrenched the steering wheel to avoid a fallen branch. She kept her teeth clenched until she got the station wagon back on course, then said, "I been thinking what I'll do if we actually catch the

ostriches, so I can sell them. I might just try advertising in the *Shopper* and some of the other small town
papers like that. First I'll go to all the local beauty
shops and find out how much they charge, then—"

"Hush!" said Ruby Bee, this time a mite shrilly.
"What?"

"I smell something burning. Unless there's a
troop of scouts near by, I'd say your engine's over-
heating."

"Me, too," said Estelle as she looked at the bright
red light on the dashboard. "I must have busted the
oil pan going over that stump a ways back. Now what
are we gonna do?"

The militia was holding a meeting in Sterling's
room. It was crowded, even without Kayleen, who'd
opted to go to church, and Judy Milliford, who'd flatout refused to go anywhere but home. Barry was
seated on the only chair. Jake was leaning against the
door, his thumbs hooked over his belt. Reed and
Sterling were both attempting to pace, which made
for some moves that might have come from a Saturday morning cartoon show.

"Watch where you're going!" snapped Sterling
as Reed bumped into him. "It's impossible for me
to concentrate with you stumbling around like this.
What's more, you stink like a brewery. How many
times have I stressed the need to be clear-headed and
alert? You wouldn't be able to see the enemy if he
walked out of the bathroom and aimed an automatic
at your head."

"Sure I would," Reed said as he tripped over the
corner of the bed and floundered into the closet,

nearly garrotting himself on a wire hanger before he hit the wall and slithered to the floor.

Sterling took a deep breath and let it out slowly. "Here's where we stand—or at least those of us who are not in the closet. I remain unable to access the electronic board. Normally, when the password is changed, I receive a coded message that allows me to determine the new password. This time I received nothing. I do not think it's a coincidence that access was denied the day after Dylan joined us on a probationary basis. Comments?"

Jake spat into a paper cup. "How do we know he was ever in Colorado or Idaho? We got no proof of that."

"Yeah, we do," Reed said as he crawled out of the closet and unsteadily got to his feet. "Remember what all he told us, Barry?"

"He told us next to nothing," said Barry.

Sterling considered reminding them to use code names, but he decided it wasn't worth the effort. "Keep in mind that the communications officer did confirm that Dylan had been in their outfit."

Barry shrugged. "He confirmed that someone named Dylan Gilbert had been a member. I never saw any identification."

"Fer chrissake," said Reed, "I've never seen your fuckin' driver's license, either. Does that make you an FBI agent?"

Barry stood up and pulled out his wallet. "You want to see it now? Hey, how about my library card? You want to see that too?"

"I don't give a shit about your library card!" shouted Reed, raising a fist. "How about we step outside and I'll put your goddamn library card in a place where the sun don't shine!''

The door opened, squashing Jake against the wall, and Kayleen entered the room. "What on earth is going on? There's a deputy in a car parked less than twenty feet from here. Don't you think we have enough problems without you getting arrested for disturbing the peace?''

They all thought this over for a moment, then Barry sat back down and Reed fell across the bed. Jake rubbed his nose in silence.

"Thank you," said Sterling. "We certainly do not wish to prolong our involuntary confinement in this flop house.''

"Or stay locked up here," Reed muttered.

Kayleen rewarded them with a warm smile. "The best way to get out of here is to get our story straight and stick to it. We really have no choice but to cooperate with the authorities in this situation. Do you all agree?''

"I ain't talkin' to that woman cop," said Jake as he went into the bathroom to see if his nose was bleeding.

She waited until he returned, then said, "I think we've already been asked about yesterday morning on the ridge. What went on Friday night up there?''

"Pizza," said Reed. "Dylan offered to go get some. He took my truck and didn't come back for almost four hours on account of the truck breaking down. Made sense to me, but then Barry and Jake got all hot and bothered because they thought they saw the truck in town.''

"What time was that?" Kayleen asked Barry.

"Around eight-fifteen, after we finalized plans for the maneuvers," he said.

Reed sat up and stared at him. "You didn't show up at the camp till way later than that. What time did you get back, Jake?"

Jake was staring at Barry too. "Close to nine-thirty. What were you doing all that while, watching the stoplight change colors?"

"I hung around the bar, hoping I could convince some of the patrons to go to the meeting the next morning. Yeah, I realize I could have spent some quality time listening to Reed complain about his wife, but I didn't have the intestinal stamina for it."

Kayleen looked at Jake. "What time did you see the truck?"

"On my way back to the camp. I thought you wanted to go to church. You'd better get going or you'll miss the chance to get your weekly bellyful of piety."

"In a minute," she said, examining them as if they were steaks in the supermarket meat department. It was hard to tell from her expression if she was finding them overly marbled with fat, but it was likely. "Let me see if I've got this right. Sterling and I remained in this room until shortly before ten, discussing recruitment tactics. The rest of you, as well as Dylan and Judy, were on your own between eight and nine-thirty."

Barry frowned at her. "So what? Dylan was shot yesterday morning, not Friday night. I've already told you where I was. Since Reed didn't have his truck, he was stuck at the camp. I don't know what Jake was doing, but I don't understand why it matters to you."

"Nor do I," said Sterling, trying to regain control of his meeting. "As long as we're forced to remain here, I think we should take the opportunity to evaluate our three potential recruits. I've made some observations about each one. Let's begin with the boy."

Kayleen fluttered her fingers and left. The deputy, who was a real sweetie, told her he thought it'd be just fine for her to go to church. He went so far as to offer her a ride, but she politely declined and left in her Mercedes.

I wanted to hash over my ideas with Harve, but I needed some more information before I could get it all straight. Or at least not quite so crooked, anyway.

As soon as I got back to Maggody, I drove to Kevin and Dahlia's house. The lights were on in the living room, but no one came to the door in response to my repeated knocks. I was on my way around to the back door when Eileen drove into yard and slammed on the brakes.

"Are they back?" she said as she scrambled out of the car.

"No one answered the door," I said.

"I don't know what to do. As far as I can tell, Kevin never came home and now Dahlia's disappeared too. I've been driving all over town, praying I'd see their car. They're good-hearted kids, but they're not the smartest folks to come down the pike. You yourself know all the messes they've gotten into over the years."

"I certainly do," I said. "Do you have a house key?"

Eileen took a key out of her pocket and handed

it to me. We went inside, made sure no one was there, and went back to the porch.

"Could the baby have decided to come early?" I asked her. "I haven't had any experience in that department, but I understand it's not uncommon."

"The hospital keeps insisting she hasn't checked in, and the clinic says the same thing. Her overnight bag's by the front door. I opened it in case there might be some sort of clue, but all that's in it is her nightgown, a magazine, toiletries, her relaxation tape, and a dozen chocolate bars. She must have decided that the instant the baby's here, her diabetes will be cured. She has some pretty peculiar ideas these days."

I patted her arm. "They'll turn up before too long. You probably should go home in case they call."

"I suppose you're right," she said discouragedly.

I waited until she left, then drove to the PD, noting as I passed that Ruby Bee's Bar & Grill was once again closed. Mrs. Jim Bob's Cadillac was not parked in front of the rectory, however, so if Ruby Bee and Estelle had gone back there for some convoluted reason, they were free to leave. What was more disturbing was that Brother Verber's car wasn't there, either. It was almost time for the Sunday morning service, and it looked as if he was cutting it close.

After all, timeliness is next to godliness (or something like that).

Larry Joe put on his coat and gloves, then picked up his rifle and said, "I'm gonna look for Roy. Are you coming or not?"

Jim Bob let him wait for an answer while he lit a cigar and took a couple of puffs. "Well, Larry Joe, it's like this. I'd like to go with you. I can't think of any-thing I'd rather do than do-si-do around the woods, getting wetter and colder till I'm shivering like a hound dog in a blizzard. If we get real lucky, we can be standing under a tree when it gets hit by lightning. I've been told your hair stands on end, but I've always had a hankering to see for myself."

"You're scared to go outside, aren't you?"

Jim Bob's eyes narrowed. "Don't start up with that shit again. If Roy wants to get hisself lost out there, it's his business. If you want to do the same, it's yours. What I want to do is get myself a beer and spend the morning looking through a couple of mag-azines that feature buck-naked girls with big tits."

Larry Joe hesitated, then jammed on his cap and left the trailer. Jim Bob waited for several minutes in case Larry Joe changed his mind. When it seemed safe, he went to the kitchen window in time to see Larry Joe's back as he plunged into the woods.

Once he'd settled down with a sandwich, a beer, and a dog-eared magazine, he ordered himself not to think about the terrifying creature he'd seen, but the image kept blotting out the simpery blonde on the page. A clap of thunder caused him to jerk so vio-lently that he bit his tongue and spilled the beer across the cushion.

"Goddammit," he said, getting up to hunt for one of Larry Joe's undershirts to clean up the mess. "Roy and Larry Joe are out of their friggin' minds, because no one with the sense God gave a goose would—"

He froze as he realized two unblinking orange eyes were regarding him through the kitchen window. He finally persuaded himself to drop to the floor and crawl into the bedroom, where he could huddle in the corner. Sweat flowed into his eyes and dripped off the tip of his nose. He wasn't exactly moaning, but he knew the strange noises he heard were coming from his own throat.

As he sat there with his arms wrapped around his knees, he realized there was only one thing to do— and that was get out to the four-wheel and get his ass off Cotter's Ridge. It wasn't easy to persuade himself to get up, but he did. After he'd peeked around the corner to make sure the creature was gone, he grabbed his coat, stuck the packet of cigars in his pocket, and pushed the button on the doorknob to make sure there was no way the creature could get inside the trailer.

He was halfway there when he remembered he'd tossed the keys to Larry Joe at some point and told him to fetch another case of beer. Had Larry Joe given them back? He slapped his coat pockets as if they were smoldering. He made it to the four-wheel and ascertained that not only were the keys not in the ignition, but that Larry Joe had locked all the doors, including the tailgate.

He hurried back to the trailer and tried to open a window, any window. Not one of them budged. He rattled the doorknob, then threw himself against the door till it felt like he'd busted his arm. A flicker of lightning was followed almost immediately by thunder.

"Shit!" he said, looking over his shoulder in case something was sneaking up on him. "This is your fault, Roy Stiver, and you're gonna pay for it. You too, Larry Joe Lambertino. I'm the mayor and I can kick you all off the town council quicker than a snake going through a hollow log. What have you got to say to that?''

If he'd had a response, he most likely would have dived under the trailer. As it was, he turned up his collar, tried one last time to beat the door down, and headed along the path to see if he could catch up with Larry Joe.

"What now?" I asked Raz as he barged into the PD.

"I've had it with that goddamn Diesel! I jest came to give you warning that I'm goin' after him like he was a rabid polecat. This here time he's gone too far and I ain't gonna stand for it no longer."

"Calm down," I said. "It's your fault, too. How many times have I told you to stay off the ridge?"

"I reckon it's a free country and I kin go wherever I damn well please. As soon as I go by my house and git a box of shotgun shells, I'm fixin' to go right back up there and teach Diesel a lesson he won't fergit till his dyin' day. That'd be today, come to think of it."

"Raz," I said, letting my irritation show, "if you shoot Diesel, you'll end up in jail. I can't see you being anybody's new boyfriend, but things may be rougher down at the prison than I think. Marjorie will end up being served with eggs and grits. I'll have a minimum of seven years to find your still. I'm sorry that Diesel continues to frighten Marjorie, but—"

"He shot her."

My hand instinctively went to my mouth. "Oh, Raz—why didn't you say so in the first place? Is she . . . ?"

He cackled at my horrified expression. "Dead? 'Course she ain't dead. I wouldn't have gone to the bother of coming here if she was dead. I'd have wrung Diesel's neck with my bare hands. Come out to the truck."

I trailed after him. Marjorie was sitting in the cab, her ears drooping and her eyes downcast. If I were into anthropomorphism, I would have inferred that she was embarrassed.

"See fer yourself," Raz said as he pointed at her side, which was covered with an orange blot. Not covered completely, mind you; Marjorie weighs upwards of four hundred pounds and it would take a gallon of Sherwin-Williams's finest to do the job.

"He shot her with a paint pellet?" I said.

"He shore did," Raz muttered, "and he's gonna pay for it. Marjorie's making out like it don't matter, but I kin tell she's so riled up she don't know if she's comin' or goin'. Jest look at her, Arly. Ain't she a helluva sorry sight?"

I nodded with great solemnity. "She sure is. Why don't you go on home and clean her up? Maybe she can be persuaded to have a little soup and watch one of those televised church services. After listening to a couple of hymns, she'll snap right out of it. Pedigreed sows are amazingly resilient, despite their delicate natures."

"Mebbe so," he said, opening the door on the driver's side.

I'd taken a step toward the PD when I realized there was something amiss with the story. "Raz," I said, "did you actually see Diesel shoot Marjorie?"

"Nope," he said, "but he done it jest the same."

"When did this happen?"

" 'Bout an hour ago."

"But where would he have gotten hold of the pellet and the pistol? He hasn't been in town in almost a year, and even if he has, these things aren't available at the SuperSaver. The yahoos in the militia had their pistols confiscated before we went to the PD."

"I know he done it," Raz said mulishly. "Marjorie's taken a strong dislike to him, and I kin tell when she's seen him."

I returned to the passenger's side of the truck, but I didn't quite have the nerve to put my hand inside. "Is the paint still wet?"

"It was purty near dry when she came squealing into the clearing. Some of it was sticky, like molasses, but it was dry by the time we got to pavement. What are you gittin' at?"

I wished I knew. "I was thinking that if the paint takes a long time to dry, she might have brushed up against a tree or rock that had been shot yesterday during the lethal retreat. But if you're telling the truth, then this must have happened this morning. Did you hear the shot?"

He took the opportunity to stuff a wad of tobacco in his cheek while he thought. "I don't recollect hearin' much of anything," he said in a creaky, puzzled voice. "I tend to keep my ears peeled when I'm up there."

"Then why did you assume she'd been shot?"

He spat out the window. " 'Cause I don't live under a bridge, that's why. I heard tell about those military folks and how they was gonna use paint instead of bullets. Marjorie sure as hell wouldn't have let herself get near enough to Diesel that he could slap her with a paint brush.''

I told him to go home and went back inside the PD. My stomach was gurgling more loudly than the coffee maker; my brain, in contrast, was anesthetized with confusion. The one thing I was sure of was that Diesel had not been recruited by the militia group. Those who prefer to live in caves are not what you'd describe as sociable. What's more, Diesel had been mistaken for Bigfoot in the past; by now he most likely resembled an ambulatory hairball.

I tried to call Harve, but LaBelle tartly informed me that he was attending various churches in order to drum up votes. This morning he was scheduled for an early service with the Episcopalians and a second with the Unitarians, who, in LaBelle's opinion, were nothing but a bunch of human secularists.

I thanked her for the insight into comparative religion and hung up, but I couldn't decide what to do. It was highly unlikely that I could find Diesel's cave, much less interrogate him. McBeen had promised to do what he could to expedite the tox screen at the state lab, but he and I both knew from experience that it could be days before we had a report. No cause of death—no confirmation of a homicide. No Ruby Bee—no chicken-fried steak, mashed potatoes, and turnip greens.

This last realization brought me to my senses, so I went to my apartment to eat a bowl of cornflakes. As I sat by the window and crunched like a brontosaurus, I saw Mrs. Jim Bob drive by, presumably on her way to church. I reminded myself that I'd promised her an official missing person report if Brother Verber wasn't back in time to terrorize the congregation with descriptions of Satan's fiery furnace. Maybe I'd throw in Ruby Bee, Estelle, Kevin, Dahlia, and the two ostriches for good measure.

Or better yet, report myself missing and make a run for the nearest border.

CHAPTER 15

"Wonder where he went?" said Larry Joe as he scratched his head, releasing a flurry of dandruff flakes that vanished almost immediately in the wind. "He's not in the trailer or the outhouse. Do you think he went to organize a search party?"

Roy grunted scornfully. "Because he cares more about his friends than he does about his own hide? Yeah, Larry Joe, he's probably at the airport renting a helicopter so he can rescue us. When he gets here, we can give him a medal."

"Well, where is he?"

"Skedaddling down the ridge. If you hadn't had the keys in your coat pocket, we wouldn't be standing by his four-wheel, either. I don't see any point in staying up here any longer. What say we grab our stuff and go back to town?"

Larry Joe shrugged. "We might as well. I was beginning to get sick of bologna and beer, and Joyce usually fixes a roast for Sunday dinner."

He and Roy went back into the trailer, threw their dirty clothes into bags, and made sure the trailer was locked securely before they got into the four-wheel and started for Maggody.

After I finished the cereal, I decided to return to the Flamingo Motel to check on the guests and see if I could find out when and how Diesel obtained the pistol.

Ruby Bee's Bar & Grill remained closed. I couldn't remember her mentioning a flea market of particular interest, but she and Estelle were always enthusiastic about the prospect of buying a chipped tea-cup for a quarter or a battered egg beater for a dime. This may explain some of my more whimsical birthday presents (and I'm sure there'll come a day when my only chance of survival depends on a bicycle pump, a muffin tin, and a 1984 world almanac).

Les was back on duty. He'd brought a book with him this time, and as I approached, gave me a guilty look as he stuck it under the seat. "Morning," he said. "I just got here, but Batson said everything's been quiet. Ruby Bee brought them breakfast trays. Right now most of them are holed up in the middle unit over there"—he pointed at #5—"having a talk, I guess. Kayleen asked for permission to go to church, and Batson didn't see any reason not to let her."

I knocked on the door of #5, and when Sterling opened it, said, "Will you please step outside? I have a question for you."

"Ask your question right here, Chief Hanks," he said. "I prefer to have witnesses. I may need them to testify in court about your abridgment of my constitutional rights."

"Fine," I said, exceedingly tired of his pet

phrase. "Did each of you bring your own pistol to Cotter's Ridge yesterday?"

" 'A well-regulated militia being necessary to the security of a free state, the right of the people to keep and bear arms shall not be infringed.' In case you didn't recognize that, it's the Second Amendment to the Constitution of the United States."

"And a most inspiring amendment it is," I said. "Would you like me to repeat my question?"

Sterling gave me an exasperated look. "I keep all the pistols in a storage box, including several extras for anyone who wants to participate. We currently have an inventory of twelve. Before an exercise begins, I distribute them. Afterwards, I return them to the box, secure it, and leave the box in a closet at my office."

I did a mental tally. "That means you passed out nine of them yesterday. Where are the rest of them?"

"In the trunk of my Hummer. Is that a crime?"

I gave him an equally exasperated look. "No, it is not a crime. Will you show them to me?"

I guess he couldn't come up with an amendment that gave him the constitutional right not to let me count his pistols, because he pushed past me and went out to the back end of the Hummer. He unlocked the trunk, pulled out a wooden box, and set it on the ground. His idea of security was a cheap little padlock that I could have unlocked with a bobby pin. However, I let him tackle it with a key.

He opened the lid and gave me a smug smile. "The sheriff confiscated nine. There are three in the box, which means all twelve are accounted for. Are you satisfied, Chief Hanks?"

I picked up one of the odd-looking things, which fell somewhere between a Colt .45 and a child's water gun. Above the barrel was a two-inch-high triangular container. "Is this where the paint pellets are loaded?" I asked.

"You want to try it?" Barry said from the doorway. "Go ahead, Sterling—let her have a pellet."

Sterling didn't look pleased as he took a pellet from the box and dropped it in the container. "Since you are a trained police officer, I assume you can figure out how to pump it and squeeze the trigger."

I aimed the weapon at Ruby Bee's unit and fired. The resultant bang might not have sent Raz dropping to the ground, but it was certainly loud enough to have caught his attention. The jagged orange splotch on the door was bleeding sluggishly, confirming Raz's comment about the viscosity of the paint. "That's all for now," I said brightly.

"Good shot," Les called as I walked back to my car, but I was thinking too hard to respond.

When I got to the PD, I called LaBelle and said, "I want you to go to the evidence room and ask to see the pistols that Harve brought in after the shooting on the ridge. Count them very carefully, then come back and tell me how many there are."

"When were you elected sheriff of Stump County?"

"Please do it," I said, scowling like a gargoyle but keeping a civil tone. "Sheriff Dorfer assigned me to this case, and he would want you to cooperate."

I heard the receiver hit the desk and the sound of footsteps as she left the office. I spread out all the statements and notes I had, reading each one and sprinkling the margins with question marks. The one statement I really needed was Kevin's, but I'd have to wait until he came back under his own steam—or was escorted back to Maggody by a couple of grim MPs, with Dahlia wringing her hands in their wake.

"I'm back," announced LaBelle as if her mission was completed and it was time for applause.

I sighed and said, "How many pistols?"

"I don't know why you care. Paint didn't kill that boy."

"I realize the paint pellets are not deadly. However, shooting one at a person without his or her consent could qualify as assault, and I've got an innocent bystander who is distraught enough to file charges. I'm trying to determine the location of the weapon that was used."

"Nine," she said, then hung up.

Even in Maggody, where math does not reign supreme, nine and three made twelve. None of the obvious suspects at the Flamingo Motel could have taken a pistol out of the Hummer and left under the benevolent gaze of the deputy assigned to watch them.

The door opened. I steeled myself for another malodorous encounter with Raz, and therefore was surprised (okay, delighted) when the process server came into the PD. He was dressed as he had been the previous day, which meant he could attend the Voice of the Almighty Lord service on his way back to Farberville. If he wanted to, that is; I never recommend it for recreational purposes.

"Looking for the Flamingo Motel?" I asked. "It's down that way, behind Ruby Bee's Bar and Grill. There's a sheriff's deputy in the lot, so this might be a good time to serve the papers."

"I'm not a process server," he said as he sat down across from me and put a briefcase on the floor.

"You're not?"

"That was your idea, not mine. It seemed easier not to contradict you."

"Then who the hell are you?" I demanded, rising out of my chair.

"My name is Tonnato, and I'm in charge of the FBI office in Farberville. Your calls to the Little Rock office and to the bureau headquarters in Washington created quite a stir. I was ordered to cut short a visit to my daughter's house and come back to Farberville."

I stared at him for a moment, then swallowed and said, "Let me see some identification, please."

He took a leather wallet from his pocket and tossed it on the desk. I gingerly opened it, as if it might explode, and found myself looking at a shiny badge and an ID card with Tonnato's somber face.

"Okay," I said, "you're an FBI agent. Does this so-called stir I created have to do with Dylan Gilbert? Was he an agent?"

"No, but we were aware of his activities and to some extent, cooperated with him."

"Well, you sure didn't cooperate with me," I said testily. "If he wasn't an agent, who was he and why did he have the serial number of a weapon used in a homicide?"

"The young man, whose name was not Dylan Gilbert, was the son of the radio talk show host who was killed by a member of a Missouri-based militia. We were indirectly involved, since we monitor these groups in the hope we can catch them in a federal offense and come down hard on them. The killer was apprehended, but the victim's son was convinced there was a conspiracy that stretched into Arkansas. We suggested he assume the identity of Dylan Gilbert, a sociopath who'd blown off several of his fingers making pipe bombs in his basement and then decided to squeal on his buddies from the sanctuary of the witness protection program."

"You can do that?" I asked.

"Oh, Chief Hanks, we can do all sorts of things. We're the FBI, not the DAR. The real Dylan Gilbert has been providing us with a great deal of useful information, including how to access the top-secret electronic boards. We allowed Sterling Pitts to get a limited confirmation of Dylan's participation in the Colorado militia, then intercepted all his messages."

I thought all this over for a minute. "Are you saying that the group in the motel is a part of this conspiracy? They don't really seem"—I struggled for a word—"*capable* of anything more sophisticated than shooting paint pellets at each other."

Tonnato shook his head. "I agree with you, Chief Hanks. I've been keeping an eye on them for several years. They share the same beliefs as other extremist groups, but they appear to be ineffective. This morning they were bickering among themselves with such fervor that two of them were on the verge of a fistfight. I was disappointed when it failed to take place."

"Wait a minute," I said, frowning at him. "How do you know what they were doing this morning? I would have known if you were skulking around the motel units."

"I don't skulk," he said primly, as if I'd compared him to a coyote. "I merely listened in on the conversation that took place in unit Number Five. Would you like to hear a tape of it?"

"How did you get into the room to plant a bug?" I asked, thoroughly stunned by now and in danger of falling out of my chair.

"I had no need to get into the room, Chief Hanks. Over twenty years ago the technology existed to overhear any conversation held in the proximity of a particular telephone. All you had to do was dial the number and sit back. It was called an 'Infinity Transmitter' and was available to the public for less than a thousand dollars. Just imagine what government agents have these days."

"But . . . how did you get the number?"

"I have resources," said Tonnato as he took a midget-sized cassette and recorder out of his briefcase. "Since this was obtained without a warrant, it's not admissible in court. I am not involved in your investigation and, even under oath, will deny the agency's relationship with the victim's son. Once you've listened to the tape, I'll need to take it with me."

His tone was affable and his smile back in place, but I had a prickly feeling that his eyes were warning me: "Don't mess with the feds."

"Okay," I said meekly. "Let me listen to it."

Ruby Bee carried the sheets as she and Estelle walked up the muddy logging trail. Lightning flickered every few minutes, and the thunder followed within a matter of seconds. Although it was late morning, the clouds were heavy enough to block out most of the light, giving the woods an eerie feeling of twilight.

"I'm beginning to regret this," Estelle said as she picked her way through a puddle. "The hissy birds could be in Mexico, like you said, or in the bottom of a ravine with their necks broke. Diesel could have caught 'em and be roasting them over a campfire. How in heaven's name are we gonna find them?"

"I don't know," said Ruby Bee, "but I don't aim to be in your station wagon when the creekbed floods and washes it down the mountain. We'll sit out the storm in Robin Buchanon's shack. After that, we can see if your engine will start."

"How far is it?"

"I don't know," Ruby Bee repeated, this time with an edge to her voice. "I'm pretty sure we're headed in the right direction, but—" She broke off and cupped a hand to her ear.

Estelle glanced at her. "But what?"

"I heard it again. It wasn't a gun being fired, but more of a hollow sound. If I didn't know those militia folks were at the Flamingo, I'd have thought they might be firing some kind of artillery weapon. Step lively, Estelle!"

They stepped as lively as they could up the road, saving their breath, and exchanged pinched smiles when they saw the lopsided roof beyond some trees. It wasn't much in the way of shelter, not by a long shot, but they scurried inside and closed the door.

Estelle was about to ask about the mysterious noise when they heard the floor creak in what had once been Robin's bedroom. "Oh dear," she mouthed, jabbing her finger at the closed door.

"A bear?" whispered Ruby Bee.

Clutching each other, they inched backward toward the front door. A second creak was accompanied by a groan, and a third by a string of pants.

Estelle stopped. "That's no bear. I'll bet it's an escaped convict that holed up here."

"Why would he do that?"

"I've never been an escaped convict, so I really couldn't say. I do know bears don't pant, though."

Ruby Bee looked at her. "Why not? Remember when we went to the zoo in Little Rock in August and that polar bear was lying on the concrete, his tongue hanging out?"

"Are you saying you think there's a polar bear in there?" said Estelle. "That's the most ridiculous thing I've ever heard."

The door opened and Dahlia came into the front room. "You got to help me," she said in a matter-of-fact voice. "Kevin Junior is coming."

Ruby Bee's jaw fell. "What are you doing here, Dahlia?"

"I *was* lookin' for Kevvie, but now I'm having a baby. I jest don't know how to do it. The doctor said to time the contractions, so I've been counting one-Mississippi, two-Mississippi. As far as I can tell, they're around two hundred and fifty Mississippis apart."

After a moment of silence, Estelle said, "Maybe four minutes. What'll we do, Ruby Bee?"

Ruby Bee stared at her. "How should I know? When I had Arly, I was in a hospital with nurses milling around like hens. When the pain got real bad, they gave me a shot, and when I woke up, they gave me a baby in a pink blanket. I think it'd be best to take Dahlia back to town."

Dahlia's face crumpled like a wet washrag. "I don't reckon I've got time to walk all that way to the county road. Besides, I ain't about to give birth under a bush in the middle of a storm."

"Then I guess we're going to find out what happened after they gave me the shot," said Ruby Bee as she set the sheets on a crudely hewn table. "Is there a bed in the back, Dahlia?"

"Yeah," Dahlia said, "but the rope rotted and the mattress is on the floor and pretty much gnawed up."

Ruby Bee thought for a moment. "Estelle, let's drag the mattress in here and cover it with the sheets. It won't be real comfortable, but it's bound to be better than the floor. Once Dahlia's settled, we can try to find some dry wood and get a fire going in the stove so we can boil water."

"And do what with it?" asked Estelle. "Have a cup of tea?"

"That's what they say to do," Ruby Bee said grimly as she headed for the back room.

I scanned the notes I'd taken while listening to the tape. Agent Tonnato, who didn't seem tremendously interested, was finishing a cup of coffee and tapping his foot as if waiting for an overdue train. I'd heard the tape three times, but the sound of my own voice asking Sterling to step outside startled me each time. It was just as well I'd been in the parking lot during the taping and missed Reed's crude remarks about my anatomy.

Tonnato set down the mug. "I need to go to the office and call in a report, Chief Hanks. I don't know if anything said has relevance to your investigation, but I hope it did. I doubt we can make the homicide into a federal crime, so you're on your own." He put the tape player into his briefcase and stood up. "If you come across anything that might concern us, don't hesitate to call." He handed me a business card. "This has my home number."

I got to the door before he could leave. "The homicide of someone you encouraged to infiltrate a militia doesn't concern you?"

"Not especially," he said, "and we didn't encourage him. Once he made it clear that he wanted to do it, we assisted him in a limited manner—just as I've assisted you."

"And he died," I said bluntly.

"Yes, he did. I took the liberty of requesting that the state lab expedite the tox screen. Your county coroner should hear something by mid-afternoon."

I held my position. "About this surveillance, Tonnato. Are you saying you can hear anything that's said in this room from the comfort of your office? You can tape the conversation without a warrant?"

"It's a very handy device," he said, assessing his chances of leaving without being obliged to resort to karate or whatever it was FBI agents utilized to knock people senseless.

"Do you eavesdrop for personal amusement?" I persisted. "Do you listen to couples in bed?"

"I monitor the conversations of potentially dangerous people. You would agree that preventing the placement of a bomb in a building is more important than a warrant, wouldn't you?"

"Do you keep files on everybody in this country?"

Tonnato gave me a disappointed look. "You've

been reading their material. A lot of it appeals to the very people who have sworn to uphold and defend the laws of the land. Good luck with your investigation, Chief Hanks.''

He made it past me and went out to a nondescript car. I was still stinging from his comment as I watched him drive away, but since brooding does not become me, I made myself go back to my desk and reread my notes.

One discrepancy was impossible to miss: Barry Kirklin had told his cohorts that he was at the bar until almost 9:30 on Friday night. I'd closed the bar at 8:30 and gone to rescue Ruby Bee and Estelle from the two ostriches. Ergo, he'd lied.

A reason came to mind. I winced as thunder rattled the PD as if it were a cardboard box, then went outside and drove to the motel to talk to him. Les acknowledged my arrival with a nod, then resumed reading.

I knocked on the door of #6. Barry opened the door, started to smile, and then caught my expression. "Is something wrong?" he asked.

"Yes, it is," I said. "Are you alone?"

"Reed's over drinking beer with Jake. Do you want to come in?"

I went into the room and sat in a chair. The telephone, once an innocuous modern convenience, was on the bedside table, but I didn't care if J. Edgar Hoover was eavesdropping from his grave. "On Friday night," I began coldly, "you arrived in Maggody and then went to Sterling's room. Once you'd been dismissed, you went to Judy's room, didn't you? You and she fooled around for about an hour before you went to the campsite."

He blinked at me. "Why do you think that?"

"Because it explains a lot of things. Jake had legitimate cause to suspect she was having an affair, which is why he was in town. Why didn't he see you go into her room?"

"I drove away, parked behind a school, and returned on foot across the field out back. She let me in through the bathroom window in case Kayleen or Sterling was watching. I wouldn't have risked it if I'd known Jake was spying on her, but we both thought he was at the camp. I lied about being in the bar, but I had to come up with something when . . ." His voice trailed off as he realized the implications of my questions.

"Don't bother to ask," I said, no doubt escalating his paranoia to heretofore unseen heights. "You found out later that night that Jake had been in town. Yesterday morning you managed to tell Judy to wait for you after the game started, and then retraced your way back to the campsite. You and she discussed this until the flare went off. At that point, she split it for the motel room and you did the same for the bluff. That's why you were so vague about your location when the rifle was fired."

"Aren't you clever," he said flatly.

"You probably should admit it, Barry. It's not going to get you a slap on the back from Jake, but it does mean you and Judy have an alibi for the shooting."

"I didn't know I needed one," he said in a voice that was oddly belligerent for someone who'd just confessed to adultery—and, if I ended up with a case of homicide, impeding the investigation.

"It can't hurt to have one, can it?" I said as I left.

I could sense his presence at the window as I paused to collect my thoughts, but I ignored him. I now knew where Barry had been Friday evening, and had a pretty good idea where Jake had been. I tended to believe their story about Reed's truck having been parked in town, which meant Dylan (who wasn't Dylan, but Tonnato had never mentioned his real name) had been in town, too.

I turned slowly and stared at #4. Perhaps Ruby Bee's would-be rapist had been someone who was more interested in listening to conversations than assaulting fiftyish women. This someone might have been equipped with the same sort of device Tonnato had used. In that there weren't phones on the ridge, an empty motel room had been appropriated.

Willing myself not to think about Ruby Bee's reaction when she saw the paint on her door, I used the key she kept under a flowerpot to let myself into her unit, and took the pass key off a hook in the bedroom. I wasn't sure I'd find anything in #4 to confirm my suspicion, but I walked across the lot and went inside.

Estelle's overnight bag was on the floor. Various items of clothing were scattered around the room and half a dozen bottles of fingernail polish were lined up on the top of the dresser. According to Ruby Bee, a chair had been moved, a lamp unplugged, and—horror of horrors—the toilet seat raised. I did not have to overly tax my deductive skills to conclude that a male had plugged in some sort of electronic apparatus, sat at the table, and at some point responded to a call of nature. If he'd been present while the meeting was taking place in the next room, he couldn't have risked even a tiny penlight and instead had relied on a tape recorder. And was aware that batteries have a knack of going dead at the crucial moment.

Dylan wouldn't have taken the tape recorder and eavesdropping device back to the camp, where they might have been discovered in his gear. The bed of Reed's truck was cluttered with junk, but stashing them there was dangerous, too. Kayleen had mentioned in the illegally recorded conversation that she and Sterling had continued to talk until ten o'clock. Dylan had returned to the camp shortly thereafter.

I lifted up one side of the mattress, but the cover of the box springs showed no evidence of being slit. I wormed my way under the bed and examined the bottom of the cover, then emerged and tried the shelf in the closet. Nothing was hidden in the medicine cabinet in the bathroom. Growing frustrated, I removed drawers, felt behind the radiator, and crawled under the table to make sure nothing was taped there. Dylan would not have disposed of his equipment on the first night of the retreat, and he had no way of knowing it would be his last night.

"Where is it?" I said, beginning to wonder if I was chasing the whiffle-bird, which is a first cousin of a wild goose. He hadn't attempted the old purloined-letter ploy, in that the Flamingo Motel doesn't bother to provide newfangled amenities like clock radios.

Discouraged, I restored everything to its proper place, checked to see that all the drawers were closed, and smoothed the bedspread. Although I hadn't disturbed the insipid print of fluffy kitties, I conscientiously straightened it so Estelle wouldn't worry that one leg was getting shorter in her old age.

As I stepped back to make sure the print was perfect, it struck me how difficult it would have been to align it in the dark. I removed it, found a recess in the wall, and removed a tape recorder and a small metal gizmo that resembled a circuit board. My ebullience faded as I opened the lid of the tape recorder and saw that the spools were empty. I reexamined the recess, but found no cassette.

Dylan must have taken it with him, I thought as I replaced the electronic toys and hung the print on the wall. If by some fluke one of the militia had found the recorder, at least there would have been no proof that someone had been bugging the room next door. Harve hadn't discovered a cassette in any of Dylan's pockets or with his camping gear. In a more cosmopolitan setting, Dylan might have tucked it in an envelope and dropped it in a public mailbox, but the town council has yet to replace the one that the local teenagers shot full of holes.

I locked the door and was heading for #1 to return the passkey when Les got out of his car. "I just finished talking to LaBelle," he said. "She said to tell you that McBeen heard from the state lab. The victim died of nicotine poisoning. It's supposed to be one of the most toxic drugs around."

I decided the passkey could stay in my pocket for the time being. "I'm going back to the PD to call McBeen. Don't let any of these wackos leave, and when Kayleen comes back from church, tell her to stay here. Got that?"

"Yes, ma'am," he said, saluting me.

It was turning into one weird day.

CHAPTER 16

Ruby Bee had busted up a chair to start a fire, but they hadn't boiled water because they couldn't find a pan that wasn't rusty and caked with grime, and they'd never quite figured out what they'd do with the water anyway. Estelle was kneeling next to Dahlia, who was panting and hooing through another contraction.

When Dahlia's heavy breathing dropped back to normal, Estelle forced herself to smile reassuringly and say, "That wasn't so bad, was it? You did real fine."

"You sure did," said Ruby Bee.

Dahlia's nostrils flared, but she didn't say anything and turned her face toward the wall. Over the last hour she'd become downright surly, glaring like she'd bite any hand that came into range. Ruby Bee was beginning to wish there'd been a polar bear in the back room after all.

Estelle got up and tiptoed across the room to where Ruby Bee was peering out the window like she thought a midwife might drive up any second. "The labor pains are coming every three minutes," she said in a low voice. "It's gonna happen whether or not any of us, including Dahlia, has the foggiest idea what to do. I always closed my eyes when it happened in a movie so I wouldn't pass out cold like my second cousin Zelda did. She hit her head and had to have seventeen stitches. They had to shave off her hair, and she walked around for four months looking like a hedgehog.''

"Was she Uncle Tooly's daughter?'' Ruby Bee said in a crabby voice, since this whole mess was his fault. And Estelle's as well, since she should have had the sense not to accept anything from a person killed by sheep.

"No, she was not.'' Estelle looked back to make sure Dahlia was doing all right, then said, "Why don't you rip that other sheet into pieces we can use for towels?''

"I bought those sheets at Sears not more than a year ago. If I'd realized that when I took them out of the closet, I would have found some old ones.''

"I don't imagine you'll be using them after this,'' said Estelle.

"I want something to drink,'' Dahlia suddenly said. "My lips are cracking and I cain't hardly talk.''

Ruby Bee dropped the sheet. "I'll go back to the station wagon and look for a cup or something. You stay here, Estelle.''

"Well, thank you, Dr. Spock,'' said Estelle.

Ruby Bee thought about responding in a suitable fashion, but the idea of getting away from the cabin, if only for a few minutes, was so appealing that she darted out the front door like a preacher leaving a whorehouse. Once out in the wind, she regretted her spontaneous offer, but there wasn't much else to do but trudge down to the station wagon.

She came close to screaming when she saw someone coming up the road. However, she managed to get her heart out of her throat as she recognized Kayleen. "What are you doing here?" she asked.

"I heard Kevin Buchanon disappeared, and I was afraid he came up this way on account of feeling responsible for Dylan's death. It was a terrible tragedy, but he should be at Dahlia's side during her last few weeks of pregnancy when she needs him the most."

"She needs him right this minute," Ruby Bee said without hesitation. "She's in labor, but not for long. Don't you have some medical training?"

Kayleen quickened her pace. "I'm trained as a nurse's aide, but mostly I worked in nursing homes."

"The contractions are three minutes apart, and Dahlia's holding up real well. She swears all her puffing and panting is what she learned on some tape and is what the doctor wants her to do. Have you delivered a baby?"

"No, but I watched several deliveries while I was a student. Did you boil water?"

"Why?"

"I don't know," Kayleen said as she fell into step with Ruby Bee.

Mrs. Jim Bob sat alone on the front pew in the Assembly Hall. Brother Verber had not miraculously appeared and proclaimed himself born again, or plain born, or anything else. Lottie Estes had played a couple of hymns, but she'd run out of steam and everybody'd left to take advantage of this unexpected free time.

She'd lost them both, she thought, her thin lips quivering. Her source of spiritual fortitude had cast his lot with the strumpet, and her source of income had taken it upon himself to spend a weekend playing poker and drinking Satan's poison. Where could she find comfort in her bereavement? Not here, in the cavernous room where the last notes of Lottie's laborious renditions lingered like a chest cold. The Methodist preacher wore blue jeans and rode a bicycle, and the Baptist preacher in Emmett was known to chase fast women.

Even the Lord had not seen fit to answer her prayers. She got down on her knees and gave it one more shot, but Brother Verber did not emerge from the storage room, nor did Jim Bob crawl down the aisle on his belly like the viper he was.

Mrs. Jim Bob stood up and smoothed her skirt, gazed sadly at the unoccupied pulpit, and went out to the porch. She was standing there, trying to decide if she should go home or sit for a spell in the rectory, when she spotted Jim Bob's four-wheel coming down the road.

Her despondency was replaced with blind, mindless rage. Without hesitating, she ran across the lawn and into the street, waving her arms above her head and shrieking for him to pull over. The four-wheel squealed to a stop at the side of the road and Roy stuck out his head.

"Are you okay?" he asked.

She lowered her arms but not her voice. "Where's that low-down, lying, adulterous scoundrel?"

Roy figured she wasn't referring to Larry Joe. "The last I saw him he was still at the deer camp. Larry Joe and me decided to come on back to town."

"That doesn't make a whit of sense, Roy Stiver,

and you know it. Is Jim Bob off with one of his women?"

Red-faced, Roy told her the whole story, although he omitted the number of bottles of whiskey and cases of beer they'd gone through in the last forty-eight hours. Once he'd finished, he realized how outright stupid it sounded, but he couldn't help it.

"I don't believe you," said Mrs. Jim Bob. "Three grown men running around the woods like chickens with their heads cut off because they thought they saw a monster? Of course their eyes were so blood-shot from indulging in whiskey that it's a wonder they didn't see the Mormon Tabernacle Choir up there too—or maybe you did and forgot to tell me. Did they sing for you?"

"It's the honest-to-God truth," Roy said, squirming in the seat as she glowered at him. "I dropped Larry Joe off at his place not five minutes ago. You can call him if you don't believe me. Are you sure Jim Bob's not at home right now?"

"Don't you think I know who's in my own house? No, there's a woman involved. I can smell her cheap perfume as I stand here. I can see her painted face and tight dress. Jim Bob arranged for her to meet him at the deer camp, didn't he? You'd better come clean if you know what's good for you, Roy Stiver."

"Look, Mrs. Jim Bob, I told you what happened. If Jim Bob was responsible for that creature, then he fooled Larry Joe and me."

She came to a decision. "Get out of the car."

"I was thinking I'd dump my stuff at the store and then drive it out to your house."

"Get out of the car!" she said, spitting out each word as if it was a watermelon seed.

Roy obliged. "What are you aiming to do?"

"I am going to the deer camp to catch him in the act of fornication." She climbed into the four-wheel and shook a finger at him. "Fornication is a sin, and so is bearing false witness. You might step inside the Voice of the Almighty Assembly Hall and beg for forgiveness."

"Good idea," said Roy. He watched her drive away, then walked down the road toward his antiques store, thinking maybe it was time to take up deep-sea fishing.

"I got your message," I said to McBeen as soon as he answered the phone. I'd considered driving into Farberville to talk to him at the morgue, but it seemed like things were heating up rapidly here in my own stompin' ground. "Nicotine poisoning, right?"

"I wouldn't have said so if it wasn't."

"Then tell me about it," I said.

"Nicotine has a rating of six on the toxicity scale, which is the top. That's a frightening statistic, since it's a legal pesticide and readily available at any garden store. There was a case awhile back when a man soaked some cigarettes in a jug of water, strained it, and used it to make iced tea for his bed-ridden wife. She died in a matter of days. Absorption through the skin or eye doesn't take near that long. Based on the witnesses' accounts, the victim in this case was sitting up one minute and dead ten minutes later."

"That's what they all claimed," I said. "Could there have been nicotine on the bullet?"

"The state lab says not. I've got the body on the

table, and we'll go over every inch of it for evidence of penetration. You might ought to have another talk with the other boy who was there."

"He's not available at the moment." I listened to him snorting impatiently while I thought. "Here's something that may help, McBeen," I added. "The victim was facing the bluff when he got shot in the shoulder. I can't see Kevin being implicated in the poisoning, so you probably should roll the body over and take a look at the backside."

After I'd hung up, I found the notes I'd taken while interviewing Jake Milliford, the only one of the witnesses who'd said he could see Dylan. He'd claimed Dylan stood up and turned around; then Kevin jumped up seconds *before* the rifle was fired. It seemed likely Kevin had reacted to something more significant than a squirrel breaking into chatter, but since he wasn't around to discuss it, I'd have to settle for the less-than-lovable Jake.

The telephone rang before I could make it out the door. I doubted McBeen had discovered anything in a scant minute, but I crossed my fingers for luck and picked up the receiver.

"Arly!" said Eileen, her voice jolting my eardrum. "I'm over at Kevin and Dahlia's house."

So the old cross-the-fingers business does work, I thought smugly. "So they're back?"

"No, but I found out where Dahlia is. I stopped at Raz's shack to ask him if he'd noticed anything out of the ordinary." She took a shuddery breath. "Dahlia showed up on his porch last night and insisted that he drive her to the low-water bridge. She wanted him to help her search for Kevin up on the ridge, but he dropped her out there and left."

"Oh, boy," I said as Eileen began to cry. "Calm down, okay? I'll go out there right now and see what's going on. She may be doing nothing more than sitting on Estelle's porch."

"It's nearly noon. If she hasn't had anything to eat since last night, her blood sugar must be way out of control by now. What if she's lying in the woods in a diabetic coma?"

"I'm on my way out the door," I said. "As soon as I find her, I'll take her to the hospital so they can make sure she's okay. Stay there and I'll call you the minute I get the chance."

I banged down the receiver and ran out to my car, but as I started to pull out onto the road, I realized there was no way I could drive very far up onto Cotter's Ridge without tearing off the bottom of the car. I sure as hell couldn't park at the low-water bridge, go on foot to find her, and then carry all three hundred plus pounds of her back down.

"Shit!" I said, shaking the steering wheel as I tried to think. It would take at least an hour to borrow a Jeep from the sheriff's department compound, and with Harve out of pocket, possibly the rest of the day. Jim Bob had taken his four-wheel to the deer camp, so I couldn't appropriate it (it would have been fun, though).

I was grinding my teeth, when a lightbulb went on between my ears. I turned toward the Flamingo Motel, and slammed down the accelerator. When I squealed into the lot, Les came tumbling out of his car, his hand on the holster of his weapon and his expression that of someone expecting the arrival of Bonnie and Clyde. I waved him off and pounded on the door of #5.

"What now, Chief Hanks?" said Sterling as he opened the door.

"I need to borrow your Hummer," I said.

"Don't be absurd. You have brazenly trampled all over my constitutional rights, but this time you've gone too far. The Fourth Amendment specifically prohibits illegal search and seizure. I insist on a warrant."

I forced myself to calm down and gave him a somewhat garbled explanation of the crisis, mentioning several times that he and the other members of the militia were directly responsible for the chain of events. I tossed in some malarkey about his personal liability should anything dire happen to Kevin, Dahlia, or their unborn baby.

When he glanced over my shoulder, I turned around and saw Jake, Judy, and Barry in the doorway of #3, and Reed out on the walkway.

"All of you will be sued," I shouted as if I knew what I was talking about. "You'll lose your houses, vehicles, machine guns, bazookas, torpedo launchers —and your goddamn paint pistols! What's more, you could face charges of—of criminal negligence!"

I really must go to law school one of these days.

"All right," said Sterling, "but I'll drive. Let me get my coat and the key."

Having used up my allotment of adrenaline, I slumped against the wall. Barry came over and said, "Do you know for a fact that this woman is up there?"

"No," I admitted, making a face as I thought about the vast labyrinth of logging trails throughout the hundreds of acres comprising Cotter's Ridge. "She should have been able to find the place where Dylan was shot, though, and she can't have gone too far past it."

"Do you want me to come along?"

"Maybe you should," I said. "Sterling and I might not be able to lift her into the Hummer. Can you get some blankets and pillows out of your room?"

Sterling came outside and unlocked the Hummer. As soon as Barry reappeared with a blanket and a pillow, the three of us managed to climb into the monstrosity. Don't assume I'm a wimp; the first step was a good two feet above the ground.

"Where precisely are we going?" asked Sterling as he drove out to the road.

I rubbed my temples. "We need to stop at Kayleen's and Estelle's houses in case she's there. If she's not . . ." I studied the dashboard, which was pretty mundane for a tank. "Can you drive this thing to the spot where Dylan was shot?"

"I can climb a sixty-percent grade," Sterling said gruffly. "The sides of the gully, however, are much steeper than that. We could attempt to use the winch, but it might take several hours."

I'd forgotten about the damn gully. "There are some logging trails around there. We can drive up the one west of the area and fan out from there."

"You should have had Jake and Reed come along," Barry said from the backseat.

"To do that," I said, choosing my words, "I'd have been compelled to bring my gun and two of my bullets, because at some point I would be unable to stop myself from shooting them. This means I'd have only one bullet left. Maggody may be a one-horse town, but plenty of jackasses come through."

"I resent that," said Sterling.

"It's good to know you're paying attention," I

said, then pointed out Estelle's Hair Fantasies on the right.

The house was locked and the garage empty. We went back to the old Wockermann place, where we found some muddy tracks that were still damp, but no sign of Dahlia. I told Sterling how to get to the logging road, then rolled down the window and called Dahlia's name as we crunched up the mountainside.

"This thing's like a tyrannosaurus," I yelled above the grinding and groaning of the engine. "The sheriff ought to get one for his marijuana busts."

Sterling glanced at me out of the corner of his eye. "He'd better stick to generic four-wheel drives. The taxpayers might object to the fifty-five-thousand-dollar price tag."

I was calculating our location when I saw Estelle's station wagon. I gestured to Sterling to go around it and continue up the hill to a painfully familiar Stump County landmark—Robin Buchanon's shack. It ranks right up there with the Washington Monument in Maggodian folklore, from fairly recent events all the way back to the beginning of the century, when Robin's great-grandpappy shot a revenuer and disappeared onto the ridge with his common-law wife and twelve feral children.

Barry tapped me on the shoulder. "We've gone too far. The bluff's back that way."

"No, we haven't," I said with a grimace. "I just didn't realize how close we were. I may not know *what's* going on, but I know exactly *where* it's going on."

Neither he nor Sterling looked particularly convinced by my remark, but we bounced up the road and into the expanse of weeds in front of the shack. Ruby Bee came out the door before I could drop to the ground.

"Thank goodness you found us," she said. "The pains are coming every two minutes, and Dahlia snarls something awful when any of us gets too close. Kayleen offered to examine her, but—"

"Kayleen's here?" I said.

"Yes, and Estelle. We were chasing after the ostriches, but—"

"Ostriches?" said Sterling.

Ruby Bee shrugged. "Sixty thousand dollars is sixty thousand dollars, even when it hisses, but—"

"When it hisses at you?" said Barry, having politely waited to take his turn.

I held up my hand. "Why don't we sort through this later? Can Dahlia hang on for another forty minutes?" I asked Ruby Bee.

"How should I know? I suppose you'd better ask her, or Kayleen, anyway. She knows more about birthing than the rest of us."

We all went into the cabin and formed a huddle by the door. Kayleen, who'd been sitting on the floor at a prudent distance from Dahlia, scrabbled to her feet and clutched my arm. "There's something wrong, but I don't know what. We've got to get her to a hospital."

"I ain't going nowhere without Kevvie!" Dahlia howled, then moaned and began to make peculiar noises, as if her lungs had been punctured.

"Forty minutes, minimum," I said to Kayleen.

"Then let's go."

I knelt next to Dahlia, whose face was thick with

sweat and alarmingly white. "Kevin's waiting for you at the hospital, along with Earl and Eileen. Can you walk, or do we need to carry you?"

"I reckon I can walk."

Kayleen and I hung onto Dahlia's massive arms as we all moved outside. Ruby Bee and Estelle brought the remains of the corncob-filled mattress and spread it out in the back of the Hummer. Halfway across the yard, Dahlia stopped and went through the "ha-ha-ha-hoo!" pattern, but eventually announced she was ready to go on—as long as Kevvie was waitin' for her.

I mumbled something, and while she was being settled in the back of the Hummer, asked Sterling for his car phone.

He stuck out his jaw. "Will I be reimbursed for the cost of the call?"

"Absolutely," I said, then called Eileen, told her what was happening, and suggested she and Earl meet us at the hospital. In response to her question, I conceded that no one had seen Kevin.

"Leave a note for him," I added. "He's liable to show up at any moment."

"Do you really think so?" Eileen said.

By this time I would have lied to Mother Teresa, so I didn't have any problem assuring her that as sure as God made little green apples, he would. I replaced the phone, did a nose count to make sure everybody was in the Hummer, and gestured imperiously to its driver.

We careened down the logging road like a boulder in an avalanche and took off for Farberville. Sterling must have been worried about the effect a birth might have on the back floor of the Hummer, because he passed everything on the road, including a state police car.

This had an impact on the decibel level, which already was high. Dahlia alternated between panting and demanding to know where Kevin had been all this time. Ruby Bee and Estelle squealed every time Sterling swung into the oncoming traffic lane. Kayleen was forced to shout her encouragement to be heard. The addition of the siren and flashing lights added to the excitement.

I leaned toward Sterling and said, "Pull over and I'll tell the trooper what's going on."

"Nonsense," he replied, honking the horn until a chicken truck edged toward the shoulder. "There's no time to waste. I'm not admitting any culpability should the delivery have been jeopardized, but people have been sued for the most idiotic things. One of my policy owners threatened to sue me because he thought his policy protected him from getting in an accident, so therefore it was safe for him to disregard the speed limit."

Somehow or other, we arrived at the emergency room entrance without running over any pedestrians or Japanese imports. The state trooper was out of his car before I could get inside to find a nurse.

"Emergency!" I shouted at him, then pushed through the glass door, grabbed the first person I saw in a white uniform, and explained the situation.

"Two minutes apart?" she said. "That doesn't necessarily mean the baby's coming any second. Can the expectant mother walk?"

"She might need a wheelchair," I said, then went back outside as Earl and Eileen drove up. The tailgate had been opened. Dahlia was still lying on the remains of the mattress, her lips pumping away. A crowd was gathering, either in response to the flashing lights and sirens, or to the massive bulk of the Hummer.

The state trooper had pretty much figured out what was going on, but he wasn't happy. "Why didn't you pull over?" he asked me. "You could have gotten yourselves and a lot of innocent bystanders killed."

"I suggested it, but the driver was caught up in the melodrama of the moment."

The trooper shrugged. "Yeah, it happens. What the hell is this thing?"

I aimed him at Sterling, watched a pair of orderlies load Dahlia into a wheelchair, and joined Earl and Eileen. "She and the baby will be fine," I said. "The doctor will have her blood sugar tested and get it up to where it needs to be. The rest just sort of happens, so I've been told."

Eileen had Dahlia's overnight bag in one hand. She looked down at it and sighed. "I hope so."

"What about Kevin?" asked Earl.

Dahlia smacked at the orderlies until they backed away from the wheelchair, then looked up at me. "Kevvie ain't really here, is he?"

"I'll do everything possible to find him and get him here before the baby comes," I said.

"I found a clue while I was in the woods," she said, digging around in her pocket. She thrust a wadded piece of paper at me. "This proves Kevvie was there."

I took her offering. "We didn't really have a chance to search for him. I'll go back and comb the ridge all night, if necessary."

"I'm comin' with you," said Earl. "The women can keep Eileen company in the waiting room."

I went over to Sterling, who was explaining all the features of the Hummer to a large group composed of orderlies, bloodied and battered people waiting to be attended to in the emergency room, and the trooper. "Are you up for a real-life paramilitary exercise?"

CHAPTER 17

I was thinking how best to organize my very own Maggody militia when Kevin crashed into the rear end of the Hummer in his 1970s vintage car. None of us quite knew what to say, so what ensued might best be described as a stunned silence.

Dahlia rallied first. "Kevvie!" she screamed. "Where have you been? Doncha know I'm having the baby?"

He staggered out of the car, wiped a trickle of blood off his forehead, smiled at her, and collapsed on the pavement. It was not a pretty sight.

There was a great to-do as a gurney was brought out and Kevin and Dahlia were wheeled away. Eileen and Earl were as agitated as fleas on a poodle, but followed the orderlies inside. The crowd, having gotten more than its collective money's worth, drifted away to treat or be treated, depending on their roles in the overall scheme of the emergency room. Ruby Bee and Estelle had scurried after Eileen, which left me with Sterling, Barry, and Kayleen.

"You might as well go on back to the motel," I told them. "Thanks for what you did today."

Sterling squared his shoulders as if awaiting presentation of the Congressional Medal of Honor. "It was the least we could do, Chief Hanks. We do not despise the government, but merely resent the perverted direction it has taken since its original founders took it upon themselves to—"

"Can it," I said, "and market it as chicken noodle shit."

This, for obvious reasons, was not well received and the three climbed into the Hummer and drove away. I went into the emergency room, where Earl, Eileen, Estelle, and Ruby Bee were standing in a corner, conversing in low voices.

"What's going on?" I asked.

Eileen stepped forward and said, "Dahlia's been admitted to the maternity ward, and Kevin's being seen to down here. I'm sure he'll be allowed to join her once his cut has been stitched up. I think he just banged his head when he hit the Hummer."

I took in the paleness of their faces. "You all go to the cafeteria and get some coffee, then go up to the waiting room on the maternity floor. I'll make sure Kevin gets to Dahlia's bedside."

Once they'd departed in the elevator, I went through another set of doors and down a corridor, poking my head into curtained cubicles in search of my quarry.

He was sitting on the gurney, wan but gaining color and holding a gauze pad to his forehead. He waved at me as I came around the corner, and said, "How's Dahlia doing?"

"She's okay now—no thanks to you. Last night she went to Cotter's Ridge to find you, and ended up at Robin's cabin. If Ruby Bee, Estelle, and Kayleen hadn't shown up, she might have given birth alone and terrified. Where the hell have you been?''

"I went back there on account of doing the right thing. Dylan was like my best buddy, exceptin' I'd only met him, and I dint think you cared about who shot him. I went into Robin's cabin to dry off, but then I got real scared and . . . well, fainted. The next thing I knew, I woke up and there was the murder weapon staring me in the face.''

"And?" I said, wondering if he'd had a concussion.

"As sure as I'm sitting here," he said grandly, "Diesel done it.''

"Diesel done—I mean, *did* it?''

"Well, it must have been him. I mean, who else is livin' in a cave on the ridge? It was fixed up real nice, considering, with some oddments of furniture and a whole shelf of books. A lot of them was poetry. I dint know what to make of that.''

"I can imagine you didn't," I said. "You saw a rifle?''

"Bigger'n life, and one of them blowguns, too. Kin I go to Dahlia now? I'm what they call her coach, and I haft to pant with her and give her ice chips and massages and things.''

I climbed up on the other end of the gurney. "In a minute, Kevin. I truly am trying to find out what happened to Dylan, and you're the best witness I have. Yesterday you gave me an abbreviated version. I need a few specifics." I immediately regretted the polysyllabic words, but he grinned at me, so I forged ahead. "What happened right before Dylan was shot in the shoulder?''

Kevin gnawed on his lip for a moment. "He

yelped. I was so bumfuzzled that I jumped up, but I hit my head and fell down. The next thing, he was gone and I crawled out and saw him on the ground."

"He yelped?" I echoed.

"Like he got stung by a yellow jacket, I 'spose," Kevin said, his hand drifting to the back of his neck. "It must have hurt something awful."

"Did he touch his neck?"

"I disremember exactly," he said apologetically. "I'd really like to be with Dahlia. She's gonna need her tape, and I got it in my pocket here. It's this smarmy woman saying how to breathe so the pain won't be so bad. I don't rightly know why makin' funny noises is gonna help, but the folks at the clinic—"

"You don't have that cassette," I said, coming out of a trance. "It's in the overnight bag that your mother brought to the hospital."

"It is?" he asked as if I'd pulled something worthy of Houdini. "I don't know how it got there, but I had it in my pocket yesterday." He rooted around for a moment, then gave me an abashed look. "Mebbe not."

"Let's move on so you can go upstairs. You went back to the site of the shooting, took refuge in Robin's shack, and ended up in Diesel's cave, where you saw a rifle. Then what happened?"

He cleared his throat as if preparing to offer a narrative rife with complexity and profundity, although in my experience, such a thing was well beyond his repertoire. "I figured out right away that Diesel wasn't there, so I took off like a bat outta hell on account of being sure he was a cold-blooded murderer. I went for the longest while, praying I'd find a road, and then, jest when I was so tuckered out I was about to drop, I saw Mrs. Jim Bob.''

I don't know what I was expecting, but this was not among the possibilities. "Mrs. Jim Bob?"

"She was driving Jim Bob's four-wheel and acting mighty peculiar. I dunno why she thought I knew the whereabouts of Brother Verber, or Jim Bob, for that matter, but I swore up and down I dint, and she finally took me back to my car by the low-water bridge. I drove home to make amends to Dahlia, found a note from my ma, and came here as fast as I could." He wiped his face with the gauze pad, leaving streaks of blood that resembled war paint. "I got to be with her, Arly. Dahlia, that is—not my ma."

"One last question," I said, "and then I'll help you find the right floor. You told me that when you were shot with the paint pellet, it wasn't fair. Why not?"

"Because he used a dadburned blowgun. What's the point of packing pistols if you don't use them? Kin I go now?"

The nurses we passed voiced objections, but I propelled Kevin back to the waiting room, held onto his arm as we took the elevator to the maternity floor, and then steered him down the hall to the sacred hallows of the delivery wing. Earl, Eileen, Ruby Bee, and Estelle were seated on benches in the hall, but we breezed by them and I found a dewy-faced nursing student who promised to patch up Kevin and escort him to Dahlia's room.

"Everything's under control," I said mendaciously as I rejoined the group. "Dahlia's in the care of doctors and has her devoted husband at her side. I, however, need to get back to Maggody and I don't have transportation." I held out my hand to Earl, who looked as if he'd rather be most anyplace else, including a dungeon, and added, "Key to your truck, please?"

He wasn't especially delighted, but he forked it over and I left them for the duration.

As I drove into Maggody, I looked up at Cotter's Ridge, speculating about my chances of finding Diesel's cave. Kevin might have been wrong about the rifle he'd seen, or even hallucinating. The cassette he'd discovered in his pocket was intriguing. Dylan certainly could have stashed it there; he'd only just met Kevin and would not necessarily have realized he was dealing with a congenital bumbler.

I reminded myself of the number of times I'd unsuccessfully tried to locate Raz's still. An idea, albeit iffy, came to mind. I drove to Raz's shack, took a deep breath, and knocked on his door.

As soon as he appeared, I said, "I ought to cuff you this minute and take you to the county jail."

"Now what'd I do?" he whined.

"You failed to tell me that you drove Dahlia to the low-water bridge last night."

"Ye didn't ask me. Listen, I got Marjorie in a washtub so's I can scrub off the paint, and I need to git back to her."

"I don't care," I said. "She'll be a whole lot less happy if I drag you out to the car and she spends the next seventy-two hours shriveling up like a great white prune. Are you going to cooperate or not?"

Raz stared at me. "It ain't against the law to fergit something, particularly seeing as I was frettin' about Marjorie. If you'd asked me, I'd have told you."

"Well, you didn't. You endangered Dahlia and

impeded my investigation. I may not be able to make the charges stick, but you'll be seriously inconvenienced if you don't agree to do something for me."

"I ain't got a still and I ain't gonna tell you where it is," he said, wiping spittle off his lips.

Sensing victory, I allowed myself a wry smile. "I'm not going to bother. I want you to go to Diesel's cave, ask him where he found the rifle, and also if he's found a cassette. Bring them both back here to your place and wait for me."

Raz looked at me as if I'd suggested he enroll in college. "Diesel ain't about to let me git within spittin' distance of him. Iff'n he hears the truck, he'll be in the next county afore I turn off the engine. That, or he'll blow my brains out."

"If he's there, it's time for you two to kiss and make up. If not, look around for the cassette and the rifle. If he blows your brains out, then your chances of a Nobel prize are diminished, but you can always try. I'll expect to see you in one hour."

"Marjorie ain't a-gonna like this."

"One hour," I said flatly. "Otherwise, seventy-two hours in the county jail."

I hurried back to Earl's truck and drove away before permitting myself to smirk. My next destination was the motel, where I found Les in his cop car and all the militia vehicles in a tidy row. Les was so engrossed in his book that he failed to notice my arrival.

"What're you reading?" I asked.

He flung the book into the back seat. "Nothing much. Everybody came back half an hour ago and went into their rooms. Kayleen said you all had found Dahlia and got her to the hospital. Is she having the baby?"

"I guess so," I said, taking a look at the book on the back seat. "*Constructing Homemade Grenade Launchers: The Ultimate Hobby*? Geez, Les, why are you reading crap like that?"

He hunched his shoulders. "General Pitts said I looked bored and loaned it to me. I don't suppose Sheriff Dorfer would be real happy about me reading on duty."

"I'll never breathe a word," I said solemnly, then went to Kayleen's room and knocked on the door.

She gave me a startled look as she opened the door. "Is Dahlia doing okay?"

"She was when I left," I said, continuing into the room. "What can you tell me about blowguns?"

"Blowguns?" She sat down on the bed and thought for a moment. "Well, they're a fad, partly because they're so new there are no restrictions. Some folks fool around with them, and others have taken to hunting with them. You can get one for less than thirty dollars. They come in lengths from eighteen inches to six feet."

"Do you sell them?"

"I've special-ordered a few of them in the last few months. Reed asked me to get him one, then proceeded to shoot Sterling with a paint pellet on Friday afternoon. From what I heard, I kind of wish I'd been there."

"Who else has one?" I said.

"I don't really know," she said slowly. "Jake said something about having a couple of them. I didn't notice one in Dylan's gear, but that doesn't mean much. Same with Barry. I guess you'll have to ask them."

Wishing I had my handy-dandy notebook, I did

the best I could to keep all this straight. "What about you? Do you have one?"

She shook her head. "Like I said, I ordered them as a favor. Down the road I may decide to stock them, but there's not much profit selling a thirty-dollar item."

"Let me ask you something else," I said ever so adroitly. "What was said in Sterling's room Friday night when you, Barry, and he were there?"

"The same old things, I'm afraid. How to recruit new members, who was in charge of distributing literature, and so on. I'm beginning to think I might just drop out of the group and get on with my life. This isn't to say I'm not concerned about the possibility of a massive social upheaval, but at the same time, I don't want to miss out on what might be the best years of my life. I'm not too old to remarry and feather another nest."

I share a certain number of genes with my mother, alas. "With Brother Verber?"

Kayleen stood up and crossed to the mirror above the dresser to examine herself. "I don't see why not," she said with a trace of defiance. "He's got a Christian heart and a gentle, trusting nature, and he seems to enjoy my companionship. That's all I ask of a relationship."

"Does he remind you of Maurice?" I asked dryly. "I met his daughter this morning, and she gave him a less than glowing testimonial. I believe she used the phrase 'crotchety old coot' to describe him. She said to give you her regards, by the way."

"Lila resented her father because she believed he was responsible for her never getting married. Whatever took place was long before my time, so I don't have any idea what really happened. Maurice was difficult, but a lot of his persnickety manner came from pain. He could also be real affectionate, and he loved to travel and meet young people. Every gun show we went to was like another honeymoon."

I managed not to make any puns, although it wasn't easy. "From what Miss Lila said, he was pretty frail."

"He could get around with his walker, and he did a few laps in the pool every day. The doctor assured me that Maurice was recovering from the surgery and was as healthy as a horse. No heart trouble, no problems with cholesterol or high blood pressure, no nothing." Her eyes began to water, and she brushed away a tear. "I honestly believed we'd have a lot of years together."

"I have a question about that night," I said. "If Maurice was all that infirm, how did he even get downstairs? I'd think the burglars could have looted the ground floor long before he reached the bottom step."

Kayleen blushed and looked away. "I don't like to talk about this, but Maurice and I weren't sharing a bedroom. He slept on a rollaway bed in his office and used the guest bathroom. I stayed upstairs in one of the bedrooms. I know it's wrong for a husband and wife not to . . . be together once they've taken their vows and been blessed by the Lord, and I was praying that Maurice might get strong enough to handle the stairs before too long."

"Sheriff Flatchett didn't mention that," I said.

"I didn't see any need to tell him about our private arrangement. I folded up the bed and put it in the closet in the hall. I feel so silly getting all upset in front of you, Arly, but I can't help it. Maurice didn't want anybody to know how feeble he was. I had no choice but to respect his wishes."

"I understand," I said softly, then gave her a minute to regain her composure. I did so not out of any great compassion, mind you, but out of a genuine distaste for emotional scenes. Divorce can do that to you. "You mentioned that Maurice left you enough to get by on and even buy property here in Maggody. Lila seemed to think all you received was the depleted gun collection, in her opinion worth no more than five thousand dollars. Did she lie about that out of spite, too?"

"There was some life insurance money," Kayleen said as she vanished into the bathroom.

I nearly keeled over as it came together like mashed potatoes and gravy. I made it to the chair and sank down, listening in awe as pieces of the puzzle slammed into each other in much the same fashion as Kevin's car had slammed into the Hummer outside the emergency room. Although I hadn't listened to the cassette, I would have crossed my heart and sworn to die that I knew what the conversation had been about.

Furthermore, I was in the wrong room.

Before I could rectify this, Kayleen emerged. Her freshly applied lipstick was a bit crooked, but her gaze was level. She went to the window and pulled back the drape, then said, "I'm thinking about going back to the hospital. All I can do is hold Eileen's hand, but that's better than sitting here, worrying about the baby. Is it okay with you, Arly?"

"Is the deputy still out there?"

"Why, yes," she said, frowning at what she must have felt was a stupid question.

I produced another one. "How much life insurance money was there, Kayleen? There's no point in lying about it. One of Big Brother's favorite offspring, the IRS, has the figures. It may not be legal for them to divulge it, but they can be coaxed, as can the insurance company that held the policy. Not the individual agent, though. He's liable to invoke his Fifth Amendment rights. God, I'm getting sick of that."

"What are you talking about?" she said.

"Sterling won't want to discuss how he can afford a fifty-five-thousand-dollar tank and a computer and other expensive equipment. If he owned a large agency with a lot of employees to drum up business, I might buy it. His agency probably doesn't generate enough income to fill the Hummer's gas tank every week." I went to the window and made sure she hadn't lied about Les's presence twenty feet from the door. He may have had the book in his lap, but he was making a show of scanning the units as if they were cells on death row.

Kayleen sat down on the bed. "Sterling and I have never talked about his personal finances. As for the insurance money, the policy was for half a million dollars. I guess when Maurice took it out, he thought he was going to get rich."

I waved at Les, then turned around. "His daughter and the sheriff both said he was a tightwad. Tightwads don't spend a ton of money on life insurance premiums so their heirs can squander it. Did he even know you and Sterling arranged for the policy?"

"I knew I would outlive Maurice, and the last

thing I wanted to do was be forced to go back to work. Is there something wrong with making sure I had security in my old age?"

"Darn right you knew you were going to outlive Maurice," I said coldly, "especially since you chose the night to kill him. It was a really good scheme, by the way. You set the stage by prowling around your neighbors' houses so everybody'd believe your story about masked men in your house. You had plenty of time to take a few weapons and hide them to give the nonexistent burglars a motive. Then you shot your husband, broke a window and the gun case, and called for help. You would have gotten away with it if you hadn't sold the Ingram MAC ten."

"You're out of your mind, Arly. I consider Ruby Bee and Estelle to be my dearest friends. They're not going to like it when they hear you said all these terrible things about me. When I say my prayers tonight, I'll ask God to help you come to your senses."

"Thanks," I said with a facetiously bright smile. "And I was wrong a minute ago. I said you would have gotten away with it, but you wouldn't have if Dylan hadn't been killed. You already know he died of nicotine poisoning. The rifle might have done the trick, but I guess you had to be sure."

She gaped at me, then stood up and edged over to the dresser. "I'm beginning to think you're plumb crazy. Why in heaven's name would I want to kill that boy? I hardly knew him, and I didn't believe all the accusations about him being a government agent."

I once again checked to make sure Les was attentive enough to gallop across the lot if I needed him (there wasn't time for him to make a grenade launcher). "He wasn't a government agent," I said, glancing at the telephone and wondering if Agent Tonnato was on the other end of the line. "Dylan was actually the son of the man who was murdered with the Ingram you let slip out of your hands. Friday night he got into the room next to Sterling's and taped everything that was said between seven and ten. After Barry left, you and Sterling discussed new recruits— but you weren't referring to your militia roster. Had you decided what to do once you and Brother Verber came up the aisle? A long boat ride, or maybe a sprinkle of this or that in his spaghetti sauce?"

"I'm just heartbroken to hear you say those things, Arly. I've had a hard life, losing two husbands and having to work night shifts, but I swear I had nothing to do with any of this."

"Ruby Bee managed to support herself and bring up a child without resorting to murdering lonely old men. I won't be surprised if it turns out you've gone through more than two husbands." I went to the door. "Get your coat, Kayleen. I'll have the deputy take you to the sheriff's office."

"I'm not going anywhere," she said in a thin voice. "All you've done is make wild accusations. You can't prove any of it. Sheriff Flatchett did a thorough investigation, and he was satisfied that I was telling the truth. Why can't you do the same? I deserve the chance to live out my life with a loving husband and caring friends. Maggody's a clean town without the kind of people who pollute the air just by breathing it."

She was damn good. Her eyes glittered with tears and her lips quivered, and she looked willing to fall to her knees and clasp her hands like a malnourished orphan. Then again, black widow spiders have a decorative red mark on their backs and no doubt find each other attractive.

I shook my head. "I don't have much proof yet, but I've sent someone to get the rifle that you hid on the ridge. The person who found it has the blowgun, too. The dart you dipped in nicotine and took out of Dylan's neck as soon as you reached his body may never be found, since you could have put it in your pocket and disposed of it."

"But I didn't," Kayleen said as she took a three-inch needle with a plastic tip out of her pocket. "It took me a long time to soak loose tobacco and then boil it down to a sticky goo. You can see some near the tip, so I assume it's still . . . serviceable, in a manner of speaking."

Did I mention I was in the wrong room? What's more, it was all my stupid, semi-arrogant fault for not leaving when I first realized she was a murderer. I could have called a cheery good-bye, gone outside, and used Les's radio to summon Harve and whomever else he could round up. Harve could have held his own press conference, impressed the electorate, and started tracking down a pair of bloodhounds.

As it was, I was obliged to settle for the trite, "You'll never get away with it, so put that thing down before you make it worse."

"Does that queer hermit I've heard about have the rifle?" she said, brandishing the dart.

I pressed my back against the wall. "Maybe."

"That's what I figured. I saw him on the top of the ridge, watching the maneuver. He ducked out of sight as soon as I fired the shot, but he may have lingered long enough to see me stash the rifle and blowgun. I was following what I hoped were his tracks when I ran into Ruby Bee." She came close enough to me that I could see the dark brown residue on the dart. "Do you know where his cave is?"

"Sure," I said quickly. "It's not too far from Raz's still."

"Ruby Bee said you've been looking for the still for several years—but you haven't found it."

It was odd the way my mother could interfere even when she was twenty miles away in a hospital waiting room.

"Earlier this week Raz broke down and told me," I said, struggling not to allow my voice to crack. I'm much better at lying when I'm not being threatened with an untimely demise. "You want me to draw you a map?"

"I don't want to hurt your feelings, but your maps are kind of hard to read. You'd better take me there. I'm sure I can reason with the hermit, or give him a few dollars in exchange for the rifle. He's one witness I won't have to worry about, isn't he?"

She actually laughed, but I wasn't in the mood to share the merriment. She kept right on smiling as she put on her coat, careful to keep the dart within jabbing distance, and then said, "We're going to walk outside and get into your car. I'll be behind you, and the dart will easily penetrate your clothes should it be necessary."

"And I'll have five minutes to tell the deputy what happened before I lose consciousness."

"Which means I'll go to prison. You'll be dead."

There was that. I shrugged and opened the door, painfully aware of her breath on the back of my neck as we went out into the parking lot. I was weighing my chances of escaping somewhere on the ridge versus running toward Les's car when the door of #5 opened.

"Kayleen! Good news," boomed Sterling, practically pounding on his chest like a silverback. "I've just spoken to the lieutenant governor, and he's going to take care of this in the next hour. Chief Hanks, it may be time for you to start practicing the phrase, 'Do you want fries with that?' "

Kayleen hesitated. In that I really, really didn't want to go back to Cotter's Ridge, I spun around and punched her in the nose hard enough to put her on the gravel. I picked up the dart by its plastic tip and started yelling at Les to get his boss on the radio. Doors opened and the entire militia came stumbling out, drunk, sober, half-dressed, clad in camouflage— the whole gamut. The only thing they seemed to have in common was outrage, but for once their paranoia had a basis in fact: cops can be brutal.

CHAPTER 18

Once Kayleen had been safely stashed in the back of Les's car, I went into the kitchen of the bar and found an empty jar with a lid for the dart. It was more than mildly tempting to pour myself a beer and sit in solitude, contemplating my near-death experience, but the neon Coors sign wasn't the light I was supposed to have seen.

Sterling was shouting at Les as I came back out. He was pretty much incoherent, although the word "amendment" was coming through on a regular basis, along with the tried-and-true "constitutional rights."

I poked Sterling in the back. "Look, buddy, you may not have pulled any triggers, but you conspired with Kayleen to murder Maurice Smeltner—and it stinks of premeditation."

"You have no proof."

"A mere technicality. When the insurance company that paid out half a million dollars to the grieving widow takes a harder look at the application, I suspect they'll find a whole slew of forged signatures, like Mo's and that of a physician who purportedly did a physical examination.''

That stopped him cold. "What do you know about that?''

"And even if Kayleen takes the rap for that," I continued, "the IRS is going to want to have a long talk about unreported income, tax evasion, and fraud.''

"I had to fund our group," he said, looking imploringly at Barry, Reed, and Jake. "No one but dedicated patriots such as ourselves will be prepared to defend the country in the face of the invasion that will lead to Armageddon. You know it's coming, don't you? Women and the inferior races have the vote, the despots in Washington burdened us with an illegal tax levy to fuel the international conspiracy, and the banks are controlled by the Federal Reserve.'' He swung around and gripped Les's shoulder. "Haven't you seen the secret codes on the backs of highway signs? They exist to aid the enemy's armies when they arrive to round up able-bodied men and execute them like dogs. Any of us who's been in the armed services or even in a hospital has a device in his buttocks that can be monitored via satellite.''

Les stepped back. "Don't go talking about my buttocks unless you want to ride to Farberville in the trunk.''

Reed scowled at Sterling. "Did Kayleen really kill Mo? He wasn't what I'd call a party animal, but he wasn't hurting anybody. I mean, we all got to get old some day, don't we? Doesn't mean we ought to be shot in the gut.''

"Sacrifices had to be made," Sterling whimpered.

I told Les to put the general in the backseat with Kayleen. When they were gone, I faced the remaining members of the militia. "Get on home. You'll be hearing from the sheriff's department, and possibly the FBI. I don't think you'll have much free time to play in the woods, since there'll be lots and lots of interrogations. Grand juries can be demanding."

Reed was whining to Barry as they went into #6. Jake spat on the ground and went into #2. They'd be gone by mid-afternoon, and the sheriff would have the Hummer and the Mercedes impounded by morning. The Flamingo Motel would regain its ghost town ambiance, and only Ruby Bee would be criss-crossing the parking lot to dust or squirt air freshener in the bathrooms.

"I cain't believe it," Raz said, nearly choking on his chaw as he surveyed the ruins of his still. "I reckon I'm gonna take this rifle back to Diesel's cave, and when he comes in, I'm gonna nail him between the eyes like the sorry sumbitch deserves. Why would he go and do this, Marjorie? I know fer a fact he takes a jar of hooch ever now and then."

Marjorie blinked, then went back to chewing on a plastic case she'd found. A strip of thin black cellophane tape dangled out of her mouth, ticklin' her chin.

"Wait jest a dadburn minute! There's something in the bushes over yonder! Iff'n it's Diesel, he's dead meat."

Raz crept closer, his mouth screwed up, and carefully pulled back a branch. "Well, look at these critters," he said. "I ain't never seen nuthin like this in all my born days—and I can smell my hooch on 'em.

You know what I think, Marjorie? These giant chickens are drunk as Cooter Brown."

It took him a long time to get the thievin' birds in the back of his truck, and he was sweating something awful. He wiped his forehead with the back of his hand, then got turned around and headed home. He wasn't real sure what to do with the birds, but he figgered they could stay out in his barn till he came up with something.

He was gonna ask Marjorie what she thought, but she was lookin' kind of green, so he fiddled with the radio until he found one of her favorite songs.

I swung by Raz's, but his truck was gone. I went on to the PD to make a pot of coffee before I headed for Harve's office. On a whim, I took out Agent Tonnato's business card, called the office and got the answering machine, then called the home number.

"Tonnato," he said.

I identified myself, then said, "Did you overhear the conversation in Kayleen Smeltner's motel room half an hour ago?"

"The only thing I've overheard today was my wife telling her sister what a sloppy paint job I'm doing on the deck. Why don't you go home and check under your bed for communists, Chief Hanks?"

He banged down the receiver, so I did, too. I poured a cup of coffee, settled my feet on the corner of the desk, and mentally reviewed my spontaneous construction of my case against Kayleen. It seemed to make as much sense as most of the things that took place in and around Maggody, and I was gathering up my notes when the telephone rang.

"Arly," chirped LaBelle, "I know you're on the

way, but this couldn't wait. Are you missing any of your local residents?"

I thought for a minute. "Not as many as I was a couple of hours ago. What are you—the census taker?"

"Well, we just got a call from the Pulaski County sheriff's office. Three days ago they raided a place outside the Little Rock city limits and found one of yours. Ruby Bee's not gonna have any trouble writing her column this week, lemme tell you."

"So tell me."

"There are certain words I don't use, but the place is called Madam Caressa's Social Club. The employees are all women, and the customers are men, if you get my drift. Most of the men were allowed to put up bail and leave, but yours was so inebriated and incoherent that they took him to the hospital for a seventy-two-hour psychiatric evaluation."

I sat down and rested my forehead on my fist. "Brother Verber, right? Hey, LaBelle, why don't you call Mrs. Jim Bob and tell her the news? She's been worried sick, so this will make her feel a whole lot better. It's real possible that she'll want to drive down there to pick him up herself."

LaBelle happily agreed, and I made it out the door before she realized what she was getting herself into and called me back.

I could tell from the look she gave me when I arrived at the sheriff's department that Mrs. Jim Bob hadn't gurgled in gratitude and thanked LaBelle for sharing the information. I hurried by her desk and into Harve's office, where he and the county prosecutor were waiting.

It took me most of an hour to cover everything.

I was unable to explain how the Ingram MAC 10 had ended up in Missouri, but suggested that an argument could be made that taking a stolen weapon across state lines for use in a felony might be racketeering, and thus a way to involve the FBI. The prosecutor was ambivalent, but Harve was so delighted at passing the buck that he offered to send a deputy back to Raz's shack for the rifle.

He also volunteered to walk me out to my car. "Good work, Arly. I'm so distracted these days that I'd probably have let it go as a hunting accident."

"Another burglary?" I asked.

"No, but the newspapers are carrying on like there's a serial killer systematically exterminating the population. Now that this militia business is done, think you'll have time to get back on the burglaries?"

"I'll reread the files," I said, then left for the hospital.

I went to the maternity waiting room. Ruby Bee and Estelle were reading magazines, while Earl snored in a corner and Eileen stood by the door, twisting a tissue into shreds.

"No progress?" I asked.

"No," Eileen said glumly. "They let me go to her room for a minute, but she was bawling because the nurse wanted to put on a fetal monitor. I don't know where she got this crazy idea that any kind of test is going to hurt the baby."

"Oh, I know where she got it," Estelle said as she opened her two-gallon handbag and pulled out a folded newspaper. "There's an ad almost every week in *The Starley City Star Shopper* that says all the tests are potentially harmful to the baby. If you send nineteen ninety-five to the address in the ad, they send you a kit to determine the sex of your baby.''

"Let me see that," I said.

"The ad's right under my column," said Ruby Bee. "I must say I'm getting a lot of compliments these days from folks that enjoy knowing about their neighbors. The folks that write the Emmett and Hasty columns must be as dull as June Bug Buchanon. She'd talk your ear off, and afterwards you couldn't recall a thing she'd said."

I read the ad. "This should have been in a tabloid between stories about coconut trees at the South Pole and man-eating rabbits." Aware that Ruby Bee was watching me, I scanned her column. "Glad to know that Petrol hasn't lost his zest. I don't remember asking you to remind anybody about hunter orange, but that's okay." I thought about telling them that Kayleen wouldn't be opening her pawnshop anytime in the foreseeable future, but it could wait.

"Here's the first column," said Ruby Bee, handing me a carefully folded piece of newsprint.

I obediently read her maiden foray into journalism. "Wow, I didn't know the Four-H club was doing so well . . . and a baby shower for Dahlia with punch and cake. Maggody was certainly on the go that week, what with Edwina in Branson, the Bidens planning their trip, and Elsie . . .''

"What?" said Ruby Bee, poised to snatch back the column if I snickered.

"I need to make a call from the lobby," I said. I rode the elevator back down, found a dime, and called Harve. "Do you ever look at those small town weekly newspapers?"

"Not in an election year," he said. "I'd like to talk, but we're kinda busy over here. Both of the suspects have lawyers falling all over themselves, and for some fool reason, LaBelle said she was going home to get drunk. Les keeps trying to tell me about a goddamn grenade launcher we can use to blow up marijuana patches, and—"

"This has to do with the burglaries, Harve, although I can't deny that I'd find ways to enjoy a grenade launcher. The newspaper I'm looking at is packed with columns written by amateur correspondents. Most of what's in them is tedious, but there seems to be a common trend—and that's to announce who's away visiting relatives or planning a trip. The burglars had all the time in the world to empty the suitable residences."

"Can we catch 'em?"

I may have been a bit cocky, but it felt good. "Have someone round up all these papers and we'll see about staking out the most likely candidates. It may take a week or two, but—"

"A week would be better, on account of the election, but just the same, nailing those bastards would make a lot of people sleep better at night."

"If you wanted to sell stolen property, Harve, where would you start?"

"Pawn store," he said promptly. "but nothing's turned up. We've got some of the serial numbers and fairly good descriptions of jewelry and that sort of thing."

"What if," I said, regretting my failure to keep track of who was where and when, "you were a fence, and had connections with fences in other states? You wouldn't have to risk selling stolen goods that were on the hot sheet, would you? You could put the stolen property in a storage facility and wait until you could move it out of state. No rush, especially if you had reciprocal agreements across the country."

Harve wasn't puffing on a cigar anymore. "What are you getting at, Arly?"

"Malthus," I said. "It's in Chowden County. You might ask Sheriff Flatchett about rental storage space. He may know all sorts of things."

"You know," Harve said, sighing, "sometimes I think about dropping out of the race and retiring to someplace like Florida."

"Hurricanes and theme parks."

"Then maybe southern California."

"Mudslides, floods, earthquakes, sinkholes, brush fires, and theme parks."

Harve harrumphed. "I'm sure as hell not retiring to Maggody. You may not have any of those things you listed, but you not only attract the strangest bunch of folks I ever met, you grow them out that way, too."

I hung up the phone.

When Jake and Judy got back to Emmet, Jake announced he was going to find LaRue. He dumped all the camping gear in the yard, told her to put it away, and drove off.

Judy went inside and called Janine to make sure the baby was fine. Afterwards, she crammed as much of her clothes as she could in a suitcase, put the money she'd been setting aside into her purse, and walked down the road to the café where the Greyhound buses stopped.

After she'd had a cup of coffee, she took a dime

from her purse and used the pay phone to call the Stump County sheriff's department.

"About those burglaries," she said without identifying herself. "You might want to ask Jake Milliford out in Emmett how he and his buddy LaRue can afford all their fancy guns."

When Reed got back to the Airport Arms, he sat in the truck and tried to come up with a way to sell Dylan's car. He was thinking he should have asked Jake about the salvage yard when a guy on a damnfine Harley drove up.

The guy pulled up the visor of his helmet and said, "You Reed Rondly?"

"Yeah, but why's it your business?"

The guy threw a fat envelope into the truck. "Just doin' my job, which is serving court orders. Have a good day."

The motorcycle was long gone before Reed got his mouth closed.

When Barry got back to his apartment, he found a message on his answering machine from an unfamiliar woman, warning him that her husband LaRue and Jake were on the way "to kick the shit out of you—and believe you me, they can do it, no matter how tough you are."

Barry decided it was time to find another group of brethren in some place like Wyoming.

When Jim Bob got back to the deer camp after six hours of being lost in the rain, blundering up and down the ridge, not seeing Roy or Larry Joe or any other living thing, he felt darn sorry for himself. To top it off, his four-wheel was gone and the trailer was still locked and by now he was so hungry he would have eaten some of that greenish bologna Larry Joe had thrown out in the grass—except something had already gotten it.

He sat on the concrete block, wiping his chin and trying to find the strength to get up and follow the logging road off the ridge, when he saw something staring at him through a bush.

It was back, he thought wildly. It looked different somehow—hairier and heftier and more like an ape —but he didn't hang around to think about the differences and instead ran down to the outhouse, scrambled inside, and banged down the latch.

He peered through a knothole and saw movement, but not enough to figure out what was going on. His heart was pounding like it was about to burst out of his chest, and his eyes were clouded with blotches of red.

He sat down to wait. It wasn't likely that Larry Joe and Roy would come back, but he wasn't about to go outside until they did.

When I got back to the waiting room, everybody was beaming except for Earl, who looked a little groggy.

"It's a boy!" said Ruby Bee, clapping her hands.

"Kevin just came out and told us," said Eileen. "Dahlia's fine, and as soon as they take her to her room, Earl and I can poke our heads in for a minute. Once the baby's been cleaned up, they'll roll him out in the nursery so we can see him. I'm just as pleased as punch!"

"Aren't we all!" said Estelle.

Eileen had to elbow Earl before he agreed, but he grunted something and we were all smiling mindlessly (there wasn't much else to do) when Kevin came to the door.

"It's a girl," he croaked, swaying like a top-heavy stalk of corn.

I caught his arm, shoved him down in the nearest chair, and held his head between his knees until he began to protest.

Earl was wide awake. "What do you mean, it's a girl? You just came in here and said it was a boy. Which is it?"

"Both," Kevin said numbly.

"Twins?" Eileen said, doing some swaying herself.

Two more Buchanons, I thought as we crowded around Kevin and began to congratulate him. Just what I needed.

The typeface used in this book is a version of Baskerville, originally designed by John Baskerville (1706–1775) and considered to be one of the first "transitional" typefaces between the "old style" of the Continental humanist printers and the "modern" style of the nineteenth century. With a determination bordering on the eccentric to produce the finest possible printing, Baskerville set out at age forty-five and with no previous experience to become a typefounder and printer (his first fourteen letters took him two years). Besides the letter forms, his innovations included an improved printing press, smoother paper, and better inks, all of which made Baskerville decidedly uncompetitive as a businessman. Franklin, Beaumarchais, and Bodoni were among his admirers, but his typeface had to wait for the twentieth century to achieve its due.